A DIARY

A Kate Killoy Mystery - Suspense
for the Dog Lover

Peggy Gaffney

Kanine Books

Sandy,
Thanks for everything.
Peggy

ISBN- 13   978-0-9770412-8-2

Cover design by the author

This book is printed in the United States of America

This book is dedicated to my son Sean and my dogs Dillon and Quinn. It is also dedicated to the wonderful Samoyeds that I have owned and bred since 1968 and the joy they've brought to my life, many of whom appear on the back cover of this book playing the roles of Kate and Harry's Samoyeds.

CONTENTS

Title Page

Copyright

Dedication

About the story

CAST OF CHARACTERS

Kate Killoy Mystery series

CHAPTER 1   1

Chapter 2   9

Chapter 3   19

Chapter 4   29

Chapter 5   42

Chapter 6   52

Chapter 7   64

Chapter 8   73

Chapter 9   82

Chapter 10   93

Chapter 11   104

Chapter 12	114
Chapter 13	124
Chapter 14	136
Chapter 15	147
Chapter 16	162
Chapter 17	173
Chapter 18	183
Chapter 19	195
Chapter 20	205
Chapter 21	214
Chapter 22	222
Chapter 23	231
Chapter 24	241
Chapter 25	249
Chapter 26	261
Chapter 27	268
Chapter 28	278
Chapter 29	287
Chapter 30	297
Chapter 31	306
Chapter 32	315
Chapter 33	326
Acknowledgement	331
About The Author	333

A word about reviews   335

FASHION GOES TO THE DOGS   337

ABOUT THE STORY

Secrets hidden in a war diary pull Kate and Harry into a battle to halt a murder's quest for power.

With two snowstorms keeping a pregnant Kate house bound, she feels safe in promising her mother she'll stay away from crime. But when an author friend of her mother's who's written a biography of a General, seeks Harry's help because of attempts made to his family's lives, it's her mother who insists that Kate and Harry save them from these killers.

Crime makes a house call in this seventh Kate Killoy Mystery of suspense for the dog lover. This story not only brings back Kate's team to help solve the mystery, but her Samoyed police dog, Dillon, who gets help from his whole canine family.

CAST OF CHARACTERS

Family

Kate Killoy Foyle—Dog Breeder/Trainer, Knitting Designer, with a talent for solving mysteries, K-9 partner 'Dillon', owner of a dozen Samoyed dogs.

Harry Foyle—Kate's husband and owner of a successful cyber security company and former math geek for the FBI.

Tom Killoy—Kate's brother, CEO of Killoy and Killoy Forensic Accountants, the family business, boyfriend of Gwyn.

Will Killoy—Kate's brother, off finishing his degree in math at MIT, is about to join the family business. He's also an extremely talented chef.

Seamus Killoy—Kate's younger brother, who's a twin, a senior in high school, a talented cyber researcher, and who works part time for Harry. His girlfriend is Satu.

im Killoy—Kate's younger brother, who's a twin, senior in high school, and an athletic superstar.

Claire Killoy—Kate's mother, who is a math professor at Yale.

Ann Killoy—Kate's grandmother.

Agnes Forester—Kate's 2nd. Cousin, who is a former supermodel, the President of Forester's Bank in NYC, and engaged to Trooper Sean Connelly.

Sybil Forester—Kate's great-aunt, who is Agnes' grandmother.

Maeve Killoy Donovan—Kate's great-aunt, who is former MI-5, and married to retired industrialist Padraig Donovan.

John and Tom Killoy—Kate's late father and grandfather who raised her and helped develop her love for Samoyed dogs.

Kate's team

Satu Mituzani—A senior in high school, a talented cyber researcher, who works part time for Harry, and is Seamus' girlfriend.

Sal Mondigliani—Retired police chief, and former MP, now manages Kate's boarding kennel, and works with her to train dogs, including police dogs. His constant canine companion is Liam, a retired Samoyed K-9 officer, who is Dillon's sire.

Roger Argus—Retired CT State Trooper who is now working as an assistant in Kate's Boarding Kennel and Training Center.

Sean Connelly—CT State Trooper, whose K-9 partner Golden Retriever 'Patrick', is engaged to Agnes Forester.

Sgt. Gurka—CT State Trooper, K-9 partner, GSD 'Teddy'.

Special Agent Deshi Xiang—FBI agent based in Washington DC Headquarters, friend of Kate and Harry.

Malcolm Bullock—Agent in Charge FBI Washington DC Headquarters, Des' boss, friend of Kate and Harry.

Dr. Gwyn Braxton—CT Forensic Pathologist, Tom's girlfriend, childhood friend of Kate.

Involved in the case

Alice Simmons—Member of the Golden Retriever Club and part of Kate's Search and Rescue team who's Golden is Lucky.

Alven Asch—Old friend of Kate's grandfather who retired from the government working with the CIA. Owns a Golden Retriever named Buster.

George Nason—Client of Harry's, whose company was robbed of a billion dollars.

Keith Harrison—Worked for George Nason.

Molly Allende—Wife of Nason's company CFO.

Ramsey Oliver—Retired FBI agent, friend of Harry.

Everet Blackler—Author writing a biography of an Army General.

Harriet Blackler—Wife of Everet and former teaching assistant (TA) for Claire Killoy, Kate's mother.

Shannon, Robert and James Blackler—Children of Everet and Harriet Blackler.

General Nathaniel Taylor—The subject of Everet Blackler's biography.

Charlotte Taylor—The General's wife.

Cory Barns—Connecticut State Police Trooper.

Billy Anders—Connecticut State Police Trooper.

Isaac Evans—Army CID Inspector, son of Vietnam War soldier Calvin Evans.

Agents Grody and Figueroa—FBI agents out of the New Haven Field Office.

Giuseppe Calamari—Also known as 'The Squid' is a gun for hire.

Gianpaolo Rapino—Hit man

Marco Weinbaum, Edward Cantwell and Alessandro Macrino—All potential presidential nominees for Attorney General.

Patience Snyder—Well known television news commentator based in New York City.

Kate's Samoyed dogs—Dillon, police dog who is Kate's companion, Quinn, Dillon's puppy, Liam, police dog and Dillon's sire who was Kate's late grandfather's dog, now Sal's companion, Rory, former companion to Kate's late father and Liam's sire, Shelagh, Kate's young bitch, Kelly, Shelagh's dam, plus older dogs and bitches retired from active showing and related to those dogs and bitches previously mentioned are Dermod, Dedre, Maud, Brendon, Shannon and Teagan.

KATE KILLOY
MYSTERY SERIES

Fashion Goes to the Dogs

Puppy Pursuit

National Security

Search

North Country Honeymoon

Guard Kate

A Diary

CHAPTER 1

Wednesday morning - early

Kate Killoy hated being in jail. She looked out onto her dog's exercise yard at her dozen hairy, arctic pups playing in the falling snow and sighed. Then, picking up her camera as a distraction from her captivity and resting her elbows on the banquette table, she focused on Quinn. He was playing King of the Mountain on the huge wooden cable spool. Snow swirled as the other eleven Sams challenged him, their excitement growing as the storm increased. This was Samoyed weather, and they loved it. Arctic dogs, whirling snow, a perfect shot. She focused in close as Dillon, the puppy's sire, leapt up behind him, knocking the puppy off, and barked his bragging rights. The close up caught his joy at the win.

These Samoyed dogs were the focus of her world. Her father and grandfather had both love the breed; raising and showing them for many years. The only girl in a family of five children, she was also the only one who didn't adhere to the family's passion for math. Kate's passions, to the exclusion of other interests as she grew up, were the dogs and knitting. When both her grandfather died, followed soon after by her father, Kate inherited the kennel, the dogs, the training barn which also held her knitting studio, the kennel manager's cottage and fourteen acres of woods. This became her entire world until she fell in love and married.

Smiling, Kate moved her lens, seeking another shot. Taking photos was her most recent distraction from being grounded. Trying to explain to the male members of her household that the word pregnant did not mean helpless was a waste of time, breath, and energy. A movement at the front window of her kennel halted her shifting lens as she slid it to the right. She zoomed in on the familiar figure standing and staring out at the snow. His face, though looking in her direction, did not acknowledge her. It was his expression that froze her hand and made her gasp. Her portrait of Salvatore Mondigliani, her kennel manager, would be one of pure despair.

Lost in thought, she jumped as her phone rang, and glanced at the screen, seeing it was Harry. She let out a breath of relief. "You're alive and safe," she greeted her husband. "I was worried. Where are you now?"

"I am where I've been for the last hour and seven minutes. I'm stuck a hundred yards from the entrance to the rest stop right before the Sturbridge exit on the Mass. Pike. A tractor trailer kept its load upright when it jackknifed in the snow, but flipped its cab. From what I can get off the police scanner, the driver is alive but injured and the tow truck is inching its way the wrong way up the Sturbridge exit to get to him. Exit traffic's halted. They're going to have to flip the cab before anything moves."

"You're not exactly having fun. How did your Boston meeting go?"

"It's right up there with this traffic for most frustrating part of the day. The idiot's company is going to be robbed blind because he convinced himself his employees are all saints. He wouldn't listen to my evidence. I've been beating myself up for giving this guy even five minutes of my day. Oh wait, a hole just opened up. Yes, I can get into the rest stop. Fantastic! There's a cup of coffee, extra-large with my name on it, waiting as soon as I park."

"I'm certain that coffee is shouting, 'Harry, come get me!' But while you're restocking your caffeine supply, and giving yourself more of a buzz, get yourself some food. Until the crane flips the cab, nobody's going anywhere so you're better off spending the time scarfing down a delicious meal in a warm comfortable rest stop, rather than sitting in traffic banging your head against the steering wheel."

"I always bang it against the headrest—it's softer."

"Smart. That mega brain of yours always comes up with the best solution."

"Well, not according to my now former client. He thinks I don't understand people. Hum, that's odd. What's he doing here?"

"He, who?"

"Oh, just someone I met at that company. The boss' golden boy."

"Well, you and Prince Charming go get some warm food in your stomachs and when your scanner says the crane has flipped the cab—head home."

"Will do, and you remember—no shoveling snow. I know you are perfectly capable, but humor me. I don't want you slipping on the snow and endangering both you and the munchkin in your belly."

"Yes sir, no shoveling, ice skating, snowshoeing, skiing, or building igloos."

"That's my girl. I'll see you as soon as I get there. Love you."

"Love you, more."

The call ended. Kate turned back to the window. Much to her surprise, Sal still stood there. Lifting her camera, she focused in on the man. His stance was rigid, and she saw his fist gripped a piece of paper. As she moved the close-up lens toward his face, a chill gripped her. Whatever was on that paper, it wasn't good news.

Sal didn't need to read the words on the paper. He knew them by heart. The postmarked envelope was from Washington, DC. As with the others, someone had typed this on plain white paper using a manual typewriter. The message never changed.

He walked to his desk, reached into the bottom drawer, took out a metal box, unlocked it, and placed the letter inside with all the other threats. He locked the box and stuck it back into the drawer of the desk. He didn't need to look hard at the letter. It was a duplicate of the others, fifty-four threats—one a year. Only this year, it wasn't the same. This time, the address was to him here, at Kate's kennel. Did that mean the threat now included his boss and her family? He rolled his chair back from his desk and stood so he could again see out the window at the front of the kennel. This time, he looked across the yard toward the home of people he cared so much about.

Kate had just lifted her camera once more when her phone buzzed with a text. *Delivery in five minutes. Can unload but can't set up. No time. Must be fast to beat this storm.*

She set down the camera and raced for the

living room. The notebook with all the details of the furniture delivery lay on the sofa table where she'd left it, thinking they would postpone the scheduled arrival of the furniture. All was ready, the rooms labeled, the lists made, markers sitting ready to mark each box. She quietly cheered and did a happy dance. At last, three months after they moved in, the second floor of the house would contain more than her old worn double bed, which she'd taken apart and stored in a closet last night. Five bedrooms now stood empty and waiting.

As she waited for the truck, she heard the kitchen door open and the sounds of men's voices coming from the area of the coffee machine. She walked back into the kitchen, and heard Sal and their kennel assistant Roger grumbling about the weather and filling their thermal mugs with strong coffee.

"Katie, you're going to have to do without me for a while," Sal said. "I don't want to leave the kids to handle plowing out that long driveway of theirs without help, especially with Sarah pregnant."

Sarah was Sal's daughter-in-law and a friend of Kate's whose young German Shepherd Kate had shown to his championship. It was through Sarah that Kate had met Sal. He'd recently retired from many years as chief-of-police in a suburb of Springfield, Massachusetts. Luckily, Sal hated retirement and became Kate's kennel manager helping her expand the dog training facility to include police dogs.

"That seems to be the theme of the day. I just got off the phone with Harry and had to swear I would not shovel or plow snow since I'm carrying his child."

"Where is he? I expected him home yesterday."

"Apparently, he had a problem making his client believe there might be a snake in Eden. After giving it one more try this morning, he's headed home, but he's stuck behind a tractor-trailer with an overturned cab. By the time he got off the phone, he was in the rest stop right before the Sturbridge exit, planning to wait out the road congestion with a hot meal. It will probably be a couple of hours before we see him."

Sal frowned and stayed back while Roger left to head back to the kennel. Looking hard at her, he said, "Kate, do me a favor and don't ask why."

"Okay, if it's important."

"It is. I want you to promise that if you're alone over the next week, you'll have Dillon and Liam at your side."

"What's wrong? Can't you tell me?"

"Hopefully, nothing. Just humor me, please."

"Okay. I promise."

They both looked out the window and spotted the big truck pulling in with the furniture.

"What's that?" Sal asked.

"That, believe it or not, is all the bedroom furniture for the second floor. It was just my luck that this was the scheduled delivery day. I purposely made it for mid-March to avoid snowstorms."

"You forget that the biggest snowstorms come in spring to New England. They'd better get unloaded and back on the road or they might spend this storm parked in your driveway."

"Then I'd better get cracking. You be careful with that plowing."

As she headed toward the living room, she glanced back over her shoulder. Sal stood in the doorway, staring at her. She almost stumbled as she saw his face wearing an expression of abject terror.

CHAPTER 2

Wednesday Morning - later

K ate watched as the large van pulled into her driveway, crawling toward the front of her house. She'd half-expected them to postpone the delivery of her furniture. But here it was, snow or no snow.

Sal stopped his truck as he headed up the driveway toward the highway.

"Keep the boys with you, Kate." he yelled.

Kate gave him a thumbs up and then turned to the man in charge of the delivery.

"We've got your stuff, lady. Lots of beds."

"My second-floor furniture. Bad timing with this storm. I hope you can at least get the heaviest pieces upstairs before you have to get back on the road. This snow is amounting to something."

Kate grabbed a clipboard and large black marker from where she'd left it on the table behind the couch. As each piece came in through the door, she marked it with a letter and told the man where to take it. "I marked the rooms with corresponding letters to make the job easy. Just get the sizeable pieces in the right rooms," she told them. "We can set them up later. It will give us something to do while we're snowbound. We can leave smaller pieces like lamps and night stands in the living room and I'll get someone to take them up later."

As four of the men hurried to get the bed frames, mattresses, bureaus, dressers and rugs to their appointed rooms on the second floor, a fifth seemed in charge of creating a forest of boxes in the center of her living room.

Dillon pushed at her leg and Kate looked at him then Liam and then at the lineup of dog faces pressed against the French doors leading out to the deck. Stepping around the two dogs, she checked off the next headboard as they carried it in and called out, "Bedroom B—left at the top of the stairs. Letter is on the wall by the door."

She decided she did not need guarding from furniture delivery men. However, trying to put Dillon and Liam out with the others where they were all parked to watch through the French doors wouldn't work. She set down her clipboard and marker and headed quickly through the house to the back hall, with them heeling at her side. When they reached the door to the yard opposite Harry's office, she quietly opened it and signaled the boys to go join the others.

Reversing her route, she headed back toward the living room when a familiar voice yelled, "Kate! Kate, where are you?"

Agnes stood in the middle of the box forest, her hands on her hips and looking absolutely gorgeous. All the workmen stood frozen in place. "Agnes," she yelled, "go into the kitchen and get a handful of your publicity shots from the fashion show. Get the ones with you and your greyhounds. Now!"

Kate gave her cousin a gentle push, then whirled around to face the men. "Yes, that really IS Agnes Forester, the former supermodel. And if we can get this job finished quickly, you will each go home with a personally autographed photo of her. This is a limited time offer, gentlemen, and the clock is ticking." Her words must have broken their enchantment because men began racing to get the last pieces into the house and all the heavy ones up the stairs.

Walking into the dining room, she faced a tragic figure holding a stack of photos but wiping tears from her face. "Kate," Agnes said, wiping a picturesque tear from her cheek, "The wedding is off."

"Does Sean know you aren't getting married?"

"Oh, we're still getting married, but I can't have a wedding. I'll lose all my friends."

"Okay, this I've got to hear." She looked back through the living room and out the front door. The truck was now empty. Turning back to Agnes, she said, "Go autograph your photos for these guys and hand each of them one of these envelopes with a bonus from me. Then we can talk."

As she pushed Agnes back toward the living room, her phone buzzed. She saw it was Alice, who was a member of her search and rescue team, along with her Golden Retriever, Lucky.

"Hi, Alice." Kate answered. "Are you enjoying the snow? Lucky must love romping in snow that will soon be up to his elbows."

"Kate, something's wrong. I can't get through to Alven. He is to speak to the Golden club tonight. Of course, we canceled the meeting because of the snow. I've called everyone to tell them not to come, but he's not answering his phone. I've been calling all morning. He always answers his cell. He's never without it. He's tough, but at his age, things can go wrong. I just know something bad has happened. He lives off the highway near you. Could one of your brothers drive over there and make sure he's, okay? Let him know we postponed the meeting. We'll reschedule it once the second storm they're predicting comes through?"

"No problem, Alice. I'll ask the twins to go check on him. Hopefully, he just forgot to turn on his phone or he had a power failure and hasn't been able to recharge it. I know the boys are home. It was an early dismissal at school because of the storm. The boys have known Alven all their lives since he and Gramps were close friends."

"Thanks. Let me know if there is a problem or anything I can do to help."

Before Agnes could return and draw her into this latest wedding drama, Kate quickly texted Alice's request to Seamus and Tim, her twin brothers. A minute later, her phone buzzed with a text. *Will do. We'll take the truck and see if he needs plowing out.*

Kate mentally ticked off this task as done. Then she stepped into the living room to see the crowd of smiling movers tucking photos inside their jackets as they headed out to their truck.

She closed the door, slipped her arm around Agnes' bent elbow and swung her toward the kitchen. "Tea!" She cried.

"And sympathy." Agnes murmured. Once Kate had her settled at the banquette, she quickly made the tea, putting the teapot with cups, saucers, milk and sugar plus a plate of cookies on a tray. The cookies were her brother Will's latest recipe. Will, though a math geek like all her brothers, loved to cook. Placing the tray on the table, she slid onto the facing bench while, taking a quick peek at her phone to see if there were any messages from Harry. There weren't.

"Okay, talk to me," Kate said, as she poured the tea. "By the way, try these cookies. Their Will's newest attempt to make healthy and delicious snacks for pregnant women. They're wonderful."

Agnes sighed and scowled at her. "I can't have a wedding."

"What does Sean say about this? I know that he's still planning on getting married."

"We've got to elope."

"It will disappoint Will not to cater your wedding."

"No, I WANT the wedding, but I just can't have it. I'll lose all my dear friends. It's impossible."

"I'm not following you. Why does the fact you're having a wedding make you lose friends?"

Agnes stared at her as though she'd lost her mind. "Kate, what have I been doing for most of my life?"

"Being a supermodel."

"And how many of the 'A-list' designers have used me as a model?"

"All of them."

"And for how many did I model a bridal gown?"

"All of them?" Kate felt a penny the size of a

skyscraper drop. "And..., if you choose one designer over another, you are going to lose all your friends. Got it. I assume these designers are coming to the wedding."

"Yes. I don't know what to do?"

"What kind of gown do you want?"

"Classic. Simple lines. But with a long train for the wow factor."

"Okay. What fabric?"

"I was thinking silk with a slight shimmer."

"Sleeves or strapless?"

"Maybe a halter? It could be backless. The lacy train could flow from the back of the neck."

"It sounds beautiful and Sean would definitely appreciate it being backless."

"But none of the designers have gowns that look like that. I can't possibly ask one of them to design me the dress I want, rather than wear one of their own creations, which are all beautiful—but just not me."

Kate pulled out her phone and checked her schedule. "You scheduled the wedding for June 10th and today is March 4th. It will be possible, though it's going to be tight. The dress will have to be a silk blend because silk stretches, but the new blends are available with a sparkle or shimmer spun right in." She paused as Agnes stared at her. Then, letting her mind run free, she looked out at her dogs. They were quickly disappearing under the accumulating snow. Quinn, sitting on top of the snow-covered cable spool, looked like a canine wedding cake topper. After a minute, she looked back at Agnes and said, "Okay, that will solve your problem and you can go back to fussing over the 5,000 other details in planning this wedding."

She stood and picked up the teapot, rinsed it out and set it onto the counter next to the kettle, after adding new tea. Then she carefully added the boiling water. When she looked up, Agnes was gawking at her in confusion and panic.

"OKAY? What's okay?"

"Your problem. Tonight, you will email your friends and tell them that your cousin, who is pregnant and is in the wedding party, threw an absolute fit saying that she was going to design and make the wedding gown as her Matron of Honor present to the bride. Tell them it would set off a whole family brouhaha if you don't agree. They'll understand. Families are like that. Plus, they'll still come to the wedding so that they can show pity that you couldn't wear their spectacular design, but they won't hate you or be jealous of one another. And everyone will have a good time."

"A gown like yours?"

"Less dog, more Irish. White? Cream? I'll have Ellen send you fabric samples once the storm is over.

We have the new lace machine and this will give my knitters a chance to practice on it."

Agnes started crying, her gorgeous supermodel tears slipping gently down her cheeks, making her look even more beautiful. "Kate. You are the best cousin ever born. It will be a one-of-a-kind Kate Killoy Original."

"As soon as this storm is over, I'll have Ellen get sample yarns and have them worked up. I'll give you a couple of designs, but you will get only two seconds to decide which one because there isn't much time to create the dress especially since we are still working flat out on orders from last month's fashion show. It seems some buyers shot videos of the show which are making the rounds. We've picked up a bunch of new boutiques who now want to carry my line."

"I will decide right away, I promise. Thank you, thank you, thank you." Agnes hugged her and then literally danced out the front door.

The door from the back hall opened. Roger, Kate's newest hire, and a retired state trooper came in and headed straight for the coffee. He loved Harry's one-cup machine with all its fancy pods.

"Was that Miss Supermodel I saw dancing out of here?" he asked.

"Yeah, I have that effect on people."

His chuckling slipped when he looked out

the window. "Looks like we're going to get a good whamming with this storm. Yesterday they talked about the storm turning east once it skirted the New Jersey coast and would line up to hit The Cape and Nova Scotia, but now it has straightened out enough to slam into Connecticut with a possible two to three feet of snow."

"Well, we're in pretty good shape here."

"Where's Harry?"

"Last I heard, he was on the Mass Pike at the rest stop by the Sturbridge exit, waiting for an overturned cab of a tractor trailer to be set back on its wheels. Traffic is horrible with everyone making a mad dash to be home before this storm gets bad. It's getting worse, and the snow has already hit Springfield and Worcester."

Kate's phone buzzed. It was Seamus. She answered, but before she could say anything, Seamus said, *"Kate, there's a problem. Alven's not here, and Kate—there's blood."*

CHAPTER 3

Wednesday noon

"Seamus, talk to me."

"Kate, when we got here, there was no answer, though there were some lights on somewhere inside. I tried the doorknob, and it was unlocked, so I went in calling Alven but got no response, even though his car was still in the driveway. I checked the living room and dining room but saw nothing. When I reached the kitchen, though, someone ransacked it. It looked like there had been a fight. They knocked chairs over, someone had shoved things off the table, the dish drainer was on the floor, a canister of flour spilled on the counter. Plus, Kate, by the refrigerator, there was a big smear of blood on the floor and fridge. I called Tim, and we went through the house but found nothing else disturbed."

"Have you called Sean?"

"Yeah, Tim just called him. We're waiting for him now."

"Have Sean call me when he can. The Golden people worry because Alven planned to speak to them tonight. They weren't able to reach him to tell him they postponed the meeting."

"I'll tell Sean to call you. Oh, I think I hear his car now."

"Find out what you can. I'll talk to you later."

Kate disconnected the call and moved to the stove to make the toasted cheese sandwiches she'd promised for lunch. She put a container of Will's homemade tomato soup into the microwave to re-heat as well.

Roger asked, "Did I hear you talking about blood?"

"Yeah. Alice hadn't been able to get through to Alven about the Golden meeting being canceled. My brothers went over to see if there was a problem since he wasn't answering his cell. What they found was a kitchen torn apart with furniture and counters in a mess. Seamus said it looked like a fight had taken place. He also spotted blood on the floor and the front of the refrigerator."

"Did he call Sean?"

"Yes. Sean had just arrived when I discon-nected. Alven is close to my grandfather's age. I'm worried that something horrible has happened to him."

"Sean will check it out. I assume Buster wasn't there. They'll check the hospitals and other care facilities. The question is, who was in the house with him, and whose blood was on the floor."

Roger went back to work and Kate, feeling restless, headed toward the whelping room to get a stack of towels. The dogs were getting buried under the rapidly falling snow and she should bring them in until their yard had a path near the fence, so that the snow didn't rise to the height that if packed down would be all they'd need to exit the yard. Also, the older dogs sometimes had difficulty walking in deep snow.

When she reached the door to the yard, she heard a phone ringing. It took her several seconds to realize that it was Harry's office phone. It rarely rang. Harry used his cell phone for communication with clients and friends. The reason for the land line was so that he could have a business listing in the area phone book. With Harry not here, she answered the call to tell whoever was on the other end of the line that he wasn't available.

She walked to Harry's desk and picked up the receiver. "Harry Foyle Cyber Security, Kate speaking."

"Thank goodness. I've been trying to contact Foyle for the last hour with no success. I need to speak to Foyle, now."

"Who is calling?"

"George Nason. I've got to speak to Foyle now. It involves a billion dollars."

"I'm sorry, Mr. Nason, but Harry isn't here. The Mass Pike has held him up trying to make it home before the storm halts all traffic."

"This stupid storm couldn't happen at a worse time. I'm going to be ruined. Foyle was right. He told me it was an inside job. I didn't believe him. Now the money's gone, and the company is going to lose all its credibility. This will destroy us."

Kate's phone beeped. She opened the app and saw Harry's car entering the driveway. She saw him turn toward the house, but then, instead, turn toward the barn. Roger must have waived him in so that he could park out of the snow.

"Mr. Nason, I just saw Mr. Foyle arrive. If you call back in about five minutes, he should have made it inside."

"I'll call. He's got to help me."

Kate figured she had a few minutes to go get dog towels out of the dryer before Harry made it into the house. She raced into the whelping room and began loading the two baskets. A slam of the outside door told her he'd arrived. She shoved the last of the towels into the basket and, carrying both baskets, headed into the hall.

Harry wasn't there. She took a couple more

steps toward the kitchen when she heard her husband's voice coming from his office. "You hired me to find out who was stealing from your firm, George. I did. That you chose not to believe me is not my problem—it's yours. The invoice will arrive tomorrow. I stand by my findings."

Kate heard the receiver slamming down onto the phone. She also heard another bang on the desk and then Harry came charging out of the office. He passed without noticing her and pushed open the door to the kitchen, then slammed it. Kate silently counted to five when she heard a yelp and a shout. "Are you kidding me? What kind of madhouse is this?" Finally came the slam of the bedroom door.

She heard a buzz coming from the office, so setting down the baskets, she stepped inside while muttering to herself, "Hello Kate. How's the love of my life?" As she approached the desk, she spotted Harry's cell phone vibrating itself across the slick desktop surface. She looked to see who was calling, not surprised that it was George Nason.

She made an executive decision. Harry was obviously in a snit from driving a two-and-a-half-hour trip in four hours in a snowstorm. But he couldn't let his temper hurt his business. Her grandfather had taught her that. Sitting in his chair, she pushed the button and answered. "Harry Foyle's Office. Kate speaking."

"Where is Foyle?"

"Mr. Foyle is not available. Can I be of help Mr. Nason?"

"Unless you can tell me how a billion dollars could be in the company's account one minute and gone the next, I don't think you can, young lady."

"Have you contacted the bank?"

"That was the first thing I did."

"What did they tell you?"

"They said that they have transferred the money to a numbered account in the Bahamas and for all intents it's gone."

"Well, that's not exactly true. Banks have to play by stricter rules than the criminals. However, Mr. Foyle works occasionally outside the box. You say it just happened?"

"About an hour ago."

"Well, if I could get some information from you, perhaps we could get it back."

Kate's phone buzzed with a call from Sean. "Mr. Nason, could you hold for just a second? One of our operatives is on my other phone. Don't hang up. I'll be right with you." He mumbled his agreement and Kate put him on mute and pressed the button on her phone.

"Kate, Seamus said he told you what we found here. We're checking all the usual places, but that will take a while. Buster isn't here either. Wherever they are,

I suspect they're together. We're going to have Gwyn check the blood, but we know nothing yet. I'll get back to you when I've got something solid."

"Thanks, Sean."

Disconnecting, she reached for Harry's phone but it slipped from her hand onto the desk. As she picked it up again, her finger touched the screen. She must have hit the gallery button, because suddenly she was staring at a photo of a man in his thirties, standing in profile with his arm wrapped around an extremely pretty woman. Why had Harry taken this photo? She checked the date and time and saw that it was today. That's when she recognized the rest stop by the Sturbridge exit off the Mass Pike. She drew a breath and took the call off hold.

"Mr. Nason. We will take some steps to get your money back. Here's what I need you to gather." Kate asked him for a list of numbers, times, names, transfer information, and all paperwork to do with the theft which she needed. "Text the information to Harry's phone. Oh, before I let you go, I'm sending you a photo. Tell me if you recognize the people in the shot." She waited until she heard a gasp and swearing.

"That's Keith Harrison, the man that Harry told me was the thief. I didn't believe him. The woman with him is the wife of our CFO, Molly Allende. She works in our finance department."

"Okay. When we hang up, call the Massachusetts State Police and the woman's husband. When you get through to the state police, send them the photo and inform them that this man is under suspicion of committing a crime against your company. Tell them someone took his photo at the rest stop prior to the Sturbridge exit and saw him traveling with another member of the corporation who is the wife of a board member. Massachusetts will notify the Connecticut State Police since that exit would bring them into Connecticut. They have ways to keep an eye out for them. I'll send the timestamp in the photo. Here's hoping the snow slows them down."

"Foyle took the shot?"

"Yes."

"That's Harrison's Land Rover right behind them, with the plate number showing. I'll call the police and her husband now."

"Do that and then, when you have the information to track the money, just send it. We'll work on the money. You deal with the problems with your CFO," Kate told him, disconnecting.

She sat in Harry's chair for a few minutes, breathing slowly with her eyes closed. When she went to stand, she realized that Harry's cat, Macbeth, had settled in her lap. A hum by her ear told her that William McKinley, who she often called 'Invisicat' because his grey coloring made him difficult to spot in a dim room, had settled on the high back of the chair. She snuggled them and then stood. Putting both phones into her pockets, she went out to the hall, picked up the baskets she'd abandoned, and carried them to the bench by the kitchen door.

When she got back to the door to the yard, a dozen pair of eyes looked back at her from under very snowy coats. She opened the door about two inches and in her firm 'command' voice said, SHAKE! There was an immediate snowstorm by the door. She grinned as all dozen dogs turned into blurs, shaking the snow off their coats. Then she opened the door and let them in. Once she was back by her basket, she called each dog by name to be toweled off and then let into the kitchen. They knew the routine, so none of them pushed ahead. Soon the mostly dry dogs were finding their favorite spots in the house. Kate carried one of the heavy baskets, now filled with wet towels, and kicked the other one down the hall. Once she reached the commercial dryer she'd installed in the whelping room years ago, she loaded the towels and pressed the button to dry them so they'd be ready for the next session.

She needed a cup of tea.

Exhaustion and frustration pushed her to plop on the banquette bench and gulp down a mouthful of tea, before she opened her laptop and pulled up a program she had written. It came in handy when she and Harry were trying to stop a thief from stealing millions and placing the blame on an old friend of Harry's.

Harry's phone dinged with a text. Opening it, she read the information and entered the numbers into her program. Quinn and Dillon snuggled her as she worked. Several hours passed as she labored to make each change to the program designed to find, grab, and retrieve the money. Finally, her program went 'ding.' She'd done it.

Grabbing Harry's phone, she called Nason.

"Mr. Nason, this is Kate from Mr. Foyle's office. We have returned the money to the original accounts. I won't keep you on the phone. You need to contact your bank right away and have the money moved into new accounts. We would also suggest you split the amounts into smaller deposits, which would make it more difficult for such a theft to ruin your company. Yes. You're welcome. I'll tell him you said so. Good luck."

Kate sighed, exhausted, and lowered her head to the table. It had worked.

"Tell me, Kate. Since when have you and George Nason become such good friends?"

Kate screamed! Harry's voice from right behind her ear made her jump, banging her legs on the edge of the table.

CHAPTER 4

Wednesday early afternoon

"Arggggg!" Kate collapsed back onto the bench, fell to her side and curled into a ball, pain radiating up and down her thighs. "Ouch, ouch, ouch that hurts."

All the dogs immediately pushed to get close to her. Quinn squeezed under the table and began licking her face while Dillon crowded in with Kelly right behind.

"Kate, are you okay?"

"Sure, Harry, I'm just dandy. This is simply my time of the day for curling up in a ball of abject pain. Quinn, stop the licking!"

"Pain. The baby? What happened?"

"It's not the baby, you idiot. It's my stupid husband, sneaking up behind me and scaring years off my life. You made me jump up and hit my thighs on the edge of the table. What's the matter with you?"

"With me? I'm not the one on the phone with strange men in the middle of the day."

Kate had just opened her mouth to argue when the doorbell rang.

"Get that." She said, while trying to straighten her legs.

Harry stomped into the living room. She could hear him talking and then he returned, his footsteps letting her know he was still angry.

"What have you been up to while I've been away?"

"What I'm always doing—working."

"Working rarely has people sending you four dozen roses. Who are they from?"

"I lost my psychic powers because of the pain. Why don't you see if there is a card?"

"They're from George Nason."

"Read the card."

Harry stiffened and huffed, but then read.

"These roses are a tiny token of what you did today. You saved my company. I hope Foyle realizes what a treasurer he has working for him. He should triple your salary. By the way, the police have caught Keith Harrison. George Nason."

Kate reached up and pulled herself into a sitting position and glared at Harry. "Well, even I know the triple of nothing is still nothing. But you could make yourself useful by getting a couple of bags of peas from the freezer for my legs, if it's not too much to ask."

Harry looked from her to the flowers and back. He then walked to the freezer, got the peas and handed them to her, then found a vase for the roses, which he put in the middle of the dining room table. Pushing the dogs out from under the banquette table, he sat and asked, "What happened?"

"Well, my husband had to drive four hours instead of two and a half to get back from Boston after he had a difference of opinion with a client. Just before he arrived, the client called, desperate to talk to him. I answered the phone and seeing your car, told him to call back in five minutes. Then I went to continue what I was doing. My husband then stomped into the house, slamming the door, he heard the phone, answered it, I suspect without listening to what the client had to say, vented his temper, threw down his phones, pushed out of his office, ignoring his wife who was standing five inches from his nose, kicked the kitchen door, exploded in rage about the boxes in the living room and then tried to destroy the bedroom door... I hope you got a good nap."

"I did."

"Excellent. The phone in your office rang

again. This time it was your cell. I answered it only to find out that George Nason had had a billion dollars transferred from his accounts to an account in Bermuda. I listened to his problem and got the information, and while I did that, accidentally opened your phone, found the photo of the bad guy, sent it to him telling him how to contact the cops, and his CFO whose wife was with the crook. He sent the information, I pulled up the program I wrote to help your professor friend last fall, and got the money back into his account, whereupon my bad-tempered husband sneaks up on me to scare what few wits I had left out of me." Kate glared across the table at him.

"I didn't see you when I got in. When I woke, I came out to hear what sounded like a friendly conversation with a man who'd insulted me just this morning. I wove my way through whatever you have going on in what was formerly my spacious living room and asked what I thought was a simple question."

"Did you have shoes on?"

"No."

"I rest my case. By the way, he's planning an article for some business magazine I didn't recognize, touting the wonders of Harry Foyle Cyber Security. Here, these peas are losing their chill. Could you put them back in the freezer?"

The back door opened, and she saw her

brothers coming down the hall. They entered the kitchen and Seamus said, "They still haven't found Alven. But Gwyn tested the blood on the kitchen floor and apparently, it's not his. Wherever he is, he's not the one hurt. Sean said they're still checking hospitals."

"Thanks, guys. Hopefully, he's hiding somewhere we haven't thought of yet. I'll see you guys at supper. It was good of you to do this for me."

"No problem. Try not to worry."

They walked toward the front door and Tim yelled back, "What's with the box forest?"

"I'm trying for a new look in the living room."

"Okay."

They heard the front door close.

"Blood?"

"My grandfather's friend was to speak to the Golden Retriever club tonight. When Alice couldn't get in touch with him to tell him they cancelled the meeting, she asked me to have the twins go check on him. Someone trashed the kitchen before we got there in what looks like a fight. Nobody was there, and there was blood on the floor and refrigerator."

Harry looked at her and then reached for her hand. "Will saying I'm sorry, help?"

"Always. But try not to sneak up on me again —at least not when I'm sitting here." She eased her way off the bench seat, standing carefully. Harry stood and scooped her up, carried her into the bedroom, and laid her gently on the bed. He then stood and went to the bathroom to get medicine.

Halfway there, he stopped and said, "I really was a jerk."

"I never argue with a man when he's right."

"I love you."

"I love you too, even when you are a jerk."

Kate eased her jeans down, trying to avoid touching her thighs. A bright angry looking red and slightly purple welt crossed both legs.

"That looks nasty," Harry said, and stroked ointment over the injured area. When done, he helped her ease her jeans on and they headed back to the kitchen. "That snow is building up."

"Which reminds me. You are now part of a traditional ritual that all who live with Shannon Samoyeds must go through each year." She gestured for him to follow her down the hall, past his office, to the rear door. Sitting outside was a sidewalk size snowblower with an electric extension cord hanging off one handle. She held the door while they pulled the machine into the hall and down to the door to the dog yard. "The outlet is up next to the light outside the door. Plug it in and then work your way along the fence all the way around the yard. Be sure you point the vent to the left. It can blow the snow to the center of the yard but the edges will then be free for the dogs to run."

Harry wrestled the machine out into what was now deep snow and got it started. A great plume of snow flew up and landed in the middle of the yard. Kate returned to the kitchen. She smiled at the sight of all the dogs lined up at the French doors in the living room to watch Harry. Kate gently eased herself back onto the bench of the banquette and opened her computer. For the next thirty minutes, she worked on the beginning designs for Agnes' wedding dress. She had some ideas to work Gaelic motifs into the lace of the train, and she wanted to get them programmed.

When she heard the door from the yard open and she saw Harry wrestle the snowblower inside, she stood and went to the French doors. "Who wants to go out and check on what Harry did in your yard?" she asked the dogs and their bouncing enthusiasm was obvious. She pulled open the door, and they raced across the deck in a competition to see who could make it around the track first.

She joined Harry at the dining-room window where they could see all four sides of the track. Quinn definitely had speed. He hadn't been the first out, but he was now at the front and pulling away. His father, grandfather and aunt were all determined to catch him, so they were really moving.

"I missed this while I was away." Harry said.

"Maybe you should try to work more from home. Next year, you'll have both Seamus and Satu in Boston. They could probably do the initial information gathering for you. They've both grown very professional looking. Give them a wardrobe budget where they can get business attire rather than jeans and a tee shirt and they can easily represent the company. I may have hinted to Nason that we have several operatives in the field that report in to us regularly."

Harry laughed. "With your business sense, my business could double in a month. But that's a good idea. I'm fed up with hotels and fast food."

"This way, you could screen the cases. You could assign those cases the kids could handle with their laptops between classes quick and dirty and you'd just have to take the ones that need the Harry Foyle touch."

"I'll talk to them. It will give them work experience that kids coming out of college rarely have."

Rather than returning to the kitchen, they headed to the library. Kate looked longingly at the overstuffed chairs, but decided that getting out of all that softness with injured legs wasn't wise. Instead, she opted for one of the wing-back chairs beside his desk.

"Tell me more about this Alven who is missing," Harry asked once he settled behind his massive oak desk that matched the wooden bookshelves and cupboards that covered all four walls.

"Alven Asch has been friends with my grandfather for over fifty years. They both started working at the same time with Alven doing something with the government and Gramps starting Killoy and Killoy Forensic Accountants. I know that they occasionally worked together. But it was the dogs that really brought them together. Alven has raised Goldens for years and is a judge. So, there was that, plus they always went on vacation together to Winter School, camping out in subfreezing temperatures and climbing Mt. Marcy using ice picks and crampons. It was the highlight of their year."

"Well, you saved my life with those skills your grandfather taught you, so I am thankful."

Kate suddenly stiffened and yelled, "I'm an idiot. It's obvious." She pulled out her phone and place a call. "Sean, is anybody over at Alven's house now?"

"No, but I could get there in about ten minutes if it's important."

"It is. Could you call me once you're in the house? I may know where Alven is."

"Give me ten minutes." He broke off the call.

Harry stared at her but didn't push for answers.

When Sean called her, she asked, "Is Buster's

bowl on the kitchen floor?"

"Buster's bowl? What does that have to do with this case? I'm now in Alven's kitchen. There is nothing on the floor."

"There is a closet to the left of the kitchen door. Can you tell me what's in it?"

"A vacuum cleaner, two brooms, a mop and bucket, and a big garbage can half-full of dog kibble."

"By the front door, there is a coat closet. What's in it?"

He headed back to the front of the house and told her, *"A raincoat, a couple of hats, some wool scarves, a bag of mittens and gloves hanging from a hook on the door, a pair of rain boots and an umbrella are the only other things in the closet."*

"Thanks, and this one is really important. There is a closet by the family room, next to the cellar door. What's in it?"

"Just a minute. A roll-away bed, bedding and extra pillows. One of those blow-up mattresses. And some puzzles and board games, actually he's got quite a collection of them. Are you going to tell me why we are touring the closets at Alven's house? I see nothing suspicious here, Kate."

"Of course, you don't. Because it's not there."

"What's not there?"

"One dog bowl, one water bowl, about a

weeks' worth of kibble, one pair of lightweight snow shoes, one pair of cross-country skis with poles, a down parka, thermal snow boots, two lightweight tarps, a full pack on a lightweight frame, a bivvy, a down mummy sleeping bag, and a metal canister filled with freeze-dried food. There should also be a small, light-weight solar generator and soft, folding solar panels. I don't know where Alven is, but I have a pretty good idea that he's unhurt, in hiding, and ready to travel fast and keep both himself and Buster safe from whoever is trying to kill him."

"Kate, how did you know this stuff was miss-ing?"

"It was a guess. It suddenly dawned on me that when you talked about the blood on the floor and finding the cell phone, nobody had mentioned the dog dishes. It didn't take that much of a leap to figure that if someone threatens Alven's life with enough violence to produce blood, that his first re-action would be to escape. With the storm coming, he correctly figured that he could use the techniques that he and Gramps had mastered in Winter School. I knew what was in the closets because they lectured me one Sunday when he and Gramps were just relax-ing and talking about the old days. Each explained that in case of emergencies, they would keep a full pack, skis, snowshoes, and everything else to be pre-pared. Gramps had the same set up in the whelping room. When I went after Harry and his kidnapper, I could get together all the gear I needed to trail him in the blizzard, in about ten minutes."

"I remember the setup you had in that lean-to. You could have lasted several days except for Harry's injury." Sean said. *"Well, this gives us a whole new area to search. However, following him while the snow is still coming down will be impossible since two-feet has already accumulated."*

"Once the snow stops, we'll have to figure out where he is and how we can help him. Seamus might help with the search using Rex. The drone can have eyes on a lot of territory from the air."

"Good idea. I'd forgotten about that drone. I'll let Gurka know what you figured out. How good was Alven at winter mountaineering?"

"Outstanding! Provided they don't run into any unpredictable wildlife, he and Buster should be fine. The danger will come when the storm ends and whoever is after him, meaning the person whose blood was on the kitchen floor, tries to find him."

Harry reached out and pressed the button on the phone between them, ending the call. When Kate reached for her phone, he took her hand and held it. "If he is half as good as you are, he's probably snug as a bug, even with all the snow. The snow is only this heavy because the temperatures are hovering in the high twenties and low thirties. There is no prediction of temperatures in the single digits or lower, so they should be fine. If they are in a lean-to, the heavy snow should also work as insulation."

Kate smiled, "Once the sun comes out, he can heat water and have something hot to drink. The last time I was at his place, he showed me a solar thermos that can boil water by just placing it in the sun. He also has some soft, folding solar panels and a powerful small lightweight power station, so he can cook and charge any equipment. He showed me the system because I was interested in adding solar to the equipment needed for the search and rescue. It's something you can carry in a pack. Now that I know he's camping rather than kidnapped, I feel a lot better."

Harry frowned at her then said, "Hopefully his hunter isn't an outdoorsman."

CHAPTER 5

Wednesday evening

Harry sat at his desk, staring at his personal laptop. That it wasn't his business computer didn't mean that it lacked all the high-tech software he used for work.

Kate grabbed one of her afghans off the back of the overstuffed chair across from the desk and, after kicking off her shoes, settled in, covering herself with the soft wool blanket.

"I get nothing but dog stuff when I looked Alven up on Google. Since you said he once worked for the government, I'll check into the database of present and retired governmental employees and see what I can find."

Quiet settled over the room and Kate let her eyes drift to the window. She took in the view through the snow across their front porch toward the house where she'd grown up. The snow was getting really deep. The steps up to her mom's porch now showed only two visible, with the three lower steps now buried in snow.

"Ah." Harry's exclamation drew her attention back.

"What did you find?" she asked.

"You were right. He did work for the government. He was a career employee, who retired about five years ago."

"What department did he work for? Does it say?"

"Yes. You say he was a friend of your grandfather?"

"Yes, he was. Why?"

"Well, according to what is in these files, which are not available to the public, your grandfather's buddy worked for the CIA. He was an intelligence operative."

"You mean, Alven was a spy?"

"From what I've learned about your grandfather, he was probably one of the few people Alven trusted with that information."

"I've known Alven all my life and I can tell you right now that he is someone I'd never think of as a James Bond type. He's mild mannered. Is there more information in that file that might give us a clue why he's disappeared?"

Harry went back to the files and checked several pages. Then he said, "Well, this is interesting. Do you remember my mentioning the guy who had the desk next to mine in the DC office? He got the cases I'd just begun when I transferred to the New York Field Office."

"Yes, he had an uncommon name—Ramsey, that was it."

"Right. Ramsey Oliver. He apparently retired quickly after I left. A few days ago, he contacted me. He said that he'd come across something in an old case, one he got when I left. Someone with my skill set should look at. He said that it was important and asked me to come down to Arlington to see him. I planned to go today, but for obvious reasons—didn't. I was going to fly down in the morning, check in with Ramsey, meet our old friend Agent Deshi Xiang for lunch, and then fly back in time for supper. The storm put a kibosh on that. I texted him this morning before I left Boston to tell him of the storm and that our meeting would have to be postponed."

"And you are bringing Ramsey Oliver into this conversation? Why?"

"Because I have found a very interesting coincidence."

"You don't believe in coincidences and neither do I."

Right. But the fact I just found which was interesting is that your pal Alven Asch had a person in the FBI with whom he liaised, and that person was my friend Ramsey Oliver.

"The Ramsey Oliver, who is worrying about something important enough to ask you to fly down to Washington, DC.?"

"The same. And now someone has broken into Alven's home, fought with him, and he's gone into hiding. You're right. I don't believe in coincidence. Something is definitely wrong." Harry said, scowling at the laptop's screen.

"Why don't you give your buddy a call?" Kate asked.

Harry pulled out his phone and keyed in Ramsey's number. It rang four times, then went to voicemail.

"That's odd. He's never more than inches from his phone. Hmm. I'll try him later." He stared across the desk at Kate, looking warm and comfortable under her afghan. "Why don't I cook supper tonight. You rest your injured legs. I'll go lay out what I need for supper and then we can bring in the dogs so that I can snow blow the yard one more time before it gets dark."

Kate smiled. "I like the way you think. Let's go get some towels and dry these snowy puppies."

Harry stood and rounded his desk, then

gently pulled his wife from her comfortable chair and into his arms for a quick but satisfying kiss. Stopping in the kitchen, Harry pulled out what he needed for dinner and then together, they then went to dry the dogs.

Kate sat in the banquette and watched the hill of snow grow in the center of the dog yard. If the amount of snow continued to grow, the hill would become a mountain. Her feet were providing cushioning for the warm fuzzy heads of Kelly, Liam and Quinn under the table. Dillon sat at her side with his head resting gently in her lap. As she watched Harry complete the last section of the yard, she let her mind drift over what they'd just learned about Alven. She remembered once when Gramps and Alven were sitting and talking. When she'd come into the room, they'd stop the conversation and begin talking dogs. She'd always thought that they were guarding their language around her since Gram would have had their heads on pikes if her naive granddaughter started spouting colorful language. But, considering what Harry found today, it was more likely that they were discussing threats against the country and how to stop them.

When Harry got back in, he took the chicken that he'd cut up before going out and put it into boiling water to stew. She watched as he worked at the island, chopping fresh herbs and vegetables. These were tossed into the big stew pot and set to simmer. The kitchen immediately smelled wonderful. Once that was cooking, he pulled out a big bowl and tore a bunch of spinach into it, then rinsed it twice. Diving back into the refrigerator, he pulled out a bunch of vegetables to chop. Next, he added some walnuts, craisins, and cut up several avocados into the bowl. He set that aside and whipped up his homemade French dressing and then put the salad and dressing back into the refrigerator to stay cool while the stew cooked.

"I vote you spend much more time at home. I enjoy watching you cook."

"You do, do you? You enjoy watching me."

"All the time. Say, why don't you try your friend Ramsey again?"

He pulled out his phone and plugged in the number. "It's ringing. Hello, Ramsey?"

"Who is calling?"

"Des, is that you? What are you doing answering Ramsey Oliver's phone?"

"Harry? Why are you calling Oliver?"

"I had a meeting with him for today, but couldn't make it because of the storm. But why do you have his phone? Where's Ramsey?" He put his phone on speaker for Kate to hear.

"Ramsey Oliver is in the hospital. He had an appointment scheduled with Malcolm for an hour ago. Someone shot him in the head as he approached the revolving door entrance of the Hoover building. He's in

critical condition in the hospital. There were no witnesses. We're trying to pull something from surveillance cameras, but so far, we've got nothing. I'll tell Malcolm about your scheduled meeting. He'll be calling you. As far as Ramsey's condition—we'll see if he comes through the surgery."

"Thanks Des. Keep me posted."

Kate looked at him. "As you said, we don't believe in coincidences."

They were still sitting there thinking when five minutes later Roger came in the back door as Seamus and Tim came in the front.

Kate looked up and asked her brothers. "Isn't mom with you?"

"Nope. We left her on a call to someone in California who wants to co-author a book with her. We made her sandwiches and left her a pot of coffee. She was settling in for the long haul when we left."

Roger began setting the table as the boys got the food ready to serve.

"Wow, fancy. What have you done, Harry, that earned Kate four dozen roses? It must have been terrible." Tim said.

"Knock it off." Seamus said, holding the card. "They're not from Harry."

Kate sat, and every male focused on her— none of them smiling. She filled her salad bowl and then looked at Harry and asked, "Do you want to explain?"

Harry frowned at her but said, "Your sister is the newest and most underpaid employee of Harry Foyle Cyber Security. Today, while this bad-tempered bear was recovering from the four-hour drive from Boston, she helped one of my business clients recover a billion—with a 'b'—dollars stolen and sent to a numbered account in Bermuda. Apparently, the owner is now writing an article for a business magazine about how fabulous my company is."

Kate smiled. "The owner of the company told Harry he should triple my salary."

They all laughed, but Seamus reached over and gave her a 'high-five' saying, "Way to go, Sis."

"Thanks, Seamus. They are beautiful roses. And before Harry forgets, earlier we were talking about the fact that he's stretched too thin and overworked because the business is so good. Especially with the need to keep companies safe from cyber theft growing daily. Harry needs to expand the active staff." She looked at Harry and asked, "May I tell them."

He waved his hand. "It was your idea and a good one at that."

"I suggested, Seamus, that since you and Satu will be in Boston for the next four years at MIT, that you both get a clothing allowance to suit yourselves out as fully professional and be the initial contacts for HFCS potential clients in the eastern Massachusetts, southern New Hampshire, and Rhode Island areas. And if that works out, we may take on some other part-timers to handle the New York and New Jersey area. You can keep your eyes out for candidates among the students you meet. You would probably be better judges of the qualifications than Harry in this kind of post. The thing is, you still have to keep up your grades, because of mom, so all it would cut into would be your wild social life."

Tim burst out laughing, and Roger grinned. Everyone knew that Tim's social life was so active that it made up for his twin having none.

"What do you think?"

"Are you kidding me? Wait till I tell Satu. She'll flip. She'll also love the clothing allowance part. She's been checking out some websites with clothes for the business woman. A chance to be professional, which she got a taste of when she went to DC with you, Kate, has had her dreaming. Let's finish supper. I've got to call her."

Harry looked at him. "We'll go over what's expected and you can try some test runs this summer before you leave for Boston. For some unknown reason, my wife would like me to work from my home office here more often, especially with the munchkin on the way. After the push of trying to cover all the bases myself these last few weeks, it seems like a great idea to me too."

"Wow! Harry, this is terrific. You are the best."

"Thank your sister. It was her idea."

Seamus leaned over and kissed Kate's cheek. "Thanks, Kate."

After dinner, there was a speed record clean up provided by her brothers. Roger headed out with the boys. He and Tim were going to watch the game on TV and Seamus to call Satu.

Kate stood and slapped the table. "Well, I'd say this has been a good day. I rescue a company from going under and make two people I love, elated. It was a job well done."

"I suggest we get these dogs fed followed by a quick trip out, and then make an early night of it."

"I like the way you think, Mr. Foyle. I like it very much."

CHAPTER 6

Thursday morning

When Kate woke, both the dogs and Harry were missing. She lay in bed, enjoying the warmth and staring up at the quilt on the wall above her head. Her grandmother had made it. Kate loved the fantasy it created involving her and Harry with the dogs in an enchanted forest. When she heard Harry's voice from the other room, she threw back the covers, put on her slippers and, grabbing her robe, opened the door.

"Malcolm, all I can tell you is that he wanted my input on something that he said required my special skills. I don't know if it is about an old case or something else entirely."

Kate did not know what Malcolm was saying, but Harry waved to her as she headed toward the kitchen to turn on the kettle for tea.

"Well, you know the date I transferred. There were a bunch of cases dumped on my desk that day. I immediately passed all of them on to Ramsey. Have someone pull those cases from the file storage. You might also find out why Ramsey's retirement steamrolled ahead by months soon after that. I'm just saying, have you ever had an agent's retirement push ahead that far?"

The quiet at the other end of the line was telling. Malcolm knew something. He might not know the reason behind Ramsey's shooting, but that silence said that he had a pretty good idea who might know—and he didn't like it. Lots of things had been happening in the Bureau that people would rather forget. Harry's scars made that impossible for her to ignore.

"Right. I'll wait to hear from you." Harry disconnected the call and stared off into space.

"I'm going to go get dressed." Kate said, as she placed a cover on her teacup to keep it warm. "We'll discuss this after breakfast. Roger will be here in a minute, and I just had a ding on my phone telling me we're feeding Sal." She kissed his cheek as she dashed for the bedroom.

By the time she'd dressed, her home was playing host to not only all her brothers, but her mother, grandmother, and Tom's girlfriend Gwyn, a forensic pathologist and childhood friend of Kate's, plus Roger and Sal. Harry was flipping flapjacks with style and the conversation had moved on to how good the spring skiing was going to be next weekend.

"If the Northway is clear, we can drive up to Lake George and stay at Camp, ski every day, and enjoy fantastic meals in fabulous surroundings," Tom said.

Gwyn added, "I think I'll go too and visit my cousin's family, and my friends in Lake George."

"It's a plan." Tim slapped the table and grinned. He quickly related the story of Kate and her billion-dollar rescue, while the women admired her roses.

Her mother and grandmother were chatting about an old friend of theirs, and soon everyone relaxed. There wasn't anything they could do about the storm. Kate looked at her mother, who had never been comfortable around her, startled to see her fitting in. Since she and Harry announced she was pregnant with her mother's first grandchild, her mother's attitude toward her had taken a hundred-and-eighty-degree turn. The tension and constant criticism of Kate for not choosing math as a focus in her life were now history. Though she still didn't understand Kate's life, her mother now seemed to accept it. Kate had her husband to thank for forcing his mother-in-law to see Kate's value.

"Kate, sit." Harry said, putting a plate filled with pancakes, scrambled eggs, and fruit before her.

"Bacon and sausage are disappearing fast. If you want some, grab it off the platter."

"Have you eaten?"

"I got mine before everyone else. As soon as we're done, I'm going to tackle the snow that fell overnight. The dogs don't like it that deep."

Kate relaxed and looked around the table. Sal and her grandmother were chatting. She was glad those two were close, though Sal seemed more subdued this morning. As people finished and stood to go, she spotted Sal reaching across the table to take some plates from her grandmother to stack in the dishwasher. As his arm reached out, his jacket rode up and Kate saw a holster and the butt of a gun at the back of his waist. Sal armed? Why?

As he passed her carrying plates, she reached for his arm and whispered, "Sal, what's wrong?"

He started, glanced around, and quietly said, "There is nothing for you to worry about. You won't be in danger. Just trust me, Kate."

She stared at him for a few seconds before nodding and letting him pass.

Kate turned to find Harry right behind her. She laid a hand on his arm and whispered, "Any word?"

He shook his head.

Her brother Tom stopped Harry and though Kate didn't hear the entire conversation, she heard 'practice later'. Harry nodded and continued loading the dishwasher. She finished her food and stood, clearing her plate and the few other dishes that had escaped the helpful hands that cleaned up as they left. Harry took them to find space in the dishwasher and she headed for the whelping room to get towels, putting worries to one side while dealing with life.

The dogs huddled by the door, not enjoying the depth of the powder snow that made walking difficult. She signaled them to wait and hurried to pull towels from the dryer. As she finished loading the second basket, arms reached over her head to stack them and then Harry carried them to the bench by the kitchen door. The whole routine had gotten so familiar to the dogs that before she knew it, they were inside, waiting for breakfast and Harry was dragging the snowblower outside at the hall door.

Kate's mind whirled with all she'd learned yesterday. Alven had been a spy and, as her grandfather used to tell her, men never stop working a job they love. They may not collect a paycheck, but they liked to keep their hand in. He had been explaining about her great-aunt Maeve and all the former agents and retired NSA and Justice Department—and apparently spies; he worked with over the years. For all she knew, Harry's friend Ramsey might have been one they knew if Gramps and Dad had lived. She wondered if her brother Tom knew about this network and possibly used them.

She was just picking up the dog dishes when Harry came back inside. She put the dishes in the sink as he grabbed a dozen biscuits and they headed for the door. Not a word needed to be said as each dog, oldest to youngest, stopped in the doorway, stacked their bodies as though at a dog show, took their biscuit and dashed out the door.

Back in the kitchen, Harry's phone rang as he reached to put his cup into the fancy coffee maker. Kate had turned on the kettle, but froze when she saw who was calling and pushed the speaker button.

"Hey, Des. Anything new on Ramsey?" Harry asked.

"Ramsey is in a medically induced coma. It was touch and go for a while. The bullet is still in his head. They need to get the swelling down in the brain before they can try to remove it. He's in a vegetative state and will remain that way until the doctors feel it's safe for him to go back under the knife."

"The interesting thing is something is going on over at main justice. They've inquired about Ramsey's being shot, but didn't give us a reason for their interest. Someone, over there, is shutting Malcolm out of meetings as well, which is unusual. He's beginning to suspect we might tie this all to one of those cases you suggested. We're going to find them and check them out. Unfortunately, when they were filed, digitalizing wasn't a priority, so he sent a team to go down into storage this morning. He said to tell you that since the people behind this might see your name listed on these cases, and to keep your head down. In the meantime, I'll keep you posted if we find anything. Just say a prayer that Ramsey pulls through and can give us some idea about what's going on."

Harry disconnected the call and sat staring out the window for a few minutes. Kate heard him mutter to himself, "I wonder if..."

"If what?" she asked.

He turned to stare at her. "When I was working in DC, I had a bad habit of scribbling my thoughts and equations as I worked on cases."

"That sounds normal."

"The only problem was I often scribbled all over the evidence or charging sheet—or whatever paper was lying on my desk."

"Ah, I can see that creating problems."

"The workaround that Malcolm came up with so he didn't have to fire me was that they did not give me the original paperwork. A clerk copied everything from the box, put it in another box, filed the original and gave the copies to me. While he was doing it, he created a digital copy which I would then upload to my cloud account. I'm pretty sure the practice wasn't legit, but it worked for years. It meant, if I woke up in the middle of the night with a workable solution for a problem with a case, I didn't have to drive across DC to check it out. Instead, I could just pull up the file on my computer, print it out, and work my idea on a clean copy."

"What you're telling me is that while your Bureau friends are digging around in the old files in the Hoover Building, you can walk into our library, sit in your comfortable chair, and pull up the same thing."

Harry looked at her and grinned. "Would you care to check out some files with me?"

"Sounds like fun." She picked up her laptop, slipped her arm around his, and they headed to the library.

When they reached the living room, Harry stopped, looked at the boxes and then at her. "Is it safe for me to ask what is going on here?"

"Actually, you know what this is. You've just been so busy that you've forgotten. I'll even give you a hint." She walked to a box beside the sofa, pointed and said, "Nightstand."

Harry looked from one box to another, judging their shapes and sizes. "The second-floor furniture."

"Bingo. It arrived yesterday morning just as the storm was cranking up. I had the men put the carpets and the heavy furniture in the assigned rooms and told them they could leave the smaller pieces for us to put away. They had an additional incentive to hurry in that Agnes dropped in. The deal was if they finished fast, they'd go away not only with bonuses but a personally autographed photo of the lady herself. It was probably the fastest unload they'd ever done. Plus, they were back on the road in under an hour, delighted men."

"You constantly amaze me."

"Your banged shin now forgives me."

"You heard that, did you?"

"Oh, yeah."

They headed into the library.

Harry settled behind the desk and immediately got to work searching for the right file. Kate settled into one of the overstuffed chairs, laid an afghan over her legs, and opened her laptop to her design program. She pulled up the digital model, which was set to Agnes' measurements, and keyed in the codes for the skirt and the top. Then, with her mouse, she made adjustments to the angle of the folds. The first dress was a backless halter sheath with a slit up to mid-thigh. The halter hooked at the back of the neck whereas the front crisscrossed giving it a 'V' neck. She was just planning out the veil when her phone bleeped, telling her she had a text.

She looked at the screen but didn't recognize the number. Clicking to open it, she read, *K. You and H keep your guard up. Don't trust strangers. Take care of EB. Buster and I are fine. A.*

Harry noticed she'd stopped working to stare at her phone and asked, "Who's it from?"

"Giving a guess, I'd say, Alven. He wants us to stay safe and to take care of EB."

"Who's EB?"

"I don't have the faintest idea."

"Well, at least that tells us that spies carry multiple phones."

"Considering the level of equipment, he took; he could also have a small tablet and be more aware of what's going on than either Malcolm or we do."

They worked quietly until Harry's phone rang. He frowned and looked at Kate after looking at the phone. "What did you say those initials were?"

"EB."

Harry pushed the button to answer the phone and put it on speaker. "Hello," he said.

"Is this Harry Foyle Cyber Security? Is Harry Foyle available?"

"This is Harry Foyle speaking, and you are?"

"My name is Everet Blackler. I received a letter in the mail this morning from a man named Ramsey Oliver, who, it seems, is a retired FBI agent. That is the reason I am calling."

"When did you get this letter, Mr. Blackler?" Harry asked.

"It came an hour ago and included this phone number and your address."

"He must have mailed it just before going to DC," Harry said, looking up at Kate. "His fear that something would stop him from talking, prompting him to put his concerns in writing. Right now, his coma may be the only thing keeping the shooter from going after him again. We need to check that he has round-the-clock guards. I've got to talk to Des?"

"Coma? Who are you talking about? Who is Des?"

"Where do you live, sir?"

"My wife and I live in Storrs. She teaches at the university. I am an historian and author and occasionally teach there as well."

"When the snow ends, could you come here to discuss this? Former agent Oliver yesterday went to the Hoover Building to talk to the FBI, apparently concerning you. Someone shot him in the head as he was about to enter the building. He is in the hospital in a medically induced coma until they can bring down the swelling surrounding the brain so they can operate."

"Shot? Because of this? What is going on?"

"That's what we've got to find out. It would help if you could come here and go over all of what information we have been able to collect. We need to figure out why your case is so important as well as find out who shot Oliver."

"Let me talk to my wife. I'll get back to you."

The call ended. Kate and Harry looked from the phone to each other.

"Did any of those three files contain something about Everet Blackler?"

"Yup. Apparently, Mr. Blackler has upset a lot of very important people."

"I want to have it on record for my mother to see, right this minute, that I have done nothing to get bad guys coming after us this time. I haven't even left the house for the last 24 hours."

Harry grinned. "Trouble has found us, anyway."

She tossed off the afghan and stood. "Well, if we're going to be fighting idiots with guns again, I'm going to need another cup of tea."

CHAPTER 7

Thursday lunchtime

Leaving the library, they headed toward the back hall so Kate could gather some towels and Harry could again pull the snowblower inside so it would be ready to go. As they passed the glass door out to the dog yard, they noticed all the dogs staring in, their heads bouncing as though watching a tennis match.

"What's with them?" Harry asked. Then they heard a ding coming from his office. They turned just as a cat went flying up in the air to catch a piece of paper that was shooting across the room. Another paper shot up and cat number two, hunched down and waiting, jumped up to catch it as it flew by.

"What in the world?" Kate and Harry stepped into his office, which did nothing to distract Macbeth and William McKinley, Kate's cats, who had become Harry's cats with the move to the new house.

Beth and Bill, as Harry called the pair, had found a replacement for hunting birds—stalking flying faxes.

The fax machine, which Harry almost never used, had a now overflowing basket, because someone had left a ream of blank paper in it rather than put the package where it belonged in the closet. Kate went to the basket and emptied it while Harry scrambled to collect all the cat's toys before they tore them to shreds. Kate separated the fax sheets from the unused paper and put the blank paper in the cupboard, then gathered the sheets, tapping the edge to align them and searched for a cover sheet.

"It's from Ramsey," she shouted to be heard over the machine. It chose that second to finish, so her announcement was really loud. Reading the cover sheet in her normal voice, she informed Harry that it was research he'd collected recently on the Blackler case. He wanted to discuss it. He must have set it up just before he went to the FBI, because according to this paper, he left instructions to send the fax at ten o'clock this morning.

Harry found a box, and they dumped all the papers inside, after checking under sofas and tables that none had wandered with the help of the cats. Then he picked up each cat to snuggle it. Though Kate had raised them from kitten hood, and named them after characters from one of her favorite children's books, they had become Harry's shadow when he began living with her. After they married and attached their new house to her old one, Harry turned

Kate's old house into his office, and the cats decided that the dogs could have the big house, but they'd stay here with Harry in his office.

With the box of papers safely in his arms, Harry headed to the dining room. Glancing out the window on his way, he decided to examined them later. Kate continued to the whelping room to grab towels yet again. By the time they needed lunch, the dogs had settled and food was ready. Sal and Roger came in talking about Alven being attacked. Sal thought they should all keep careful guard in case there might be some connection through Alven's friendship with Kate's grandfather, Tom Killoy, when he was building his Killoy and Killoy Forensic Accountants business. He mentioned Ann said they were very close and may have worked cases together.

Kate nodded and laid out the food, but her mind was on the box of papers in the dining room. When everyone had eaten, the former cops left for the kennel. Harry told Kate that he had to see Tom about something but would be back in about an hour.

"Would you like me to see if I can redo the cat's sorting system of the papers that Ramsey sent?"

"That would be great. I'll call Des when I get back and see if there is an update on Ramsey."

Two minutes later, silence filled the house.

Kate made another cup of tea and settled down to work at the dining room table with the box on the chair beside her. She first located the papers, which hadn't been part of the cat's game. Placing the cover page to one side, she checked the stack that followed to see if there were page numbers. No such luck. That meant that every page had to be read, understood, and assigned their specific place in the document. She looked back into the box and noticed that it was about a third full, maybe fifty or sixty pages. This was going to take a while.

The first sentence of the document Ramsey sent said that this was for Harry's eyes only. He had then begun talking about one case Harry handed to him when he left. The case wasn't a standard crime, but it was a case against a man who was writing a biography of a general, apparently now dead, who had fought in the Vietnam War. The premise was that the author was going to publish information that various members of the government would rather not see the light of day.

Kate had finished sorting the organized part of Ramsey's information and was trying to figure what would come next, when she heard plowing going on in the driveway. She glanced out the window and saw that the heavy snow had ended, and what fell was barely flurries. The sun was even struggling to make an appearance.

She stood and stretched. She needed another cup of tea and should thaw out some of the muffins she'd made last week. Using one of the new recipes that Will had created that were both good for pregnant women and delicious, she'd made enough for a small army. There would be many people in and out with all the snow. Having muffins on hand would keep them happy in the battle against this weather.

Looking out, she saw Tim behind the wheel of the truck, plowing the driveway again. It looked as though Roger had finished plowing all the outside runs for the boarding dogs, because they were now outside enjoying the first peeks of sunshine. When she looked out the front window, she saw Seamus had almost finished plowing the sidewalks. He had stopped to shovel the front steps of mom's house. Having no school today had worked out well to allow for cleanup, especially since her weather app was giving them no chance to avoid the next storm. It was coming from the west rather than the south next time.

Kate made tea and put a muffin on a plate, then settled back at the dining room table. Setting the organized work to one side, she stared at the papers, which were now roughly covering about half the table. She studied them for a minute and judged by the pile that all but one bunch seemed to have fallen into clumps. The other papers, which were slightly wrinkled, seemed to have been the victims of the 'catch the paper birdies' game the cats had been playing.

Using that as her guide, she began making

separate piles of likely groupings. The most messed-up bunch she set to her left, and after leafing through it quickly, found Ramsey's name at the bottom of a page. Carefully working to associate the first group of words on one page with the last group of words on another, she could slowly build a stack out of the most cat imprinted pages.

Apparently, sitting still for long periods was not something that the baby enjoyed. A round of kicks and movement told her to get up and take the kid for a walk. She headed for the living room intending to check that the movers had placed the rugs, beds, bureaus and dressers in the correct rooms, when her phone beeped telling her that a car had entered the driveway.

The living room windows gave her a good view of a black SUV that was pulling up in front of her porch. Glancing left and right, she noticed that none of her relatives appeared to be anywhere around. Remembering Sal's warning, she quickly dashed to the French doors, using hand signals to get Liam and Dillon to come and let them in before the other dogs joined whatever game she had in mind.

The sound of footsteps on the front steps had Kate opening the front door, and locking the security storm door Harry had the builders install. As the heavy bolt fell into place, a man wearing no coat but in a dark suit, white shirt, and conservative tie walked across the porch.

He approached slowly, checking out their surroundings, but then focused on Kate as he reached the door.

She could tell when he spotted her, and saw two white dogs, their tails not wagging, standing still and focused beside her. Kate did not smile but tilted her head, waiting to hear what he had to say.

"Excuse me, mam, does Harry Foyle live here?" the man asked, his tone firm and businesslike.

"Who's asking." She said as she studied the man before her. His coloring was as dark as Malcolm's, but his eyes were almond-shaped with a slight upward tilt. They appeared dark brown, almost black. He wasn't tall, about her size, but he was arresting in his appearance. The word 'dapper' came to mind. His beautifully cut suit, and his stylish shoes were probably Italian, as well as his shirt silk. He not only appreciated high style, it seemed he had the pocketbook for it. She judged he was probably in his late forties. His cultured speech showed no noticeable accent.

"My name is Isaac Evans, mam. I'm a CID Inspector and I need to speak with a former FBI agent, Harry Foyle. Does Mr. Foyle live here?"

"I'm afraid that Mr. Foyle is not here at the moment. Do you wish to leave a message or perhaps check back later?"

"Are you Mrs. Foyle?"

"Yes, I am."

"Well, mam, I will check back. When you speak to him prior to my return, tell him that Oliver sent me." He turned and walked back to his car, and left.

As she closed the door, she pushed the button on her phone, hit speaker and after two short rings, someone answered, *"AIC Bullock's office, who is calling?"*

"My name is Kate Killoy and if possible, I'd like to speak to Malcolm."

"One moment please, Miss Killoy."

Kate heard someone put her phone on hold, but only a few seconds later, she heard Malcolm Bullock's voice ask, *"Kate, what's up?"*

"Malcolm, I've just had a man drive up in a government issued SUV, and ask to see Harry. He identified himself as Isaac Evans, a CID Inspector. When I told him that Harry wasn't here, he said that he would return later. He also said something strange. He said to tell Harry, 'Oliver sent me.'"

"Oliver? As in our Ramsey Oliver? Give me some time to look into this. When Harry gets back, tell him about this, and that'll I'll be talking to him after I do some checking. Thanks for the call, Kate."

"You're welcome. Keep us posted about Ramsey."

"Will do."

She wove her way through the box forest and sat in the middle of the living room sofa as both dogs defied her rule of no dogs on furniture, and bounded up to settle next to her. They pressed in close and she hugged them, asking, "What in the world is going on?" Their response was face-licking.

Kate's memory began itching. Somewhere, she he remembered seeing the name Isaac Evans. She stood, pushing the dogs to the floor, and went to make tea. As she passed through the dining room, the box of papers that Ramsey had sent caught her attention. The memory stirred and. she reached into the box to grab a fistful of papers. Tapping the ends of the sheets on the table, she started flipping through them, scanning each as it went by. She was three-quarters of the way through when something caught her eye. Backing up a few pages, she checked each paper until she spotted the name. It was on the first sheet of the charges against Blackler alongside those of Harry and Ramsey Oliver. Isaac Evans was not only an investigator, but they had assigned him to analyze the charges against Everet Blackler. Why was the army interested in this investigation?

CHAPTER 8

Thursday afternoon

Dillon pressed tightly as she pulled out a chair and sat with Liam glued against her other side. She brought out her phone again and texted Harry. Where are you? I just had a visit by a man named Isaac Evans, who is a CID Investigator. He was looking for you.

It took less than a minute before her phone buzzed with a reply.

Did he say what it was about?

No, but I just found his name on the charging document that Ramsey sent.

Sit tight. I'm coming.

It was less than five minutes later when Kate heard clumping steps on the front porch. She headed to the door, following the dogs, so she could unlock and open it, as well as flip the lock on the storm door. It surprised her to see Harry and Tom removing snowshoes from their feet before they came in.

"Since when did either of you know how to snowshoe?"

Tom looked at Harry, who said, "Kate, when you came after me during the snowstorm last fall, you saved my life. That wouldn't have happened if you hadn't known how to use these snowshoes. Tom and I got talking after that. He told me that though he used the new style of shoes on that occasion, he didn't feel confident on them. We both decided that you shouldn't be the only one who had the skills to do rescues in deep snow. We ordered the snowshoes and have been practicing. When the snow stopped earlier, we decided we'd put on the snowshoes and practice today."

Tom broke in. "What your tactful husband is trying to say is we would all feel guilty if the only person in this family who could do that kind of rescue with all these storms, would be the pregnant lady."

"You guys do know pregnancy is not a crippling disease, don't you?"

Tom winced but said, "Kate, this is mom's first grandchild. You've seen what that sole fact has done. She's had an entire personality change. She would completely freak out if we asked you to trek out and do a rescue again while you were carrying her grandchild. Math degrees or not—we would all be dead."

Kate laughed. "You're right. And to tell the truth, I get tired more easily these days. Next winter after the baby is born, we can all go out together on a hike at one of the state parks or up at camp and make a day of it."

Harry added, "I figure if Alven can do it in a full pack, including a solar setup at his age, it's something we can learn. What's this about a CID Investigator?"

Tom told them he had a job of his own to do. He and Harry decided that if they could, they'd get in another session, maybe with the others, that afternoon.

"Others?" Kate asked,

"The twins, Satu, Gwyn and even Agnes, are getting into it. By the time we're done, winter rescues will be easy."

Tom left and Kate showed Harry what progress she had made with the cat's flying paper adventure. "The beginning of the message was intact. The batch I was working on when junior decided I needed to do a walk-about, are from the end of the message. It is definitely from Ramsey. Working from the end forward, I'm matching the end of each page to beginning of the next page. I haven't been stopping to read, so we'll have to review what it says once it's back in order. It was on the first page that I found our CID man's name."

"Look, lunchtime is coming up. Why don't I take over feeding whatever masses show up while you continue on your system? If you're not done when we finish eating, I'll take a section and try to follow your pattern."

Kate settled at the table again, though this time she had Liam and Dillon doing bookend imitations at her sides. She had completed another section when the back door opened and both Roger and Sal strolled in, intent on the coffee machine. They talked about the pair of Siberian Huskies kenneled together. The dogs had not wanted the snow removed from their run. "Ryder and Buck were practically wallowing in it. It got to where they were moving the snow around so effectively, I thought to hitch them up and tell them to clear the sidewalks."

When the laughter died, both Harry's and her phones dinged, announcing someone in the driveway. It seemed the subject of the investigation had arrived just in time to eat.

"Set another place at the table, Roger." Harry told him. "We're about to have company. My newest client is coming to the door."

Harry held open the door and waited for the man to get out of the car and mount the porch steps. Everet Blackler looked less like an academic, and more like a member of the Olympic weightlifting team. The man was as tall as Harry. But where Harry's muscles were lean and toned, Blackler's bulged. His down parka was open over a rugby shirt that outlined every curve of his chest and it was a massive hand he held out to shake with Harry as he came in the door.

"Mr. Blackler. I'm Harry Foyle and this is my wife, Kate. I hope your drive wasn't too bad. I assume they plowed the interstates."

"Actually, once I got to the interstate, it was easy. Ah, what beautiful Samoyeds," he added as Dillon and Liam came forward to meet the visitor. "I knew someone who had dogs like these. I thought I recognized this address. It was one of your neighbors, but I don't remember this house being here the last time I was in the area."

"No, it went up in December. We've only been in the place since Christmas. It came in on five trucks and they bolted the whole thing together in two days. We were just about to have lunch. We can talk about your case after we eat." Harry guided him through the dining room on the way to the kitchen. The pile of paperwork caught Blackler's eye.

"Is that about me?"

"Yes. And a very confusing mess it seems to be. Perhaps once we all eat, you could give us a quick overview of the problem which led to this case."

Blackler stopped short at the view out the dining-room window. "Oh my, there are more Sams, lots more."

Kate went through to the whelping room, grabbed towels, and invited all the dogs into the hall. She hurried through the routine and dried each pup, with Sal giving her a hand. Then, after throwing the final towel into the basket, she opened the kitchen door, let them in, and followed behind while Sal took the towels to be dried.

As the dogs milled around, their guest settled at the table, greeting each white fluffy by giving good firm rubs on their heads. Harry made him coffee while Kate fixed herself some tea and they served lunch.

"Mr. Blackler," Kate asked. "I'm told you are writing a book. Can you tell us something about it?"

"Well, I was writing a book. Since this problem has cropped up, that entire part of my life has been put on hold."

"I'm a reader. What kind of book was it?"

"A biography. It is a story, which began in Vietnam, of a soldier who rose through the ranks until he became a general."

"It sounds interesting." Sal put in. "I served in Nam, though it's not my favorite part of the world."

Kate listened as the men discussed different wars and the chaos inflicted on places around the world by the use of massively destructive armaments. She realized that the world her child would inherit had many dangerous flaws. However, as she listened, she heard arguments she'd heard before—word for word. Several times, when she was with her grandfather and Alven, they had held those exact conversations. Kate looked at Blackler. There had to be some connection.

Harry asked him about the case which was created against him. "Did they have you sign anything, or did they record any of your statements?" Harry asked.

"No. I didn't make any statements. I barely got a word in edge wise. I also signed nothing. In fact, I did not know why I was there or what was in the papers they were waving in my face. It didn't matter, though. Word got out that I was in trouble with the government and my publisher dropped me. They trashed my reputation. My ability to earn a living was impaired. My life dropped into the toilet. I don't know why, but my wife and family stuck by me and we've been surviving. A relative of my wife's retired from the government, has been looking into what happened and he told me to keep a low profile. I have and things had been quiet—until now."

"I have a couple of questions for you before we get bogged down in details," Kate said. "First, if that information in your research which is locked away became known, would I see it on the front page of every newspaper in the country?"

Everet looked at her for a minute and then said, "Probably. What's your other question?"

"Do you know who attacked Alven Asch?"

Kate had never seen a person's face actually lose all color the way Blackler's did at that minute. She worried he would pass out. He tried to stand, muttering something about having to leave, and almost knocking over his chair.

The dogs hindered his exit. Realizing something was happening, they all stood and crowded around his legs.

"Would it help?" Kate asked as she laid a hand on his arm, "if I told you I've known Alven since I was in diapers and he texted me to make sure you were safe?"

"You know where he is?"

"Relatively—to within a half mile or so."

Blackler stared at her in confusion.

"Kate," Harry said as he walked around Blackler to stop him from leaving. "Stop confusing the man."

Turning to Blackler he said, "Kate's friend Alven is camping out somewhere in the acres of woods between his property and ours."

"Camping—oh right. Winter school," Blackler muttered.

"You've heard the stories of his romps up to Mt. Marcy's summit in the snow and ice, too," she said, grinning.

"He took me a couple of years ago. He'd lost the friend who'd used to go with him and he decided I would do as a healthy if inexperienced replacement. Alven is my wife's great-uncle."

They put their conversation about Alven on hold as Sal, and Roger returned to work. Harry theorized that this project might take a few days, and Blackler said he'd made reservations at a motel nearby. Harry suggested Blackler go check in while it was still light and plan to come back for supper. By then, hopefully, he and Kate would have the paperwork organized so that they could start working to undo the destruction this case had brought to his career. s

Blackler agreed. After he left, both Harry and Kate went to work putting the last pages of Ramsey's message back in order. With their new client's livelihood hanging in the balance, it was vital they do it and work fast.

Kate looked at Harry. "Mr. Evans will be back later. I wonder what he has to say about this threat against Everet? I think you and he need to talk."

CHAPTER 9

Thursday evening

With the departure of their guest, they settled in at the dining room table to bring order to the piles of papers. Before Harry began, he called his assistant Sadie and filled her in on the CID Investigator who had talked to Kate.

"It sounds, from Kate's description, that Mr. Evans might have a heritage that could include Vietnam. Many black soldiers met and married Vietnamese girls, and though they couldn't bring them with them when the government airlifted all the troops and personnel out of the fallen country; many Vietnamese later escaped using small boats." Sadie chuckled. "It would be interesting to know why the Army is getting involved with what was initially FBI business. Let me do some checking and I'll get back to you later."

"Oh, while I've got you on the phone, Kate came up with the idea to use the kids once they're settled in Boston as the initial approach to new cases in the greater Boston area. We could give them a wardrobe allowance, and I thought we could try some dry runs this summer. Kate would like me to be closer to home more of the time with the baby on the way."

"Well, at last. You're finally thinking like the head of a company. All this running around, leaving your wife to manage the home fires, so to speak, has been ridiculous. If this works out, you might check out some non-students as well. Every so often I come across someone who'd be perfect for the bureau, but because of life commitments, can't apply. I'll keep my eye out. That's how Tom Killoy grew his business at the start. Talk to Ann. She'll give you some ideas. Her husband involved her completely at the beginning."

"That sounds like a brilliant plan. I think she's coming to supper tonight. I'll tell her what I want to do then. She might have some perfect suggestions." Harry ended the call and turned back to the table. Kate's pile of sorted pages had doubled while he was on the phone.

For the next hour, they worked quietly, matching up information until finally, all the pages were in order. "At last, we can know what Ramsey wanted to tell us." Kate said, standing and stretching. She headed to the kitchen to make another cup of tea and use the bathroom while Harry sat and read the information that Ramsey had sent. When she returned, he was not looking pleased.

"What does he say?" Kate asked.

"Apparently, the subject of Blackler's biography was a man with a secret. He kept diaries all his life. Blackler has those diaries hidden, and he isn't giving them up. The problem with the case against our author is that he has the books legally."

"Hm, I wonder how he managed that?"

"I'll leave it to you to ask him after supper."

As they got supper organized, they found their numbers growing. They were soon up to a dozen for dinner. Harry baked some chops and had several vegetables available, along with applesauce. Ann would bring a few loaves of freshly baked bread and dessert.

Everet Blackler returned just prior to supper, and Harry told him they had organized the information that Ramsey Oliver had collected about the case. As soon as they finished eating, they would go over it with him because they had a good number of questions.

Sal and Roger came in the back way as Ann, Gwyn, and Tom came in the front. Kate took the bread from Ann and put the loaves in the warming oven. Sal joined Ann at the table. They were all chatting about the timing of when the second storm would come when Kate's brothers, Satu and her mother arrived.

Her mother walked into the kitchen to see who was there and cried out, "Everet. What are you doing here?"

"Claire, I could ask the same of you. I didn't know you knew Harry Foyle."

"Know him. He's, my son-in-law. Kate is my daughter."

"I knew you had sons, but I didn't know you had a daughter."

Claire paused, embarrassed, as Kate and everyone else in the room looked down or away from her. Then she glanced at Kate, saying, "Well, that's my fault. I have neglected my daughter all her life because she was independent and I wanted her to be just like me. I am just finding out what a wonderful daughter I have."

Startled, Kate looked up at her. It was all she could do not to drop her jaw in shock. Her mother reached over and squeezed her hand, and for the first time, Kate squeezed back. It was going to take work to build this relationship, but she was beginning to think it might be worth the effort.

Kate took the papers which had been on the dining room table, set them aside, then she laid out a cloth while the others helped set the table

"What are those papers?" her mother asked.

"They're to do with Mr. Blackler's case. Someone sent them to Harry, hoping the information would help. We'll be looking them over following this delicious dinner Harry has made." She encouraged everyone to sit.

"What does she mean, your case, Everet? Does Harriet know about this? What is going on? Is Harriet, okay? Are the children safe?"

"Claire, I know you don't pay any attention to politics or what goes on in the news, but this has something to do with the mess about my research, which Harriet must have mentioned."

"Oh, Harriet told me about that. It was all a big mistake, wasn't it?"

"Well, it is coming back to haunt me. Harry and Kate are helping me straighten it out."

Kate, impatient to get some of her questions answered, frowned and said to him, "What strikes me as odd, Everet, is why this is becoming such a big deal now? Harry left the Bureau a couple of years ago. He had barely looked at the evidence in your case when he left for Manhattan, and that was the last he saw of your case. He ended up working on another project where a rogue agent shot him. If it hadn't been for Sal, he'd be dead. Thank God he survived, but following that incident, he left the bureau and set up his own company. Your case went to the agent, Ramsey Oliver. According to his note, he was then told it was over and it never went to trial. He retired soon after and Harry assumed the case was dead."

"However, yesterday, Harry got a call saying that something was blowing up in Washington involving this case. Last night, he heard someone shot Ramsey in the head on the steps of the Hoover Building, and was in a coma. Plus, Alven, who perhaps is involved with the case, has disappeared under very suspicious circumstances."

"What I want to know is why did a simple case, uncontested and filed away, bring a CID agent here this morning looking for Harry, to 'assist' him? Why now? What has raised this case from the dead, to where someone is attempting murder?"

Everet stared at her, getting more upset by the minute. "I don't know. I deal with history, not the present day. I feel this whole thing is racing out of control, and I'm frightened for myself and my family."

Claire laid her hand on his arm. "Then it's good you came here. If anyone can figure this out and stop these people after you, it's my daughter and her husband."

She turned toward Kate as the timer went off on both the microwave and oven. "However, Kate, eat before you do anything else. You have my grandchild growing inside you and you must take care of that baby. You two sit down. Sal, Roger, Ann and I will get the food on the table."

As Kate watched her mother talking to Everet Blackler, Sal and Roger, she was shocked to find that the single-minded woman who had raised her could be charming. Conversations with her children while they were growing up rarely strayed from the subject of mathematics. It convinced Kate that math was everything her mother thought about. She couldn't understand what her father saw in her mother. He was not only a loving parent, but one interested in a broad number of topics, even though his work revolved around mathematics. Her brothers were interested in math, so they were safe from criticism. At least most of them. When she'd chosen to get her degree in fashion design, it took both her father and grandfather to get her mother to agree. However, she never accepted it. Three months ago, her younger brother, Tim announced he wouldn't be attending MIT with his twin brother in the fall, but would study political science at Boston College, it took the whole family plus their parish priest to calm her down and get her to agree.

As Kate grew up, she shared with her father and grandfather the hobby of breeding and showing dogs. Her mother fought against that because she wanted Kate's total focus to be on math. She didn't win. Nor did she win when Kate chose a career studying Fashion Design. This split led to not speaking. Her skills had developed into two successful businesses, her own fashion house, and a career raising and training dogs. This war with her mother had led Kate to avoid her as much as possible, and made her life painful since they barely spoke. Now, as Kate looked across the table at the person chatting amiably with the others, it was hard not to wish that somewhere during those growing-up years, she could have met this woman.

As the others were finishing their coffee after dinner, Kate decided to try an experiment. Following her father's death, her mother declared she wanted nothing to do with the dogs. She'd avoided them ever since. Kate stood and went to fill the dog bowls. Using the island her brother Will had encouraged her to include in the kitchen of this three-month-old house, she pulled open a bin which held their kibble, and the small refrigerator which held their fresh food. She quickly mixed it, adding water for those who wanted their food wet. She nodded at Sal, who left the table and walked into the living room to open the French doors.

Immediately, the house filled with excited dogs, some barking, and some like Quinn, racing around bouncing from person to person, looking for love. Everet gave him a snuggle.

Kate watched her mother stiffen, but then something caught Kate's eye. Rory, Quinn's great-grandfather, was among the last to come in. He stopped for a minute in the doorway, looking around the room. Then, pulling his body into an alert stance, he trotted around the table to the place where her mother sat, and stood, perfectly stacked, looking up at her. Taking a step forward, the magnificent old dog then lowered his head onto her lap. The gasp from her mother turned into a sob as she reached out her arms to encircle his head and laid hers on top. Tears streamed down her face as she cried out, "Rory, Rory."

Gasps filled the room as the members of her family watch Claire hugging this dog who had been her husband's constant companion. Kate realized that since Rory had been with him constantly, he'd also been with her mother. Fighting back the tears that were suddenly filling her eyes, Kate drew a long shuttering breath and said, "The old guy still loves you, Mom."

Her mother looked up, her face covered with tears, and said, "I didn't realize that the day I lost John—I lost Rory too. I told myself that it was too painful to be around him because he reminded me so much of your father. I should have seen it for what it was, another loss. I couldn't even admit to myself that I missed this dog. I fought you and the dogs because I couldn't take the hurt. The boys talked about how they worried about you, Kate, sitting in that yard surrounded by the dogs for days on end. They said it was the only way you could deal with your father's and grandfather's deaths. I resented you, but didn't know why. I realize now you were finding a path through grief that I couldn't." Claire sat up and patted Rory's head, which had turned as Kate stacked up the bowls and, after hugging him once more, said, "Go eat."

Harry stepped up next to Kate and grabbed one stack of bowls while Kate took the other. As she stepped away from the island, the dogs moved to form a semi-circle, Rory slowly taking his place. Kate started at one end of the group and Harry at the other, placing a bowl of food in front of each dog. Once the bowls were down, Kate signaled them to eat. They finished quickly and again sat. After they picked the bowls up, Kate grabbed two fistsful of biscuits, stuffing half into her pocket and headed down the hall. She opened the door, and each dog, from oldest to youngest, repeated their routine, received a biscuit, and dashed out into the yard.

The emotional evening settled, and conversations moved on to be more about Everet's case. He and Harry put off until morning, examining the documents Ramsey Oliver sent. The day had been too eventful for them to wrap their heads around what was happening and come up with viable solutions. Soon, everyone decided they needed a good night's sleep and headed out.

Harry let in the dogs. Kate watched Rory move to heel position as Clair stood and picked up her knitting bag. He moved at her left side to the door. She stopped when she got there and he sat, looking up at her.

Kate had a thought and asked, "Mom. Would you like Rory to spend the night with you? You're coming to breakfast so I'll feed him with the others and he can play in the yard all day."

"Could I? I'd really love that, Kate." She smiled down at the dog stroking his head, then stood straight, opened the door and said, "Rory, heel."

As her mom and Rory went down the porch steps, her younger brothers followed, grinning. Ann stepped forward to hug her. "I don't know how this happened today, but I love it. I'm so proud of you. I haven't seen Claire that happy and relaxed in years."

"It has been an interesting day all around," Kate said, hugging her grandmother back as she, Tom, and Gwyn then headed out. Everet also left, saying he'd see them in the morning.

Suddenly, the house was quiet. Kate leaned into Harry, allowing the stress of the day to fall away. "Go get ready for bed while I lock up," he told her as he kissed the top of her head. "Tomorrow may be even more stressful than today when we finally find out what this case is all about. You need your rest to get ready."

He kissed her again and then turned her toward the bedroom as he headed for the hall to lock the doors and to say goodnight to the cats and dogs.

CHAPTER 10

Friday, early morning

K ate woke slowly, warmth surrounding her. A large hand was resting possessively on her stomach. She stared across the room and out the large window that faced the woods across the driveway. The sun had not yet made an appearance, but there was an early glow of twilight providing a faint grey shine. It was enough to let her see the snow had stopped. All was quiet, and she sank back into sleep when two things happened. First came a need to use the bathroom and second, she remembered what awaited her outside this room today.

"You just remembered what we've got on the agenda."

Kate twisted and kissed Harry's bristly cheek as she rolled from the bed, saying, "You're right. Plus, Baby has just stomped on my bladder." She dashed for the bathroom as Harry reached out to run his hand over the warm spot that had held his wife. He closed his eyes and smiled, only to feel his hand nudged by a cold, wet nose. "Coming," he called as he rolled onto his back and swung his feet to the floor while grabbing some sweats to throw on. The dogs lined up at the French doors facing the deck. He rubbed each of the three heads, then opened the door. Their white bodies shot across the deck toward the path he had made yesterday. Moving quickly, Harry went to the living room. As he reached the French doors, the full crew of eager Samoyeds watched the first three round the corner of the great snowy mountain. He opened the door and all the new competitors joined the race.

Next, he headed to the kitchen. He turned on the coffeemaker, the oven, and the teakettle. Then he pulled a mixing bowl from the cupboard in the kitchen island. After that, he took a dozen eggs, along with some tomatoes, mushrooms, and cheese from the refrigerator. He broke the eggs into a bowl and chopped everything else. Combining everything, he added spices, poured the bowl's contents into a large casserole, and when the oven buzzer sounded, he slipped it in and set the timer. Next, he grabbed a pound of bacon, which he laid out on a baking sheet and put into the second oven on a low heat and set that timer.

Kate was just leaving the bathroom when he got there. Showered, and dressed, her skin was pink from the warm water, and her hair still damp and very curly. He leaned in for a kiss as he passed her on the way to take a shower and dress. When Kate got to the kitchen, she pulled a loaf of bread from the refrigerator, sliced it, and was just loading slices into the four-slice toaster as she heard the kitchen door unlock and Roger walk in.

"I just had a text from Sal. He'll be here for breakfast. Apparently, Sarah has made yogurt smoothies for breakfast. That daughter-in-law of his doesn't realize that men need more than fluffy food to start the day."

"Sarah is getting strange cravings because she's pregnant again. Unfortunately, she doesn't realize that her husband and father-in-law will not thrive on her mother-to-be diet." Kate'sphone went ding, and she glanced out the window, spotting Sal's car entering the driveway. She heard steps on the front porch and the sound of Harry opening the front door to her brothers. Their voices, along with her mother's, called a greeting.

Sal came through the back door, and everyone gathered in the kitchen. They sat, and they passed plates of food around. A companionable silence settled while everyone ate. Tim told Harry he'd finished plowing everything but Gram's driveway where it circled the house to her garage. Harry said he'd take care of it after breakfast. He realized Tim and Seamus had to leave soon, because if the roads were clear, school would be open.

Claire thanked Harry for the breakfast, saying she was heading out for work. Yale would be open and she had classes. She hugged Seamus for bringing her car up to the porch and, on her way out the door, called back for Kate to take care of the baby. Kate shrugged as she realized her mother's attention was far more focused on her grandchild that her own child, then laughed at herself. She better learn to accept what would probably be the best she could ever hope for from her mother.

Once the crowd left and Sal and Roger returned to the kennel, Harry and Kate quickly let in and dried the dogs. Harry pulled the snowblower down the hall again and went to work. It took more work to blow the snow this time as the dogs had packed it down, but Harry soldiered on as the dogs watched. Kate was just starting the dishwasher when her phone buzzed with a text that startled her.

B. & I are safe. Warn H old case dangerous. Protect EB. Beware FBI and JD. Don't search. Contact soon. A. A.

As she stared at her phone, Harry's phone, which was lying on the kitchen counter, buzzed. He had a text from Blackler telling them to expect him in thirty minutes.

She was still staring at the phones when the dogs began circling and she realized Harry was finished and these guys needed food. After shoving her phone into her pocket, along with Harry's, she laid out the bowls and quickly filled them with dog breakfasts. She had just finished piling the bowls when Harry came in and grabbed the first pile. The dogs moved into position without being asked, and they quickly completed the meal. After gathering dog's dishes, she saw that Harry's large hands held a dozen biscuits. She opened the door to the hall and strode to the yard door. Then, taking the biscuits and without having to tell them anything, the dogs lined up in order, stacked, got their treat and bounded out to inspect the newly cleared path.

Closing the door, Harry moved past her, saying he was going to plow out the last part of her grandmother's driveway. She stopped him to say that Blackler would arrive in about thirty minutes. Kate handed him his phone and showed him hers with the text.

He stared for a minute and grumbled, "This text answers the question of whether he had not only an extra phone but probably his tablet. This whole situation is getting weirder by the minute. We need to know more about Blackler and Alven's connection."

"That's one thing we need to ask him when he arrives. In the meantime, I know you'll want to check up on Ramsey, but be careful what you share with Des."

Harry pulled the keys off the wall by the back door and hurried across the driveway to the truck.

Back in the kitchen, Kate filled a cup with tea and then uncovered the piles of paper they'd organized yesterday. She opened her laptop and found the file Harry had sent her with Blackler's case. She checked to see the size of the file, then hit print and headed into the library to be sure there was enough paper in the printer.

Her phone buzzed with a text from Harry. *Tom and I are taking twenty minutes to practice snowshoeing. When EB comes, find out exactly who is after him—if he knows.*

Kate returned to the dining room table and set the pile of paper Harry had in his file on the table next to the information that Ramsey had sent. She decided she would check out both stacks of the paperwork and label them by topic. Obviously, if there were charges, they had to be about something someone thought was a crime. Job one was to find the crime or crimes.

A cup of tea appeared at her elbow. She hadn't heard Harry return, though he now sat across from her and picked up the papers she had finished reading. "I see you've started with the case. What do you think?"

"Well, I'm not a lawyer, as they say, but even a layperson can see that the case is bogus. It's quite obvious that they don't want Everet to write his book. However, according to what I've read so far, Blackler should have said, 'Tough,' and walked out. They admit he owns the material they're after."

"What I would like to know is how Everet got involved with this topic. I think we need to sit him down before we study any more case material and hear his story. Did you even look at this case before you handed it over to Ramsey?"

"Not really. They put it on my desk just when my phone rang, telling me to get downstairs immediately. That's when I found I was being reassigned to New York. Since they listed me as a person who worked on the material, they gave me my digital disk, which I sent to the online file server, and then I quickly handed over the files. I told Ramsey that I hadn't had time to check the file out, but the case was his and I had two hours to pack and get a flight to New York."

"I vote." Kate stopped talking as her phone dinged. She stood and looked out the window to see Blackler now getting out of his car, "We talk to Blackler first and then see how it fits with the paperwork."

"Good idea," Harry said as he went to let the historian in. Kate heard them chat over the condition of the roads until they reached the kitchen. Kate stepped up and said, "Mr. Blackler, I think if we start with the case and the stuff Ramsey sent, Harry and I will work half blind. What we need is the story of how you got involved in this mess. What gave you the idea to write the book? What were the steps you went through to gather your information, et cetera, et cetera? What is the entire picture from your point of view with as many details as necessary? We need to find reasons why they charged you and feel endangered now." As she spoke, she placed a plate piled with scones she had thawed out and kept toasty in the warming oven, along with several types of jam in front of the men at the table.

"Well, if you're going to bribe me, using scones, something I haven't eaten in ages, is definitely the way to do it." He smiled as they all sat. Kate grabbed a legal pad out of the drawer under her laptop, and a couple of pencils, as well as a scone, before she joined them.

"Believe it or not, the story started when I was a freshman in high school. A bunch of my friends had gotten ten-speed bikes and would ride around the neighborhood or go to an old track behind the high school and race. I really wanted a bike like that. I had enough trouble fitting in being a geek and being scrawny."

Harry and Kate stared at him, and he laughed. "I grew up. Later, I joined the army and went to college on a wrestling scholarship. Let's just say I had a growth spurt. However, back to the bike. My dad and I had a long discussion about my thinking about myself as opposed to thinking about others. He said, if I only think about what I want, I won't be able to take on life. I could tell I disappointed him and bottom line was I wasn't getting the bike."

"Well, a few days later, I was with a bunch of kids walking home from watching the bike crowd race around the track, when we passed a house that was set back from the street two blocks over from my house. The place looked run down, and the yard was a mess. The kids said that the woman who lived there was a witch and haunted the place. You know, usual kid stuff. But as we passed, the front door opened and an old woman came out carrying a watering can. She trudged to the edge of her porch where she had two flower pots and bent to water them. The pots had geraniums in them and they looked great. When I hurried to catch up with the others, I looked back and watched her slowly walk back into the house. When we turned onto my street, I looked at all the smaller houses with their neatly mowed lawns and thought of what my father had said. The woman was doing what she could to make her place look good."

"After the kids left, I told my mom I was going out for an hour. I went out to the garage and got our lawnmower. Then I pushed it down the street and around the corner to the lady's house. When I got there, I started the engine and mowed. It took about forty minutes to mow the front and side lawns and the backyard. When I finished, I pushed the mower back to the front. The woman was waiting for me. She had a tray holding a pitcher of lemonade, two glasses and a plate with cookies. She asked how much she owed me, but I told her she didn't owe me anything. While I drank a glass of lemonade, I told her the entire story and what my dad had said. 'He was right, I feel better doing this for you, rather than for money.'"

"Well, that was the start of a friendship that lasted for years. I would mow her lawn and fix things in her house. And she would tell me about her late husband Nathaniel Taylor, or 'The General' as she called him. He'd begun army life as a soldier in Vietnam and then made it his career, rising through the ranks. Mrs. Taylor told me stories about Vietnam battles he'd fought in and how difficult it was when much of the country opposed the war. People often disparaged soldiers. But the most interesting thing she said to me was that he kept diaries, journals really, in which he wrote what happened to him because in that way, he'd be forced to think about each day. She said it gave the day some value. Sometimes, it even taught him a lesson."

"After graduation, I joined the army, mainly to pay for college, since the recruiter had stressed that benefit when he talked to students. Maybe it was all the stories she'd told about 'The General' that gave me the idea. She was happy and thanked me for arranging for someone keep up her place while I was away."

"The day before I left, I went to do her yard work. When I finished raking her leaves, Mrs. Taylor came out and handed me a glass of cider and a package. In the package, I found a blank journal. She suggested I write what was important each day, as The General had. That night I began and I still write in my journal every night. I have many volumes, but it was the best training for becoming an historian. To record my story which people might read some day."

"When I returned from the army, the first thing I did was visit Mrs. Taylor. We talked about my life as a soldier. I'd risen to the rank of lieutenant. She was so proud of me. I read to her from the journals I'd kept about my army experience. I then told her I was going to college and studying to become an historian because of her. This delighted her. Little did I realize how much this friendship would affect my life. What happened two years later is the reason we're sitting here."

CHAPTER 11

Friday early afternoon

We put Blackler's story on hold when Kate heard Sal and Roger talking to the dogs as they walked the fence line, expecting to eat a lunch that didn't exist. Harry sprinted to the refrigerator and yanked open the door and different drawers within calling out, "Cheeseburgers, my special home fries and green salad."

"Done," called Kate as she pulled out the large frying pan and the medium-sized one. Harry slid the plastic container with the hamburger patties across the counter and Kate whipped off the lid and started slapping hamburgers into the now hot pan. Containers holding chopped mushrooms and onions flew across the counter at her and she added them. By the time the two men walked into the kitchen, they sniffed and sighed. Harry slid in next to Kate, where the second frying pan she had heating was now filled with sliced raw potatoes turning golden brown in oil.

Kate looked over Harry's shoulder and saw Everet putting the last of his chopped vegetables into a bowl along with the spinach and curly lettuce. Harry reached into the refrigerator and pulled out a bottle containing his home-made dressing and slid it down the island to Everet. Roger put a stack of plates next to Kate and took a bag of Will's rolls from the refrigerator, pushed the button for the quick warm setting on the warming oven and then when it beeped, began loading them on the plates as Kate laid slices of cheese on top of each burger.

Within two minutes, they were all seated at the table, chatting about which teams would make March Madness. Roger and Tim had been following the early competitions on the large-screen TV at Claire's house. Much to Sal's delight, he found Blackler had competed in wrestling, as he'd wrestled when he was much younger. Kate smiled at the efficiency of the meal prep and relaxed, letting sports fill the conversation.

Following lunch, the three of them again sat at the table and Everet picked up his story. "The guy I had tasked to take care of Mrs. Taylor was former army. He'd left the service when his wife got pregnant with their third kid. He had inherited his father's garage in town, which gave him a steady income. Like me, he enjoyed talking to Mrs. Taylor about The General."

"I had taken some advanced classes online while in the service so, when I got to college, I found I needed only two years of classes to get my degree. Following graduation, I went to visit Mrs. Taylor, only to be told that she had died two days earlier following a brief illness. Dean Avery, the former soldier, was at the house along with a lawyer. The lawyer was happy that I'd arrived because both Sgt. Avery and I were mentioned in Mrs. Taylor's will and he could do the reading right then."

"Mrs. Taylor had several bequests to organizations, but the bulk of her estate was to go to Dean and me. She left Dean the house in which to raise his family. He was also left her old car which he had kept going for her even though it was over thirty years old."

"The lawyer informed me that Mrs. Taylor had left me a substantial amount of money to allow me to marry and raise a family without worry. She also left me all of The General's diaries hoping I would one day write his story. And the last bequest to me was a beautiful ten-speed racing bike. Dean said that she had him find the bike for her. She'd told him I would understand."

Kate smiled. "I know that I would have liked Mrs. Taylor."

"You would," he agreed.

Harry looked at him and said, "So you've had the diaries for quite a while."

"Yes, and during that time, I have used a chunk of the money she left me to follow up research on uncommon events The General spoke about during his his career. I uncovered several things that do not shine a flattering light on a few prominent members of the government and the Pentagon. Whereas the diary would state certain facts from The General's point of view, I could find proof."

"But what I think brought this hell tumbling down on me was The General's story of something that happened when he was a private in Vietnam. Apparently, a crime occurred, which forced him, under a threat of death, against him and his new wife, to keep it secret. He wrote the pages following that statement in code. Hidden in the binding I found two small black and white photos. They looked as though he took them late in the day, by the slant of the sun. The first showed what looked like a group of huts burning. The second showed a man, a lieutenant by his uniform, standing watching the place burn, holding his rifle in his arms with a big grin on his face. I couldn't solve the code. I showed it to some people with that talent and was told that I needed the key to figure it out. A note written on the page following the photos simply said he had to keep his Charlotte safe, but hoped that someday someone could follow up on the crime and bring about justice. Since I could not fulfill that wish, I did what I was good at. I sat down and wrote a biography of General

Nathaniel Taylor."

"Is the book finished?"

"Yes."

"My publisher dumped me when this case came up. They had originally agreed to publish, based on my proposal. However, following the FBI investigation, they backed out. The government never told me what the charge was. Essentially, important people didn't want a dirty little secret exposed."

"Where are the diaries and the book?"

"They are in a bank vault, along with all the supporting documentation. The people who questioned me never said, but I assumed that their goal was to destroy all the evidence. The thing is that the diaries belong to me legally, thanks to Mrs. Taylor. She had inherited them from her husband and left them to me specifically to be used to create his biography. Since it was in her will, they could not question her intentions."

"Now whoever is behind this has upped the stakes beyond trying to get rid of the evidence, but to get rid of the man who knows everything," Kate said. Standing, she walked to the table and returned with the papers comprising the case against Everet that she'd printed out.

She set down the stack and lifted the front page. "Shouldn't this page set out the charges? The charge listed here is 'classified'. Does this mean that they are charging you with a crime they won't name?" she asked.

Harry reached across the table, saying, "Let me see that. That's ridiculous. I'm glad I didn't work on this. How do you prove the evidence leads to guilt when you do not know the charge?"

Harry leafed through the papers, handing each to Kate, who passed it on to Everet. Two hours later, they'd finished going through the paperwork but were not any farther along understanding how the government planned to charge Blackler with a crime.

The three of them sat in silence and stared at each other. Then Kate frowned and reached across the table to take the stack of papers from Everet. Tapping the edge of the stack to get the pages aligned, she picked up the charging sheet from next to Harry and placed it on top. Then, staring at that page for a minute, she turned to the men and said, "We need to talk to Isaac Evans?"

"Where do you see an Isaac Evans in this case?" asked Harry.

Everet asked. "Who is Isaac Evans?"

"Isaac Evans is the third man assigned to the case behind Harry and Ramsey. See. Isaac Evans, inspector CID."

"CID is the Army's investigative team, like the

Navy has NCIS," Harry said.

"Well, Evans was here yesterday and said he'd be back. Hopefully, when he arrives, he'll not only tell us his connection to the case, but maybe give us some clue why such an obviously bogus case found its way onto your desk." She looked across at Harry.

"Wait!" Kate said, then stood and raced into the dining room to find the letter from Ramsey. Back in her seat, she scanned each page. When she reached the end, she scowled. "I think that we're going to need some help she said, shoving the papers across to the men and pulling out her phone and tapping a few keys."

"Sadie. I've got a question."

"And, hello to you too, Kate. You sound upset."

"Frustrated with the fresh case Harry and I are working on. Yesterday a man showed up at the door. He said he was an Army CID inspector by the name of Isaac Evans. Harry wasn't here when he came, so he said he'd be back. Could you run him through your computer and see if anything pops up?"

"Hum. Do you know if he is active duty now?"

"I don't have a clue. I'd say he's in his late forties or early fifties. We found his name on a document from Harry's last case at the DC Field Office, the one he handed over to Ramsey. Evans was the third name on the charging sheet."

"Okay, I'll do some digging. He could still be active or retired. He could have risen in the ranks. I will check the latest listings I can access."

"Thanks. How's the snow near you?"

"We got about half of what you did. But I'm waiting to see what this next storm brings since instead of coming from the south and heading north, it's moving on a west to east trajectory. We may both get slammed, so you take care."

Kate told the men that they must wait until Evans came back.

"Somebody had to accumulate all the 'supposed' evidence. And I wonder if this man Isaac Evans was the one."

As Kate went to gather up the papers, they heard the front door open and the sounds of her mother and brothers arriving, including Tom. "Does anyone want to get in some snowshoe practice before it gets dark."

"Sure." Harry said. He walked over to the French doors and noticed that the dogs were pretty dry, since most of them were sleeping on the deck. He opened the door, and they all flooded in with tails wagging. Dillon and Liam ran straight to Kate, Quinn ran to meet his new friend, and Kate smiled as Rory pushed his way through the crowd and moved around her mother and sat in heel position at her side. Though her mother was talking to Blackler, her hand fell to her side and rested on Rory's head, gently scratching his ears. The dog leaned into her side, with his big fluffy tail waving back and forth in a ticktock motion.

Kate was watching the dogs as they settled when Blackler's phone rang. He pulled it from his pocket and smiled, looking at her mom. "It's Harriet."

"Hi, love. What's up. Remember Claire's husband's dogs? Well, guess what? It turns out... Harriet, honey, what's wrong? What happened? Threatened you. Tell me what happened. Hon, you've got to stop crying. I can't understand you. Shannon, what's wrong with your mother? Kill you? Who wants to kill you? Hang on, Claire is trying to tell your mother something."

Her mother grabbed the phone and said, "Shannon, listen to me now. You and your brothers go pack one bag each. Then you go pack a bag for your mom. Put them by the garage door while I talk to her. Now give her the phone... Harriet, listen to me now and stop crying. Tears will just get in the way. Your kids are packing. You are to get everything you need, close up the house and be in the car in ten minutes. You are coming here, understand. Everet will be waiting and I have people who can protect you. Once you are here, nobody can get at you. Okay, quickly. Go! Have Shannon text Everet once you are on the road. Hang up! Now! Go!"

Everet reached for his phone to talk, but

Claire stopped him, ending the call. "Don't!" she said. "If you talk to her, she'll start crying again. There's no time for emotions. I heard Robert yelling in the background. Your family just got a murder threat. They have to get out of there."

CHAPTER 12

Friday Evening

Everet stood staring at his phone, white faced and shaking. Harry stepped in front of him. "Claire is right. We've got to get your family here. It's a safe place and we can take care of them. It's not an obvious place for people to look for you. You don't know what you're fighting and neither do we. Give us a chance to figure what we're up against, before you panic."

Kate was thankful when her mother placed a hand on Everet's shoulder and said, "Listen to them. Kate and Harry are your best chance toward removing this threat and being able to return to life as normal."

"Normal? I've forgotten what normal is. I don't want to endanger my family."

"Is there another place where Harriet and the

kids can go? A place that few know about?" Claire asked.

"I would have suggested them hiding with you, but with this investigation going on, I don't think it would be safe."

"Actually," Kate said, "I think it is a perfect idea. Our security system is excellent, and we are not a relative to be traced through your employee files. There are even enough bedrooms." Kate looked around. "Unfortunately, the rugs need to be laid down, the beds assembled, and the other furniture moved into place. That's what's in all those boxes scattered about the living room."

Kate's mother looked at her for a minute and then they both smiled. Her mother then pulled out her phone, and a hit speed dial series of numbers. "Boys, I want you back here at Kate's within the next half hour with hand tools, prepared to work." She then ended the call and turned to Everet and said, "Go check out of your hotel and come back quickly. You want to be here when they arrive."

Then, reaching for her daughter, she said, "Kate, let's open boxes. Bring your post-it notes to mark where each piece will go."

Harry and Everet stared at each other for a minute and then Harry said, "Claire has spoken. You'd better go get checked out now. I'll be upstairs rolling out rugs and, if I know my wife, and I do, there will be a map with instructions in each room telling people exactly where everything goes."

The next hour and a half was a whirl of activity. But by the time people began thinking about supper, Claire and Kate could walk through each room and see Kate's vision come to life. "You did a wonderful job creating each room slightly different so that you can visualize the perfect place for a guest, and in years to come, the perfect room of each child."

"Thanks for the help, Mom." Kate said and hugged her.

"Oh Kate, all those years wasted. I was such a fool. You are a wonderful daughter."

"Gram once told me, looking back does not get you moving froward. I'm glad I've got my mother now."

"And you are going to make a wonderful grandmother, provided you don't push your grandchildren to choose math above all things, Claire." Harry said as he came up behind them. "It's an enormous world out there changing every day. By the time our children grow up, most of the careers they'll be in aren't even on the horizon yet."

"You remind me of Kate's father. He could always see the big picture. That's what made him so successful at what he did."

"Showing dogs," he replied innocently.

"No. That's not what I meant," Claire argued, swatting him.

"I know. I'm just teasing." He smiled and gave her a hug. "Seamus wants to know where the sheets, blankets and pillows are."

"I put them in the closet of each room."

"While we finish up here, why don't you go down and pull one of those casseroles with sausage, cheese and spinach out of the freezer and thaw it. We can make tacos to go with it."

Kate kissed his cheek and said, "I like the way you think."

"I'll stay and double check everything is perfect for your guests," her mother said.

Kate headed down the stairs, pausing on the landing to enjoy the sight of her living room without a forest of boxes. She should take some chicken out to thaw for tomorrow. She can make chicken stew with dumplings to feed a crowd. It will fill everyone up.

She checked on the dogs, who were back outside, but they seemed happy. Quinn had found one of his tug toys buried under the snow. He and Shelagh were about evenly matched in their game. The rest of the dogs were sleeping, snuggled together in small groups. Dillon, Liam and Rory had staked a claim to the spot on the deck in front of the living room door. The family resemblance running through them was striking.

Opening the freezer, she checked the labels

on the various casseroles stored there and pulled out the one they would use for supper. She put it into the microwave to defrost and made sure she had all the ingredients for tacos. Sliding onto the bench of the banquette, she sat to rest for a minute and looked out the window at the dogs. Kelly, who took over playing with her daughter, had stolen the toy. Quinn, not about to challenge the older bitch the way he did her daughter, decided he was tired and climbed the few steps onto the deck to add himself to the pile along with his dad, granddad and great-granddad.

As she leaned back and closed her eyes to rest after the busy day, she felt the flutter of the baby. This was its first time today. He or she must have enjoyed having its mom run from room to room to make sure there were no problems. She had only just relaxed enough to doze lightly when a flutter in her pocket sounded with a beep. Kate pulled her phone out and saw she had a text. Though she didn't recognize the number, she opened it. It was Alven!

Kate. We are well and safe. Your grandfather would have enjoyed this adventure. However, I have to warn you. The man who came after me is also after EB. His family needs protection. EB knows more than he thinks and someone is out to make sure he doesn't realize what it is and share it. Even with those at the bureau —trust only Malcolm. Keep your guard up.

A.

Kate had to smile at the thought of Alven and her grandfather, hiding from the bad guys in the deep snow. They would have loved sharing this type of adventure. Wherever they had camped, she was sure that Alven and his golden Buster were snug, happy.

The rest of the message made her thankful that her mother had demanded Harriet Blackler bring her children to stay here. They would be safer here than anywhere else, plus her brothers could entertain their kids. She was reviewing the rest of the message as the microwave dinged, telling her the casserole was thawed. Standing, she went to the stove, set the oven to preheat and began chopping the tomatoes and laying out the other ingredients for the tacos.

She'd been working for a while when a pair of hands reached around her. One hand took the knife and the other, an olive. A kiss landed on her cheek as Harry whispered, "You've worked hard enough today. Go sit. I'll make the tacos."

Kate leaned back against him, resting her head on his shoulder for a minute. Then, after putting the casserole into the oven, she smiled at the growing crowd. "Thanks, everyone. You made magic this afternoon by taking that monumental job and getting it done in under two hours. Everet, good. You're back in time to eat."

"Yeah. My kids will love that you have a dozen

dogs."

"The dogs are always a game changer. Quinn will make himself dizzy, bouncing from one to another, trying to love everyone."

Sal and Roger came in and joined the line, getting tacos and dishes for salad, as well as a serving of the now hot casserole. Claire came down from the second floor and thanked the boys for helping.

Tim asked Everet, "How old are your kids?"

"Shannon is a senior in high school and will go to Boston College in the fall. Robert is a sophomore, and he's the jock, playing basketball, softball, and running cross-country. James is twelve and a tinkerer like his father. He's got his mother's head for math."

As they sat around the table, Harry filled Sal and Roger in on the threat and the plan for the Blackler family to stay with them until they can be secure from danger. Roger noticed that the forest of boxes had disappeared from the living room and Kate told him about the whirlwind furnishing of the second floor.

Seamus, who had taken over making the tacos as people headed back for second helpings, said that his mom had cracked the whip and had them all working at warp-speed to get the upstairs rooms finished for company.

Harry's phone rang. He answered, but before

he could even say hello, Des yelled. *"Malcolm got a tip this morning from someone who signed himself, 'Friend of Kate.' He warned there might be another attack on Ramsey, which is why we went to the hospital. Malcolm wants to know who this is. What isn't your wife telling us, Harry?"*

Harry frowned. "What happened at the hospital?"

"Someone disguised as a doctor got near enough to Ramsey's room to take a shot at the cop guarding the door. Luckily, as he fell, the guard pressed the panic button on his phone, which sent out a call to all of us. We stopped the shooter." Harry looked at her and Kate shrugged her shoulders. He pressed a button and told Des he was on speaker and Kate was there."

"Kate. What is going on? Who is this friend of yours who is getting involved in FBI business? What's his name and where can I find him?"

"Des, I have friends all over the country. Since I've never met Ramsey Oliver, I don't know why someone sent you a request to check on him using me as a reference."

"Why don't I believe you?"

"I don't know, Des. Why don't you?"

Kate let her inner snark seep into her voice. *"I'm stuck in a blizzard in Connecticut right now and getting ready for another storm while I'm dealing with installing the furniture in the second-floor bedrooms of the new house, oh, and designing a wedding dress for Agnes. With nothing to do with my day, I'm sure that I woke up this morning thinking 'what can I do to make Des' life more difficult."*

Harry spoke up. "Whoever warned you about Ramsey's safety has probably encountered Kate in the last year, during a case of our cases. They know you guys know her. Using her as a reference, they figured would get your attention quickly. It seems they were right."

Silence stretched on the other end of the call. Finally, Des said, *"Okay. But Kate the Bureau expects your cooperation."*

"And I would like to remind you I have done nothing but cooperate with the Bureau over the year, whereas the Bureau has loosed multiple killers to murder me. If I come across information that I feel applies to the attempted killing of former agent Oliver, I shall be in touch."

"Um, I guess. Thank you, Kate. Malcolm will keep you updated on Ramsey, Harry, since his new location is undisclosed even to us, but hopefully he'll be safe." The call ended.

"Two agents? I thought it was only the man who tried to shoot you during your wedding," her mother said, while staring at Kate.

Harry stepped up and wrapped his arm around Kate's shoulders. "On the case where we met. There was also an agent who tried to kill Kate. Luckily, Dillon saved her life both times. Those agents are now serving prison sentences."

Claire stood straight and walked up to Kate. "Kathleen, you are not, under any circumstances, to put yourself or my grandchild in danger. Do you understand?"

"I don't go looking for people to shoot me."

"Do you understand?"

"Yes, mom."

CHAPTER 13

Friday later that evening

Everyone in the room stared at Kate.

"What?"

"Did you just tell off an FBI agent and accuse them of sending killers after you?" Roger asked.

"Yes. Next question."

"Kate," Sal asked. "Did you just lie to the FBI?"

"No. I don't know who sent that message. I have many friends and have no proof that any of them contacted the FBI in the last twenty-four hours."

"Because it's a crime to lie to the FBI."

"Really?"

"Don't get snarky with me, Missy. You know the law as well as I do."

"Right. And I also know that they base the law on FACT not guesses, suppositions, or flights of fancy."

The two of them stared at each other for a minute, then Sal nodded. "Agreed. But if any of your flights of fancy work themselves into the fact column, I want you on the phone to Des immediately." Having gotten the last word, he nodded to Roger, and they headed out.

Kate turned, noticed her mother and Everet staring at her and said, "Sorry about that. I rarely fight with Des or Sal. They're upset because of what almost happened to former agent Oliver."

Harry caught Kate's hand as she went to sit next to her mother. He wrapped his arms around her. Resting his head on hers. He nodded as her brothers quietly left before their mother could blame them for people shooting at Kate. After holding her for several minutes, he whispered, "Go sit. I'll get your tea."

As Harry sat opposite Kate and Everet at the table, Everet's phone rang. He smiled as his daughter's photo filled the screen. When he answered the phone, all could hear was screaming.

"Shannon, baby, I need you to calm down and tell me what's happening."

"They're following us and trying to kill us." Shannon yelled as her brothers screamed and called for their father.

Before Everet could answer, Kate reached over and pushed the button for speaker, and pulled the phone toward her.

Speaking loudly and with authority, she said, "Shannon. My name is Kate and I need you in work mode. You can panic later. First, did you say that someone was following your car?"

"Yes. They began following us as soon as we headed out of town toward the interstate. They have stayed on our bumper ever since. They're way too close."

"Okay, you and your brothers must work together. First, you must have your brothers figure out what kind of car is following you and if it's that close, try to see if they can get the license number. Now, your job is to give us your exact location on the interstate. The way you are going to do that is to check the mile markers as you go by."

"What are mile markers?"

"On the side of the road, you will pass poles with a string of numbers running down them. These will tell the cops exactly where you are."

Kate looked at Harry, who already had Sgt. Gurka of the Connecticut State Police on his phone. She heard one boy yell as the pole was coming up. Shannon called out the number and Harry repeated it to Gurka.

Kate turned back to Blackler's phone. "Shannon. I am going to talk to your mother now. But before I do, I want you each to make yourselves as small as you can and squeeze down into the footwell. Harriet, I'm Claire's daughter."

"I didn't know Claire had a daughter."

"Well, she'll introduce us when you arrive. My husband is in contact with the state police. They are on their way to your location. What I need you to do is to stay safe until they arrive. Your kids said that the car is right behind you. Has it tried to move to the left and pass you?"

"Yes, I sped up, and it pulled back in behind us and rammed the bumper."

"That is exactly what I need you to do. If the car tries to pass you, accelerate so that you remain in front. If he rams you, don't break. Let the shove which their car gives you lose its effectiveness by pushing you forward. Your job is not to let it be anywhere but directly behind you. If it gets to the side, it could send you flying off the road or crash you into the traffic on your side."

The sound of sirens came from the phone, followed by the sound of a shot, breaking glass, and screams. "Harriet, are you okay?" Everet screamed.

"Yes, but they are shooting at us. They shot out the back window. The police are coming up behind us. The car is trying to pass me."

"Don't let it pass. They are desperate. They'll shove you off the road." Kate yelled.

"The police are now surrounding us. They're slowing all the cars down. Kids. Stay down. I'll tell you when you can sit up. James, down! I'm following the police car that's moved in front of me. We're being moved to the side of the road... We've stopped, but I can't get my hands to let go of the steering wheel."

The next thing they heard was the sound of a car door being opened. *"You are okay now, ma'am. Tell me, is anyone injured."*

"Kids, are you okay?"

"Yes, mom," the voices came from the phone.

"My name is Cory, ma'am. We're going to get you safely wherever you need to go. We'll need to impound your car as evidence of a crime. You'll get paperwork that will have the information on who to contact and the schedule."

"Cory Barns, is that you?" Kate asked. "It's Kate Killoy."

"Yes Kate. Are these people friends of yours?"

"Yes, they are. In fact, they were on their way to my place just now."

"Well, Billy Anders is going to take them where they need to go. He knows how to get to your place. They'll probably be leaving here in about fifteen minutes and will be at your place in half an hour after that. We'll take good care of them, Kate."

"Thanks, Cory. "

Everet stood and walked through the living room and outside, followed by Kate's mother, who grabbed their coats.

Kate leaned back, closed her eyes, and breathed slowly. Harry placed a fresh cup of tea in front of her at the table. Then he slid into the chair Everet had vacated, lifted her into his lap, wrapped his arms around her, then rested his head on top of hers. He held the cup steady as she lifted it and took the first few sips.

"Chamomile, vanilla, and honey. It will calm you and will hopefully calm junior as well," he muttered. "It's a good thing that you've trained most of the cops with police dogs in the state. You probably know the entire force." They stayed that way until they heard the others return.

The chair Kate had been sitting in moved and Claire slowly sat, still shaking as she reached forward to take Kate's face in her hands. "You were wonderful. I was so frightened for them, but you didn't panic. You just made sure that everything worked the way it should. Harriet and the children are safe and alive because of you. Kate, your father and grandfather would be so proud of you." She spread her arms and held on to her, sobbing quietly.

"I don't know what to say." Everet said as he stared at them, his eyes full of tears as well. "Thank you isn't enough."

Harry had taken her in his arms. Kate lifted

her head off Harry's chest and smiled. "Thank you is always enough."

***

When the state trooper's car pulled up in front of their house, the front door flew open. Everet raced down the stairs to reach his wife and children. He swept them all into a massive hug. Right behind him was Claire, tears in her eyes, desperate to hold Harriet and the kids.

The trooper walked to the back of the patrol car, opened the trunk, lifted out suitcases, and began putting them on the porch. Harry went to help him, patting his shoulder and shaking his hand.

"Thanks, Billy." Kate shouted from the porch. "These people have been through a scary time. You guys did a fantastic job catching the car chasing them. Did the guys who drove the car say anything?"

"Glad to help, Kate. No, they said nothing. They were screaming for their lawyers before we could get their doors open."

"Well, that's how it goes. Pass on my thanks to the guys and gals when you get back. I much appreciate it. These people are my mother's longtime friends."

Billy saluted and then turned, got back in his car, and drove off.

"Mom," Kate whispered. "Could you take over and get the Blacklers settled in their rooms? We'll have supper once we settled everyone. I'll be out in the kennel if you need me."

Kate slipped into the house and pulled on her coat to ward off the chill she'd gotten standing outside with only a wool sweater to block the cold. Quietly slipping out through the kitchen, she moved down the hall. When she reached the door to the yard, she spotted Dillon. She called him using hand signals, and quietly let him in, and headed for the kennel. Sal was on the phone in the lobby chatting with one of their suppliers when she came in. She waved at him and headed for her office.

Shutting the door, she sank onto the dog cushion under the window, lowering herself and wrapped her arms around Dillon, and let tears flow as the shakes gripped her. Dillon snuggled close and his big Sammy tongue licked her face, happy to taste the salt and catch each tear with his tongue. His voice whined in sympathy. Eventually, her tears ceased. Kate felt a shove and a huge white fluffy tail swiped her face. Hecate, her 25-pound white, Maine Coon Cat had, wonder of wonders, left her favorite spot on Kate's desk chair to push in front of Dillon and get Kate's attention. Overwhelmed by the mass of hair that both animals produced, Kate had to fight to breathe.

She gave them each a massive hug, then freed herself and stood, beating her cat to her chair, and settled in front of her laptop. She opened it, staring at the screen for a moment, then pulled up a game of solitaire and began moving the cards around. As she moved each card into place, she felt a tiny piece of order slide back into place in her life. Three games later, the vivid scene of a car being chased, hit, and almost run off the road yielded a little of the real estate it held in her brain.

By the time she had fit the last piece of a 300-piece online jigsaw puzzle into place, the vision of the shot and breaking glass which kept repeating in her head, replaced the wave of relief she had felt when the troopers got all the cars to stop. Kate stared. After placing the last piece, the complete picture came together: a lovely castle on a hill overlooking a lake.

She closed her eyes and let the stillness replace screams, gunshots, breaking glass, grinding metal, sirens and panic. She waited. Stillness remained. Dropping her head forward, she rolled her shoulders. Pain in her neck and shoulders was sharp at first, but soon eased. She leaned back and embraced the peace.

That's when she realized that the pain in her shoulders wasn't the only discomfort she was experiencing. Hecate had slipped back onto her lap while she was decompressing, and now, Kate winced as she realized that pins and needles were setting in, her legs quickly losing all circulation. Closing the laptop, she lifted the cat from her lap to her desk and worked her hands into her thick white coat from her tail all the way to the cat's head and finished by scratching her between her ears. Then she started working down from her head, massaging the cat's body slowly until she reached the magnificent plume of a tail. While all this attention was being dealt out, Dillon placed his feet on the desk and began licking the cat's head. The room reverberated with a sound similar to trucks rumbling over a corduroy bridge. Sal opened her door and smiled.

"I figured either we were having an earthquake, or the grand lady was enjoying some snuggling," he said.

"She is, but the session is over. I've got to get back to my company."

"You feeling better?"

Kate stared at him, and then asked, "Billy?"

"Yeah. Only you could go through a high-speed car chase while sitting at your kitchen table, and NOT be playing a video game."

"I don't play those kinds of games. They're too hard on my nerves. I play solitaire and put together online jig-saw puzzles. It's a great way to get rid of the noise of crashes, shots and screams in my head."

"So, it worked?"

"So far, so good."

Harry walked in and sat in the wing chair which faced her desk. "You better?"

"Yeah."

"Good, because it's suppertime. Were you planning to use that chicken for stew?"

"With dumplings. I figured that comfort food would be the best way to end this day."

"Is Hecate ready to let you and Dillon leave this love fest?"

She gently shifted the cat to the floor and let Harry pull her out of the chair. Before they reached her office door, Hecate was back settling into her favorite spot and Dillon moved to heel position. Harry wrapped his arm around her shoulders, letting her lean on him.

They had almost reached the back door when both their phones dinged, announcing a new arrival. They moved down the hall to the kitchen and Kate crossed to the window to find who had arrived. Harry frowned, but Kate recognized the visitor.

"We are hopefully about to get some answers we need. Come and meet Inspector Isaac Evans, CID."

They reached the living room just as he rang the doorbell. Harry opened the door. Isaac Evans introduced himself to Harry.

"I would like to talk to you about a case involving Everet Blackler, sir. I wanted to talk to one of the other agents assigned to that case, but he did not keep our appointment and I've since heard that someone shot him. It is vitally important to get answers to crimes that took place in Vietnam during the end of the war. From what I have from my source, is a series of murders and a massive theft took place and the killer could go free because he threatened and intimidated the witnesses."

"It sounds as though you've got some valuable information for us. We're about to cook supper. Why don't we plan to discuss this following the meal? There's coffee or tea while you wait." Kate and Harry settled their guest at the table and got to work. While Kate finished cooking, Harry got Evans' help in opening the dining room table to its full length, got the tablecloth spread out and the chairs in place, then with a smile at Kate, began laying out the plates, glasses and cups and saucers.

Checking the pots, Harry whispered to Kate, "The only one missing tonight is Hercule Poirot."

"Your little gray cells can handle it, Mr. Foyle," she whispered back.

CHAPTER 14

Friday night

By the time Kate's three brothers, her mother, her grandmother, Gwen, and all the Blacklers, plus Roger and Sal and their guest, joined Kate and Harry to eat, it was a rather full table. Luckily, Kate had made plenty of stew with dumplings. Everyone was hungry. Harry didn't need to explain to the men the presence of each other once introduced. They quietly agreed to talk after supper.

The kids were still getting over the excitement of the afternoon's car chase. They were repeating the details for Roger and Sal when Kate heard a beep on her phone and stood to look out the kitchen window.

Though darkness had settled, it wasn't pitch black. She could make out the shape of a sedan which had stopped at the top of the drive. As she opened the security app on her phone, she typed in a code which would save a photo of the car's license plate. When the car backed out of the driveway, she instructed the camera hidden there to take multiple photos and try to get a picture of the driver's face. Once he left, she reached into the warming oven and took out another loaf of bread, and brought it to the table.

"Ah, you read my mind," Tim told her as he sliced off a chunk of the bread. Kate sat and ate, though after a few minutes, Harry reached for her phone so that he could open the security app. He scrolled through the photos Kate had taken.

Most of the shots were in profile or the back of the man's head, but one had him looking directly into the camera. Harry quickly keyed in another code, sending the photo to the printer in the library. The photo would be available after the meal ended, so he printed several copies to hand out to all concerned.

Following the meal, the group split up. The kids went with Seamus and Tim up to the playroom on the second floor. There are two computers up there loaded with video games that Kate had designed. Claire and Harriet went off with Ann and Gwen to visit. Then Kate and Harry quickly fed the dogs and put them out. With Sal and Roger joining them, they moved to the library to talk to their guests.

The first thing Harry did was to pass out

photos of the man whose car had stopped at the end of their driveway during dinner, however nobody recognized him.

Roger said, "Send me the photo and license plate. I'll forward it to Gurka. After what happened earlier today, he'll want to be kept in the loop."

Harry settled in at his desk with Kate in the wing chair beside it. Their two guests took the over-stuffed chairs, leaving Sal on the other wing chair and Roger the widow seat.

Harry looked at Isaac Evans and said, "Since we know the least about you, perhaps you can explain where you fit in this whole undertaking."

"I am Inspector Isaac Evans of the CID. That's the army's investigative arm. I am listed on the case concerning Mr. Blackler because I requested the assignment when I learned it had to do with General Nathaniel Taylor's diaries. Those diaries are import-ant to me, so I asked to be placed on the team. How-ever, almost before the case began, it disappeared. I found you reassigned Foyle and that Ramsey Oli-ver had left with early retirement. Assuming that the bureau works in a similar manner to the CID, I reasoned that was unusual and I assumed the case was being covered up."

Sal had stiffened when he heard Taylor's name. Kate saw it upset him. "Did you say Nathaniel Taylor?" he asked. Evans nodded and Kate looked in his direction.

"Over the intervening period, I've been doing research into you, Blackler, and into a certain incident included in those diaries. Though I didn't make it widely known, I have a personal reason for the investigation. My father was part of the patrol that went out that night. Taylor was a private. The lieutenant in charge, I'm still investigating. My father just called him 'the Bastard.' Apparently, everyone under him hated him. He was an Ivy League type who liked to talk down to everyone below him in rank, especially those of color. His racism and hate extended both to the enemy and the Vietnamese on our side. His treatment of their women was disgusting. It was an open secret that he'd tried to rape the women who worked in the camp."

"Apparently on the night in question, he took the patrol out to look for a machine gun nest of snipers which had been giving patrols problems. The patrol had been advancing, clearing each area before going in, when the lieutenant told them to stop and wait while he went to take care of some business. One of the new guys made the mistake of asking him where he was going and was threatened with insubordination. They all settled in, posting one man to keep watch and catch what rest they could. Taylor followed the lieutenant. The others told him not to, but he didn't trust the man. If he was doing something illegal, he didn't want all of them dragged into the problem."

"According to my dad, they didn't come back

for two hours. Taylor returned first and feigned sleep. When the lieutenant reappeared, he rousted the men and told them he found a camp which had burned. There were bodies that needed to be buried. He told them to get up and bury all the bodies they found. He also ordered them not to say anything about what happened this night if they valued their lives and those of their families. He advised them he had contacts who could make accidents happen. They did as he asked."

"When my father was dying a few years ago, he told me of the men on the patrol that night. He pointed out that several had met with accidents over the years. He wouldn't name the lieutenant. He said, for my safety and my mother's. If the Bastard found out he'd told, both my mother and I would die since the Bastard hated the Vietnamese, especially the women, and that he had the power to do it."

Harry looked at him and asked, "So your dad never named the lieutenant?"

"No."

"Have you been able to find out who it was? I would think you could have tracked down the records and learned who the lieutenant in charge was."

"I found the listing for the unit, but all information about them they classified about ten years ago."

"Do you know which department classified it?"

"The Justice Department."

"Not the Pentagon?"

"No."

"That's strange."

Turning to Blackler, Evans said, "I don't know about you, but I have a pretty good idea what is on those coded pages now. We need to figure out the key —and fast."

Roger stood and nodded to Harry. "I'll be here if you need muscle or an extra gun, but this is where you brainiacs take over. I'll go to bed down the kennel dogs and see you in the morning."

Kate looked at Sal. He hadn't moved since he heard Taylor's name. He stared at Blackler and Evans, but didn't say a word. Suddenly, he stood, nodded to Kate, and left. A few minutes later, his car pulled out of the driveway. Turning to her guest, she said, "Everet, I think The General wouldn't leave those coded pages without some hint to the key somewhere. I need to read that diary."

"I'll give you access to download the first diary. That's the one that dealt with Vietnam. If it's in there, I missed it and I've been over that book with a fine-tooth comb many times. But it's better with more people looking, I suppose."

"Good. We'll each download the diary tonight and begin tomorrow." Harry said. "Evans, where are you staying?"

"I'll go find a motel. I saw some when I drove up here."

"Well, if you want a room, we've got one left upstairs that doesn't have Blacklers in it. You're welcome to it. If we're being watched, the less they know about who occupies this place, the better."

"Well, I appreciate that. I'll get my things out of my car."

"Good." Kate said. "I'm going to have some tea and a bedtime snack. The kitchen is open for whoever wants anything. Your kids may want something before bed, Everet."

"Always." he said and headed up the stairs.

Two minutes later, the thunder of footsteps racing down the stairs warned of hungry kids and adults. Kate had a couple of pies, apple and blueberry, and a tub of ice cream. A line formed with Harry dishing up slices of pie and Kate topping them with ice cream. They settled at the kitchen table with the kids sitting at the banquette. Kate sat next to Everet and once they'd eaten most of the dessert, she asked him to tell her what he knew about Nathaniel Taylor.

"What do you need to know?"

"Well, where was he from? Did he marry before going to Vietnam? Did they have any children? If we are going to solve the code, it would help to know the man."

"Good point. Well, he was a classic New Englander. He and his wife grew up in the same town as I did, Sturbridge, Massachusetts. They married young, straight out of high school. The house they lived in had been in his wife's family for two hundred years. They didn't have any children of their own, though they both came from good sized families with ancestors who had settled in the Sturbridge area prior to the Revolution. Mrs. Taylor remained living with her parents while Nathaniel was away in Nam. When he returned, he announced he planned to make a career of the army. Much to the dismay of both families, the young couple began living on base and following the drum. Eventually as he rose in the ranks, they settled in DC. Nathaniel had become a general, and ended up teaching at the National Defense University. It is at Fort Lesley McNair in Washington, DC. The school is funded by the Defense Department and facilitates training, high-level education and professional development for leaders in national security. They remained at the college until Nathaniel's health forced him to retire. They returned to Sturbridge, to the home his wife inherited from her father. It was that house, with the lawn that needed mowing, that began this whole adventure."

"I think I would have liked the Taylors," Kate said.

"I feel as though I have gotten to know The General by working with his diaries over the years.

He was an honorable man. The only blot on his record, and only he knew it, was the mysterious action of the unit he was part of that ties to this coded entry in the first diary. Slight mentions of that time, in later diaries, let me believe it weighed heavily on him over the years."

"Apparently, it was of significant importance that it is now threatening you and your family, even though you don't know what it is. We need information, especially the name of that lieutenant who led the unit."

"But they sealed that information," Evans said.

"Hmm." Kate pulled out her phone and quickly dialed. "Hi Maeve? How's the snow in the city?" Kate and her great-aunt chatted away about the weather in New York City as opposed to Connecticut and various family members. But eventually Kate got to the point. "Maeve, I was wondering if you might help Harry on his latest case. Since you know everybody, I was wondering if you'd ever met a General Nathaniel Taylor who taught at the National Defense University? You did. I was told that his wife was a really nice person. What has come up is a need for information about the start of his career during Nam. We've been trying to identify members of his unit, and though we've come across some names, we haven't been able to locate the name of the lieutenant who led them. All I can derive is that he was less than popular and referred to by his men as 'the Bastard.' When we checked the unit information, they had classified the names of those involved, which we thought strange. Harry's trying to help the author of Taylor's biography check his facts. It's a really interesting project and the professor who is writing it married one of my mom's former TAs. You know someone who was close to him? Great. Call me if you can find out anything." Kate laughed. "It's a different mystery. Hopefully, with fewer bullets flying. Thanks, I'll look forward to hearing from you."

Harry came up to her and said it was time for bed. Kate told him about calling in reinforcements. He glanced at the phone and smiled. "Maeve?"

"Of course."

He grinned at Blackler. "Maeve Killoy Donovan is my wife's great-aunt, also former MI-5 and one of the best sources of information on anything and everything criminal on either side of the Atlantic. She and her husband Padraig live in New York City and are part of what Kate calls 'The long arm of the law club.'"

Kate said, "She knew your general and his wife during the time they were at the University. But still better, she knows a retired officer who knew him well during his career. She may get that name."

"Great," Harry said. "But that is for another day, because you and Junior have got to get some sleep." They wished Blackler goodnight and headed to bed.

When they reached their bedroom, he walked her to the bed, helped her change into pajamas, and tucked her in as Dillon settled on the floor beside her. Then, kissing her goodnight, he went back to let in the rest of the dogs and lock up.

Liam and Quinn were sitting at the bedroom door, waiting to get in, when he secured the final lock. He opened the door and followed them in. Without waking her, they checked on Kate, bumped noses with Dillon, and then each went to his favorite spot. Harry smiled, and turning out the lights, shed his clothes and lifted the covers and settled into his favorite spot. After waiting to see if there were any aftereffects from the strain of that car chase, he decided, thankfully, that she apparently needed people actually shooting at her to set off her PTSD.

He pulled Kate tightly against him and slept.

CHAPTER 15

Saturday morning

Half-awake, Kate rolled on her side, her arm slipping over the side of the bed, when her hand felt only air. She opened her eyes and looked down at the carpet. Where was Dillon? She turned her head and spotted all three dogs standing at the door to the living room, their ears on alert but not showing signals of danger. Gently swinging her legs over the edge of the bed, she grabbed her slippers from their shelf, slipped them on and pulled on her warm robe while checking the time. It was only five o'clock. When she opened the door, the dogs shot past her as Kelly and Shelagh came running up and nudged her legs. Then they ran back to the group of dogs gathered in front of the sofa.

"There were only eight, but now there are eleven. Mom said there were a dozen. Eleven isn't a dozen."

"You must be James, the number cruncher." Kate said to the boy lying in the middle of a pile of dogs as she settled on the sofa.

"Who are you?"

"My name is Kate. This is my home."

"You were the lady on the phone who told us what to do. The one that is friends with the policemen." Robert said as he patted both Teagan and Maud's heads, which rested in his lap.

"That's right."

"How come you know the policemen?" Robert asked. "It did not surprise them you told us what to do."

"I train their police dogs and then teach the policemen to work with the dogs. It's part of my business and I've trained a lot of them. I know most of the cops in the state."

"How come you have so many dogs?" James asked.

"Well, I breed and show dogs. That means every few years, I add a puppy to the group of dogs I have here. All of my dogs are related to one another, and once they are part of our family, they stay. See, this is Quinn. He's the youngest. His father is Dillon, sitting next to me. His grandfather is Liam, who is sitting next to Robert. Liam's father is Rory, who spends the nights at my mother's house across the driveway."

"My mom said she didn't know that Mrs. Killoy had a daughter."

"Well, my mom and I sometimes have had trouble getting along because I didn't have a career in math."

"That's a dumb reason for forgetting she had a daughter."

"Well, you'll have to take that up with her." Kate hid her laugh.

"Now what are you guys doing up so early?"

"We couldn't sleep. It scared us that the evil men who chased us would find us. Or the man who was watching our house," James muttered, holding onto Quinn.

"The men who chased you are in jail and should stay there for a while. Who's the man who was watching your house?" she asked.

"We don't know. He showed up a few weeks ago. But he's there most days. We tried to tell mom about it but she said it was probably a new neighbor or someone looking for a house to buy. But, it's always the same guy." James growled, his frustration at being treated like a child obvious.

"Okay. What does this guy look like?" Kate asked.

James nudged his brother. "Show her. She works with cops."

Robert studied Kate for a minute, then reached into his pocket and pulled out his cell phone. Opening the gallery app, he hit some keys and then turned the phone for her to see the photo of a man. Kate reached for the phone and scrolled back, finding two more shots. One was a good view of his face.

"Excellent. You'd make a brilliant detective," she told the boy. He smiled.

Before returning the phone, Kate looked at the boys and said, "I know it's early, but I'm hungry. Would you like some breakfast?"

The boys shot to their feet and followed Kate to the kitchen, where she put the kettle on to boil. Then she whipped up some cocoa for the boys to ward off any chill. Hitting some keys on Robert's phone, she transferred the photos to her laptop and sent them to her phone. Returning to his phone, she used a shortcut and reached into the freezer for the leftover pancakes she'd made last week. She grabbed some sausages and checked the refrigerator for a container of chopped fruit.

Setting the boys up at the banquette, she let the dogs out into the yard, and put the pancakes and the sausage into the microwave. Before she could even make her tea, she had breakfast for three on the table with butter and syrup. She scooped the fruit into small dishes, and she placed a container of whipped cream within the boy's reach.

Telling the boys to dig in was all the encouragement needed. While they scarfed down the food, she sent the photo from her laptop to the printer in the library so that she'd have copies to show to Sal and Roger in case the man tried to breach their security.

She sent a copy of the photo to Sadie, telling her what the boys had passed on to her. Then she sent a text to Alven telling him that the Blacklers were all safe and staying with her. She attached the photo and told him this was a stalker who the boys spotted watching their house.

Harry walked into the kitchen dressed for the day. He greeted the boys, made his coffee, and slid into the banquette. Kate opened her laptop and pulled up the photos of the stalker Robert had taken. She asked Robert to tell Harry about their stalker. The boy glanced at his brother with a worried look.

"Did you know Harry used to work for the FBI? He now has his own cyber security company and tracks down bad guys all the time."

"Why don't you work for the FBI anymore?" James asked.

"I got shot and almost died."

Both boys nodded. Then Robert screwed up his face as though thinking hard and asked, "Do you ever get shot at in your new business?"

"Yeah. But I've gotten better at ducking."

They all laughed and, after kissing Harry's cheek, Kate went to get dressed.

Roger had joined the others eating by the time Kate got back. She'd stopped by the library to grab the photos. When she'd joined the party, her mother stood and walked to her. Looking Kate in the eye, she turned to the Blacklers and said, "I need to introduce you to my daughter, Kate Killoy Foyle. Kate was the one on the phone with you yesterday. Much to my shame, I am just learning to value the skills of my very talented daughter. I know that her father and grandfather would be extremely proud of the girl that they alone raised."

"Harriet, Shannon, it's nice to meet you. James and Robert are already my friends. If there is anything you need during your stay, just let me know. Harry, have you explained about the security?"

"No, I was waiting for you. Do you have the photo?"

"Yes. Now this property and especially this house have an excellent security system, because of Harry's job and various threats we've had to face. Harry, Sal and I have our phones synchronized to the system. If anyone tries to access the property, we will know it. If we perceive the person to be a threat, we have the technology to take their photo and a picture of their license plate. Don't worry about people sneaking up on you." She smiled at the boys.

Then, stepping behind them, she placed a hand on Robert's shoulder and said, "Robert has proved himself to be an asset to this investigation already. His ability to observe things out of the ordinary led to the photo identification of a man who has been stalking you and watching your home." She placed the 8 1/2 x 11 enlargement of the head study from the photos that Robert had on his phone, on the table, and handed one each to Sal and Roger. "We don't have a name for the man yet, but I've sent copies to several investigators Harry works with and they should have a name soon."

Roger turned to her. "Send the photo to my phone and I'll make sure that all the troopers see a copy. Gurka will run him through the database and see if anything pops up."

Kate nodded. "Tell them to keep an eye out to see if he tries to contact the pair who tried to run the Blacklers off the highway. This is a dangerous situation, and the family needs it cleared up fast so that they can return to normal life."

Roger stood. "Thanks for breakfast Kate, Harry. I'm going to get the kennel dogs out and then I'll send this to Gurka and see if we can spot him. If he tries to come here, we can get a license number on him."

"Why do you have a photo of the Squid." Kate heard the question coming from behind her. She looked over her shoulder to see Isaac Evans staring at the photo on the table.

"Who's the Squid?"

"Giuseppe Calamari. He is a gun for hire to whoever has the biggest pocket book."

"Hang in. I'm going to hook you up with Sgt. Gurka, since he's going to have every cop in the state looking for this guy. But first, go bug Harry and get some breakfast. You are going to need your strength today."

The group divided. Claire and Harriet went to visit with Ann. Seamus took the kids up to the area at the top of the stairs to challenge them to a competition. Sal's car pulled into the driveway and he came into the kitchen to check with Kate on her plans for the day.

Returning to the kitchen, Kate and Sal found Everet, Harry, and Isaac settled at the banquette to go over the charging document. She told him her plans, but when he turned to go, she asked him, "How do you know General Taylor?"

Kate walked Sal into the library. As they sat in the wing chairs, she asked, "Why is the name Nathaniel Taylor familiar to you?"

"Anything to do with Taylor can be dangerous."

Kate looked at him for a minute and then asked, "What did you do in Nam?"

"Same thing I did after Nam."

"You were a cop?"

"They call it Military Police."

"And you know Taylor because you investigated this crime?"

"Tried to."

Kate stared at the now silent man across from her. Then she remembered the look on his face when she took his photo, and his warning for her never to be alone. She also remembered the letter he'd held. "Do you get threats too?"

"Yeah," he muttered.

Kate kept her eyes on him, trying to think of a way to break through his reluctance. "Sal, we're trying to find who did this crime and stop him from killing again. I will tell no one what you've told me. If you decide to help, it will be your choice. I'm going to sit in on what the guys are working on. Watch and see what they're doing. What you do beyond that is up to you."

Sal looked at her for a minute. Then he nodded and stood.

As he headed for the door, Kate grabbed his hand, holding him back. "We're not done. You've received threats which include your son, Sarah and your granddaughter."

He nodded, clinching his jaw, determination to fight for them all over his face.

Kate pushed him back into the chair. "We've got to get them to a safe place so you can think about helping us stop this bastard. When you go home, you're going to talk them into taking a few days at Camp. Helen and Otto will be there cooking and taking care of everything. There are 12 guest rooms, so they can invite their friends. There is a security fence around the place and skiing is only an hour away."

"Sarah can't ski. She's pregnant like you," he grumbled.

"Did I mention the heated indoor swimming pool?"

A corner of Sal's mouth tilted up. "You fight dirty, Killoy."

"I win?" Kate grinned.

"Yeah. You win."

"If they watched their home, have their friends come to borrow skis, etc. And they can slip their suitcases into their car. Then your kids, plus their dog and the munchkin, can go to the store for groceries. In the parking lot, they can switch to a friend's car and leave theirs there. You can pick it up and bring it home while they are heading for vacation in Lake George."

"The Army could have used you to plan maneuvers during the war," Sal told her, chuckling. They walked back to the kitchen. Sal waved goodbye to

Harry as Kate went to make more tea.

Kate heard Isaac say, "They hint at it, but they don't outright accuse Blackler of the theft of documents from the late General Nathaniel Taylor."

"They mean the diaries, which, since I inherited them legally, their claim is invalid. The General's and his wife's wills are proof of that." Blackler argued.

"The charges also hint that you planned to use materials in your possession to blackmail high-ranking members of the government. I assume that there are statements made by the general that accuse people of being less than choir boys."

"No, actually. The book follows the general's career from the time he was a private until he retired. It encompasses Vietnam, the Gulf War, and the beginning of the Iran-Iraq conflict. The general recorded what he saw, the good, the bad and the ugly. He was a man of great intelligence and compassion. He was also honest and forthcoming about the mistakes he made along the way. He calls out the poor advice and orders he had to deal with. Though he was critical of several military decisions, the case was not about those, but about what happened in Nam."

"What about the part that is in code?" Kate asked.

"Well, in the first diary, he talks about the crime. The code is there, but without a key, so it's useless. Knowing a crime had happened, he wanted to report it, but he knew if he tried to tell what he'd seen, his life would be worth nothing. The criminal would take revenge. He said it described the crime on the following page, but in code. I wasn't able to break the code. Those pages were what I sent to Alven. He said he needed to figure out the key. He was recruiting an old friend to help. Plus, there were the unlabeled prints of the photos I found hidden in the binding of that diary."

"To your knowledge, Taylor told no one?"

"I haven't been able to find any record of a crime in any of the sources I've checked or any mention of it in any later diary."

"What did you find out about the other members of that unit?"

"Many of them are dead. Some died during the war, others died of supposed accidents, and some of age-related problems. The only survivors are the lieutenant whose name is unknown, a sergeant who owns a restaurant with his son in northern California and another private who recently retired from teaching high school in Missouri."

"But the criminal could be one of these people. You are assuming it is the lieutenant."

"Right."

"Do you only have the one copy of that diary that's locked up, or does it exist in digital form?"

Harry asked. "The reason I'm asking is that it would be a lot easier to spot potential enemies, if we read what he wrote and who the major players were."

"I scanned the diaries and they exist in a file Alven had me set up on the dark web. My biography is in digital form there as well. The part about the murder was not in the synopsis sent to the publisher. Since I was hoping to include that, neither my editor nor my agent have read that part of the book. I told them I'm still doing revisions."

"Well, I'd say that a biography about someone who was there when the murder occurred, is making somebody very nervous." Kate said.

"I hadn't thought of that."

"Was it one of the big five or a university press?" Harry asked. He had several friends who were authors and had heard their tales of working through contract negotiations, with rights issues for the different publication such as e-books, audio books, paperback, hardbound, and foreign rights. He knew it could be overwhelming for a novice author.

"It was a small press, with no advance paid. I worried they wouldn't be able to market it to the right readers. By the time I'd finished writing all 985 pages, I was pretty confident I knew my target audience and how to market it. But getting back to Harry's question. If it speeds things along, I will download an e-book copy as it stands for you from my cloud storage and a PDF of the appropriate part of the diary." Everet pulled out his phone, pressed some buttons and soon both Kate and Harry's phones buzzed, announcing they had a new download.

"Okay," Harry told him. "I suggest you go upstairs and spend some quality time playing computer games with your boys. They've earned some 'dad' time. And if anything jumps out at us while we read, we'll call you."

Blackler nodded and headed upstairs. Kate and Harry stared at their phones. "Why do I feel I have an unexploded bomb in my hand?" Harry asked.

"Because you do," Isaac said.

"Wonderful. It must be a day ending in 'y'. I had hoped we could get through this next storm at least before people started shooting at us. Why am I staring at pages of documents on my phone when I'd rather be out snowshoeing?"

"Because, handsome, you need to use your mega-brain and your code-reading talent to figure out what he hid in this diary that is bringing down chaos and danger and life-threatening actions on our new friends. You can still go snowshoeing, but you need to read the diary by suppertime so that we can come up with some plans after supper. We both know that somewhere in this diary is the answer to not only who—but why someone wants Everet to disappear from the face of the earth."

Kate kissed Harry's cheek as he got up to go find her brothers to get some practice. She then gave Isaac the link to download his own copy, then opened the download on her phone, took a deep breath and read as fast as she could. Time, as they say, was of the essence.

CHAPTER 16

Saturday afternoon

B y the time Harry finished training with her brothers on the trail behind the kennel, the snow seemed to have moved to just threatening. There was even a hint of sun. He changed his clothes and joined Kate and Isaac, who had gotten comfortable by moving into the library. Picking up his tablet, he joined their study of Everet's book. As he had passed the dining room table, he'd also picked up the box of papers sent from Ramsey.

"I vote that before we get too far into the book," he said, "we go through these papers that Ramsey sent. Someone must have figured out what he was doing. Perhaps from some checking he did. Since Alven apparently sent him the coded entry in the diary, we should check to see if he could decode it."

"I suspect it was why he asked you to come to

DC and meet with him. He knew about your ability to decode," Kate said.

Harry divided the gigantic pile. "Here, you take this stack, I'll take the next and Isaac, why don't you take what's left. We can skim this. Hopefully, we can see if we can find a coded message."

"He apparently dug deep into the three survivors from the unit," Isaac said. "That might have set off red flags to the person in question that he was about to be exposed."

Harry grunted but didn't look up. Kate finished her pages without finding the code.

However, Kate had picked up her tablet each time she came across a reference that seemed somewhat explosive and bookmarked it for further research. This wasn't Harry's usual type of case, and the book she'd noticed, though she had read little, how well written it was.

Harry looked over at his wife. She sat with her feet up on the chair's hassock, her phone in her lap, her tablet on the table next to her chair, and a pad stuffed into the crack next to the seat cushion. He watched her read, stop and make a note, then pick up her tablet to check it out. She was pushing herself, and it showed. Frowning in frustration, he must have made a sound because her head snapped up. "What have you found? Anything?" she asked.

Harry stood and took the tablet from her hands. He took her Kindle and notepad as well. Then he walked to his desk, placed them in a drawer, and locked it. Finally, he walked back to lift her from the chair and said, "Excuse us, Isaac."

She let Harry steer her to the bedroom. He made her sit on the edge of the bed, pulled off her sweater and took off her shoes, telling her, "You were up way too early this morning with the boys. Take a nap and let junior rest. You'll feel much better later."

With a smile, he tucked her in, collecting a kiss for his troubles.

Kate was tired but didn't think that she'd sleep with all she'd read still spinning around in her head. However, she quickly lost the battle to keep her eyes open, not even hearing Harry close the door.

When she woke and opened her eyes to glance at the clock, she saw it was almost three o'clock. She lay still, feeling too relaxed to move. Her glance strayed to the window and blinked at the brightness of the sunshine bouncing off the snow. She grinned as she remembered all the solar camping equipment Alven had taken with him. When this mess was over, she definitely needed to talk with him about which they could work pieces of equipment into her search and rescue program. He seemed to know a lot about the new technology for someone buried in the woods. She wondered if he had a portable hot-spot with him. That and a tablet in the hands of the old Spook could make it easy to keep track of what was happening in DC. She hoped he'd keep her updated.

The bedroom door opened and Dillon and Quinn came in to check on her, followed by Harry. "I figured I'd send in your favorite alarm clocks to inform you it was time to wake up."

"No problem. I was already awake and marveling at the glitter of the sun on the snow. It is a beautiful day which seems to hold off worry about the next storm. I'll get my shoes on and join you in a few minutes." Harry walked in and lifted her shoes down from the shelf above her nightstand, out of reach of puppies looking for a nice shoe-chew. He pulled off the quilt which was covering her and helped her sit.

"I'll go put on the kettle for tea," he said, again collecting a kiss for his trouble.

Kate bent to tie her shoe and noticed that there was more of her belly to work around for that operation than there had been last week. Soon the job of shoe-tying would need to be farmed out, or she'd have to switch her footwear to loafers. She felt a flutter as she sat up and smiled at the thought of junior agreeing.

Her sweater slipped easily over her head, and down her body as she headed for the door. Then she stopped. Looking in the mirror, which showed her being further along in her pregnancy. She tilted her head as ideas filled her; she took the knitted fabric and, using her fingers, pleated it, turning left then right to judge the effect. Then she pulled the front into a box pleat. Both ideas looked good on her when she was barely showing, and would also work when she was well along in the pregnancy. She'd have to have her manager, Ellen, research the market for maternity sweaters within their boutique market. She could create a couple of styles that would show off the different dog breeds, be flattering while wearing a bowling ball at one's waist, but would still look good once the baby weight disappeared. Hmm. More designs to play with in her nonexistent spare time. She left the room chuckling to herself at the thought of Agnes, possibly pregnant by then, striding down the catwalk modeling pregnant dog owner fashions during her next fashion show.

She was still laughing to herself when she entered the living room. Everet was standing with her mother in the living room. "Your family will get to meet our whole family at supper."

Harry and Sal were standing together. Harry handed Kate her cup of tea and said, "I came to pick your brain on what to feed the five-thousand since it seems everyone is coming to supper."

"Loaves and fishes?" she asked, grinning.

"I was thinking like a couple of vats of chicken stew or a mass of meatloaves. I'm trying to come up with comfort foods that will relax the adults and appeal to the teenagers."

"I thawed out some chicken, but I can save that for tomorrow and thaw out some hamburger instead and make some meatloaves. We can have mashed potatoes, broccoli with cheese sauce, hot rolls, or bread, and I think I still have some of those fruit pies I have in the freezer. We could thaw them out, warm them up and serve them with ice cream."

"Okay, you're making me so hungry you'll be hearing my stomach growl soon. I'll see you two at supper." Sal said as he took the fresh cup of coffee he'd just made and headed back to the kennel.

Kate's phone buzzed with a text as she slipped into a banquette seat. She pulled out her phone, opened the text, she skimmed it.

Is B's family, OK?

A

Kate looked at Harry, who was peering over her shoulder, then typed.

Yes. They're safe.

K

Harry, "Kate, was Des right? You know who gave the warning about Ramsey." Harry said as he leaned over her shoulder.

"Not really."

"Okay. But maybe I should get in some more snowshoeing practice tomorrow." He said, while raising one eyebrow.

"It's always good to practice an important skill," she replied, smiling.

Kate finished her tea and then went to the freezer to pull out ingredients for dinner. Harry checked and saw only one pie. He headed to the basement to bring up more from their back-up freezer. He had gotten the second freezer for half-price at a going-out-of-business-sale and it was proving a lifesaver like this when their two-person household suddenly expands and normality becomes creating meals for a crowd.

Kate stepped to the cellar door after checking her supplies and called down for him to bring up more hamburger and bacon as well. A few minutes later, Harry placed a box containing the food that Kate needed on the kitchen island.

"I heard you did a virtual Indy 500 on I 84 earlier, Kate." Satu said, grinning as she came in with Kate's brothers.

"You'll have to ask the kids about the real thing. I was just a voice on the phone. If you want to help, open the dining room table all the way and get out the longest tablecloth and the good China. The count is seventeen for dinner at the latest tally. You may have to pull in some of the extra kitchen chairs if anyone else shows up."

Preparations moved along quickly and Kate mentally thanked her brother Will for including the large island in the middle of her kitchen as part of the house plans. She could assign the jobs of mashing potatoes, or making salad, or filling small divided dishes with pickles, olives, and other nibbles to anyone who wandered into the kitchen. The smell of meatloaves must have reached the second floor because soon footsteps sounded on the stairs. The doorbell rang, and voices filled the living room.

Kate's grandmother pushed through the sea of bodies carrying several of Tom's spinach casseroles to fill out the menu. Kate kissed her cheek and thanked her while placing them in the warming oven. Ann looked at the long table and raised an eyebrow.

"Seventeen for dinner. You'll meet the Blackler family any minute. They will stay with us for a while. The second floor is now furnished, which was timely. Point of reference. Mrs. Blackler is one of Mom's former TA's."

"Ah. Math is on the menu then."

"I'm hoping to keep the conversation general, but since we've upped the number of math geeks, I don't guarantee it."

Roger and Sal came in from the back hall as everyone else filed in to the dining room. The Blackler family settled at the table with Kate's mother assigning seats and everyone else filled in wherever they wanted. Sal held Ann's chair and then took the one beside her. Tim had taken the chair next to Shannon Blackler and introduced himself. He would head to BC in the fall, so they could talk about their college year ahead. Harry sat at the head of the table with a spot saved for Kate on his right. Just as all the food had arrived at the table, Kate, Harry, and Sal's phones dinged. Kate jumped up and quickly pulled out her phone as she stepped around the corner to look out the kitchen window at the entrance to the driveway by on the highway. A blue, late model sedan had turned into the driveway, but stopped.

Kate opened her security app and recorded the car's license plate. Whoever was behind the wheel seemed to be more interested in the place's layout than in driving in. Kate was about to ask Sal and Roger to check them out when a state trooper vehicle pulled in next to the car. The sedan quickly reversed and swung around to exit back onto the highway. Kate's fingers flew across the keys on her phone entering codes as the sedan paused before entering the highway due to traffic. By the time the car sped off down the highway, Kate was sending the head shot she'd captured using the camera at the entrance to the driveway, to the printer in the library, and to Harry and Sal's phone. She'd fetch the photo later. Then smiling as the patrol car pulled up to the porch said, "Satu, add two more place settings" She pulled two chairs from the kitchen table and handed them to her brothers.

Sal stood and went to open the front door. Conversation, which had paused when she dashed into the kitchen, picked up again to be joined by voices coming from the living room. Sal returned and sat as her cousin, along with her fiancé, filed into the room. What had been busy talk with all the Blacklers talking about their day, stopped? Silence filled the room. Their guests just stared at the new arrivals.

"Hi you two, we've saved you seats and your timing is perfect." Kate said, waving at the two empty chairs next to her. She noticed the Blacklers were all transfixed. "Oh right, introductions are necessary. Guys, this is the Blackler family who will stay with us for a while. Blacklers, let me introduce my cousin Agnes Forester and her fiancé trooper Sean Connelly." She silently counted to five and then added, "Yes, she is THE Agnes Forester, former supermodel, presently a bank president, and you'll be happy to know, another math geek," she said grinning.

As Agnes began chatting with Mrs. Blackler, introduced as Claire's former TA, Sean leaned over to Kate and asked. "Did you get a license plate on the car at the entrance to your driveway? He sure was in a hurry to leave when he spotted the patrol car."

"I'll send it to you. I also could get a head shot on the driver. There will be a printout for you after supper, but I've just sent the shot to Harry's, yours, and Sal's phones. Just in case."

Sal stopped the conversation he was having with Blackler when his phone buzzed. He pulled it out and laid it on the table while he finished the point he was making. Then, he hit the button code to open what Kate sent him. He was just about to look at it when Blackler's silverware came crashing onto his plate and he gasped. Sal immediately grabbed the man's shoulder to see what was wrong. The man he'd been looking at only seconds ago had lost all color and now twisted in an expression of horror. Following Everet's line of sight, he looked down at his phone and saw that Kate had sent him a photo captured by the camera at the top of the driveway. He reached to grab his phone, when Everet took his arm and yelled, "It's him. It's the man who grabbed me and took me to DC for this supposed trial."

CHAPTER 17

Saturday evening

Everyone began talking at once. Nobody was eating, and the kids were trying to get everyone's attention to find out what was going on when suddenly, an ear-piercing whistle silenced them.

Kate took her fingers out of her mouth, and in a very calm voice, said. "I have cooked a dinner that is going to be consumed while hot. Any discussion of criminals, crimes, car chases, etc, shall wait until we finish this meal." She looked at the staring faces around the table and asked, "Who knows the timing of the next storm?"

Roger piped up, "Sunday night into Monday morning was what I heard."

"Great," Tom added. "That will give us time to get in a little more snowshoeing practice. We should meet behind the kennel about 10:30 tomorrow after Mass and breakfast. That way, we can all have time to practice both in the open areas and on the circle trail. We can even practice with the snowmobile and make sure the trail is clear."

Kate looked around. "One thing we haven't done, despite all the snow, is to get out the sled. Liam, Dillon and Quinn used it when we were at Camp. I bet the bitches would love pulling, as would some of the veterans. For those who are not snowshoeing, lessons in dog sledding are now scheduled for the afternoon." Kate looked at the Blackler kids. The ragged fear that had been on their faces only moments ago, now had given way to excitement at the thought of riding in a sled being pulled by dogs.

Kate smiled quietly to herself and picked up her fork to continue eating. The meal settled down and soon everyone relaxed and enjoying the food. Kate noticed that Harry now had the main conversation flowing around an article in the latest AMS journal, which held all the mathematicians enthralled. Sal and Everet were in a quiet discussion about growing up in Massachusetts, and Tim was talking to Shannon about BC. She heard Satu explaining to the boys that the computers at the top of the stairs held new games that weren't even out commercially, ones that Kate had only designed this last Christmas. She touched Harry's arm and signaled she was making a trip to the bathroom and then stood to head for their room.

Once she finished, she pulled her phone from her pocket and sent the photo to Alven with the message. This man threatened Blackler. She was running a brush through her curls when the phone buzzed with a text.

Gianpaolo Rapino, a hit man for hire, originally from New Jersey. Ask Sadie.

A

She quickly sent a text to Sadie, Harry's assistant, with the photo and the info from Alven. Sticking her phone back into her pocket. She opened the bathroom door and ran straight into Harry's chest.

"Should I worry my wife is carrying on with still another man behind my back?" Before she could move, his hand shot out, pulling her phone out of her pocket. Opening the text app, he saw that she'd sent the photo and gotten a reply. Also, that she'd sent the information to Sadie.

"Kate, this is Bureau business."

"No. Let them do their own research. I'm a private citizen chatting with friends and trying to keep a house guest and his family alive. Tell me, Harry. Which of the people at the bureau would you choose to know that your wife has information about a potential killer? At the moment, I'd prefer to do my homework before I trust any of them."

"You trust your spook."

"My spook is 80 years old and has spent his entire career keeping this country safe. I've known him since I was a baby in diapers. I prefer letting him know that we've got some information rather than the person who shot Ramsey. Can we find out what Sadie knows before you put your wife in the line of fire."

Harry turned pale as what she said hit home. She was right. All those years being loyal to the Bureau had caused him to put his wife in danger twice already. He'd sworn never again. Yet here, the first challenge to that promise, all his bureau training filled his brain and his knee-jerk reaction was to play by company rules. He felt sick to his stomach. One word to his old colleagues could get Kate shot.

"You're right. I'm so sorry. Years of training have brainwashed me and it is a hard habit to break. Kate, I love you. You know that. Next time, don't even argue, just hit me in the head with a brick."

"I love your head too much to hit it, but I will fight you on this. Our responsibilities are different this time. We're not just guarding ourselves and our family, we have the Blacklers and their children we must keep safe. At least for now, we should keep this whole thing to ourselves and our trusted allies."

"Agreed." He reached out and pulled her into his arms, kissed the top of her head and then rested his cheek on it. His body was still fighting the shock of his wife's hard truths. It would take a while for that panic to fade.

When they returned, Ann and Gwyn were dishing up pies and ice cream for everyone.

"You okay, Kate?" Agnes asked.

"Yep. Pregnant lady strikes again. Um. That pie is just what I need."

"Good, because my next question is…"

"I've got two designs. I'll work up a third if you don't pick one of these."

"Now! I've got to see them now." Agnes shot out of her chair and raced around the table. "Do you have the designs on your laptop? Can I get it for you?"

Kate laughed. "You're worse than a four-year-old. Bring the laptop over and I'll pull up the sketches."

"What sketches?" Claire asked, upset that the conversation she'd been having was being interrupted. "What work is Kate doing for you?"

Agnes ignored her and rushed into the kitchen to grab the laptop. Gwyn came up behind her and moved Kate's food out of the way so she could get to the keyboard. Kate shook her head, laughing, but knowing how important this was to Agnes, and pulled up the first design. She enlarged it so that it filled the screen.

Agnes froze with a gasp. Sean stood, but Ann

told him to sit and not look. Agnes' hands were grasping Kate's shoulders as she minimized that screen. Then she clicked on a file and the second design came up. Agnes wrapped her arms around Kate and then reached out with a finger to trace the flow of the wedding dress and the delicacy of the veil.

There were tears in the eyes of the women standing around Kate when Claire and Harriet Blackler stood to see what all the excitement was about. Kate pulled up the first sketch, so that both were visible side-by-side.

"Oh, my goodness. You're designing Agnes Forester's wedding dress." Shannon gasped. "They are beautiful. The detail is incredible."

Kate leaned her head back and looked up at Agnes. "I'll send you both designs. Show them to Sybil and see what she thinks. Your grandmother has good taste."

"They're perfect. I can't decide."

"Study them. We'll talk after you get Sybil's input."

"You are wonderful, Kate."

"Don't let Sean see them. It's bad luck."

Everyone laughed. "I won't. I think that Sean and I will head out. I can't wait to show Gram." She hugged Kate as Sean got her coat and helped her into it. Then, kissing Kate on the cheek and waving goodbye to everyone, they left.

Shannon, who'd been part of the crowd behind Kate's chair, said, "I can't believe I got to see the designs for Agnes Forester's wedding dress. They were mind boggling. I can't wait to tell everyone."

"Sorry, Shannon." Kate told her. "It would devastate Agnes if anyone leaked information about her dress. You need to keep it to yourself. I'm sure you'd rather tell your friends that Agnes Forester sat next to you at dinner and is becoming your friend than that you betrayed her secret."

"Oh, no. I'd never do that. She is so beautiful and so nice. You're right. I'd much rather have her as a friend. I'll keep her secret. Thank you, Kate, for letting me see the dresses. They are unbelievable."

Harriet reached over and hugged her daughter, mouthing the words 'thank you' at Kate. Ann leaned in and whispered into Kate's ear, "You're going to be such a wonderful mother."

Kate grabbed her hand and squeezed it, and then rescued her pie, which was swimming in a lake of melted ice cream. She gobbled down the dessert while everyone else cleared the table. Her brothers and Satu took the Blackler kids up to the playroom at the top of the stairs to try out the new video games.

Harry pulled out Kate's chair and suggested that the adults retire to the library for a discussion of the problem at hand and for a phone consult with his assistant. He took her hand and led the way, settling Kate in one of the wingback chairs before taking his seat at the desk. The others settled into the chairs, and Roger stretched out on the window seat leaning a pile of pillows.

Harry swiveled his chair around and took a stack of photos from the printer behind his desk. He passed the stack to Everet to share with the others.

He looked at Kate and nodded to her to begin. "The man in the photo is the one Everet has identified as the man who took him into custody. We have been able to identify him as Gianpaolo Rapino, a hit man for hire originally from New Jersey. First question is who, at the Justice Department, is using hired killers to bring in suspects and second, is... I take that back. There is no second."

"I have sent the photo and information to Harry's assistant, Sadie. She is a retired FBI agent and analyst who may have more information on him and hopefully we will speak to her."

Harry had been dialing his phone while she spoke, and Sadie answered. He put her on speaker. But before he could say anything, the voice from the other end of the phone yelled, "Are you two out of your minds?"

"Sadie, you're on speaker in a room which includes all the usual players plus Kate's mom, and Everet Blackler and his wife Harriet, and Isaac Evans, a CID Inspector. Everet just informed us that Gianpaolo Rapino was the man who snatched him, supposedly taking him into custody."

"Congratulations, Blackler, you're lucky to be alive. Rapino rarely treats his targets so well."

Kate spoke up. "I've been thinking. He might have been told to keep him alive because they needed information from him."

Harry spoke up. "Going with the obvious, I would say that the snatch had to do with the information he will reveal when his biography of General Nathaniel Taylor comes out."

Sadie broke in, "I met The General once when I was just getting started. He had a reputation for being pure gold. Straight as an arrow."

"Well, from what I've been able to learn from Everet's research, he was good at keeping secrets, until all those he loved were safe from retaliation," Harry said.

"Everet," Kate asked. "Can you tell Sadie how you got this information?"

"The General's wife lived nearby and needed her lawn mowed. For years I mowed her lawn, did repairs, shoveled snow and kept the place up. After each job, we'd snack, and I'd listen to her stories of 'The General,' about all he had done over the years. She inspired me to go into studying history. Later, I had just finished my PhD in History. Harriet and I had just married, when I learned that Mrs. Taylor, had just died at age 87. She left me all her family records, photos, histories, bibles, everything. Source material for a career as an historian. It was a treasure. But the best part of the bequest was all her husband's diaries. I immediately changed my thesis topic and finished my degree by basing my thesis on research from those books."

CHAPTER 18

Saturday night and Sunday morning.

"**M**r. Blackler," Sadie's voice interrupted the discussion and filled the room. "You are lucky to be alive. Our friend Gianpaolo is a hired killer, trained by the mob. He hires himself out to the highest bidder, usually to eliminate people. This case seems to be a more elaborate job for him. Finding his puppeteer might take a little time, especially with the government connection. The photo looks like you took it at the end of your driveway, Kate. Who ID'd him?"

"Alven."

"How is the old fart? He always was one of the best spooks in the business."

"I think Gianpaolo went after him earlier this week and ended up bloody for his trouble. Alven and Buster have gone underground," Kate said.

"He's smart. Ramsey may know something about what's going on."

"Did you hear what happened to him?"

"Yes. Now that we know Gianpaolo is a player, everyone is going to have to keep a low profile. Let me do some searching. I'll get back to you."

"Alven suggested the answer is in the information in Taylor's diaries."

"Well, if he said it's there, it's there. Get busy going through that paperwork. I'll talk to you tomorrow."

Blackler looked at Harry. "That man, Gianpaolo, didn't sound like a mobster."

"Part of his training would have been to develop a sophisticated accent. We've had that occur with different criminals that we've encountered in the past."

"Harriet, I'm sure you've had a hard enough day to deal with today. So why don't we plan on getting together after lunch tomorrow." Harry said. "Some of us will train on snowshoes for an hour, but then we'll come in and get to work going through the files. We'll be going to the 7:30 Mass and breakfast will follow that, so work your schedules around it. Kate will get the sledding going later in the afternoon."

Everyone stood, though Harriet, who had been sitting in one of the overstuffed chairs with the hassock, swore she was comfortable enough to fall asleep there. Her husband boosted her up and wrapped his arm around her as they headed upstairs, followed by Isaac, who'd been silent through the entire session.

Sal and Roger headed out. Sal said, "The kids left on their trip today. I'll be bunking in the kennel."

Kate nodded, "See you in the morning."

Harry went to the French doors and let the dogs in. Sal had fed them and put them out after supper. The dogs greeted everyone who was still around, but soon settled. Kate went into the bedroom, followed by Dillon, Liam and Quinn. She heard her mother talking to Rory as they headed down the porch steps to the driveway with her brothers and Satu. After changing into her pj's, she went to the window to check the weather. The moon was visible clearly in the night sky, but there was a faint ring around it. More snow would be coming. She hoped they could get through everything that needed doing outside before that happened.

After saying her goodnights to the three dogs who settled around the room, she crawled into bed a and waited for Harry. She could hear him chatting with the other dogs in the living room as they settled for the evening. For the thousandth time, she told herself that Harry was the perfect husband for her. His bonding with her dogs was one of his most endearing traits. She chuckled and thought, 'love me

—love my dogs'.

Though she was tired, she put off sleep. Harry secured the house and joined her in bed, happy to hold her and give her something better to think about to distract from the horrors of the day. He lay awake for a time after she slept, waiting to see if the stress of the car chase would set off her PTSD. But eventually he relaxed. He guessed it took being shot at to bring that on.

***

The alarm woke them both to the realization that they had church and much to do that morning. Kate dressed while Harry let out the dogs. Then, while he got ready, she went to the kitchen to fill the kettle and turn on the coffee pot. She set a timer on the warming oven and put two coffee cakes in to warm. Pulling out a bowl, she cut up fruit and combined it with some walnuts and roasted almonds in the bowl. She tucked that into the refrigerator, figuring those things would hold anyone until they returned from Mass. She would feed the dogs when they got back.

Harry had her coat ready when he reached the kitchen. They ducked out the back door, and told the dogs that they'd be right back, and got into the car which someone had cleared of snow. The drive to church was short and uneventful. Inside, they stopped only to say hello to Fr. Joe. They nodded and waved to neighbors and friends, then found a seat.

When the sound of a bell rang, Mass began, and Kate let peace flow over her. Harry took her hand and squeezed it gently, and she let herself relax. When Mass ended, they made their way slowly down the aisle. Sean was waiting by the door to say hello before going on duty. Kate reached into her coat pocket and pulled out a copy of Gianpaolo's photo with his name and license written on the back and gave it to him.

"I got confirmation that this is the guy who went after Alven." Kate told him.

"Do you know where Alven is?"

"No, and I didn't ask. He and Buster are fine. He passed on that information, so don't get greedy. It would be great if we could pull him in, but I will warn you that Sadie says that this guy's a mob trained professional killer. Tell your guys to be extremely careful."

"Fun. You always come up with the most interesting killers, Kate."

"He's not after me, as far as I know. But he is around and is apparently after Blackler."

When they arrived home, breakfast was in full swing with her brothers, Ann, Tom and Gwyn, Sal, Roger, Isaac and the Blacklers all gathered around the kitchen table and banquette. Everyone was in a good mood. As soon as they ate, the group split up. The kids went over to Kate's mother's place with Claire and Harriet. They were going to a later

Mass and then would spend time in Mom's computer room. They loaded the computer room in that house with many games Kate had developed over the years as presents for her brothers. They weren't on the market because writing code was only her hobby. The kids were eager to try them.

Harry and the others who wanted to become proficient in snowshoeing, bundled up and headed out. Sal and Roger went to work on the kennel. When Kate looked up from where she was fixing dog food, all she saw was Everet and Isaac settling in at the dining room and taking papers out of the box.

"It looks as though it's just us, gentlemen, to attack this mess." The dogs who'd been competing for the men's attention recognized that the bowls were now ready and headed for Kate. When they were sitting, she passed out the bowls and then told them to eat. They finished quickly and when the last one sat, she gathered the bowls, picked up a dozen biscuits. She imitated the Pied Piper by heading down the hall to the yard door. The dogs quickly exited and Kate returned to put the bowls into the sink full of soapy water. Once she washed the bowls, she joined Everet and Isaac as they began unloading a box. Then she stopped and asked, "How much do you two know about what went on in the Vietnam War? I mean, what it was really like on the ground."

The two men looked at each other and shrugged. "Not much," Isaac said. "I've studied it along with other wars, but as far as what it was like and how it was different. It was a guerrilla war, fought in the jungle. Methods used by the enemy to fight differed vastly from those taught in basic training. We lost that war because we never should have been in it. It was unpopular at home and if it weren't for the draft, there would not have been the numbers of soldiers available to die."

Blackler stared at him for a minute then said, "I've only got what my research told me and that was strictly academic."

"Since none of us have a clue of what was happening on the ground during the actual fighting, I vote we talk to someone who was actually there. Hopefully, we'll get a better feel for what the situation was like and how The General's diary entries fit in. We might even find a clue to his pages of code."

"And how do we do that?" Isaac asked.

"Come with me," Kate said, standing and grabbing her coat as she led them out the back door. It delighted the dogs that a parade of their favorite people was walking the fence line. Every head needed patting as they stood on their back legs, stretching for hands to give them a special stroke or cuddle.

Kate spotted Sal at the main desk in the kennel, making entries in the kennel calendar. "Hey Sal. Will we be able to work the pickups around the next storm?"

"Yup. They've all called for extensions. Smart

people don't want to get stuck on the way back from their vacations by being caught in a blizzard. The two drop offs for tomorrow, have put their travel off for another week."

"Great. If you've got a few minutes, I think you might help us with some research we're doing on this case."

"Sure. Let's go to your office. You can give Miss Hecate a snuggle."

Kate led them into her office, pointing to chairs for the men, while she lifted her the massive bundle of white fluff from her chair and sat. Hecate did the rounds, rubbing against the legs of each of the men, and then returned to climb up onto the back of Kate's desk chair. Kate shifted her position as the cat settled her twenty-five pounds on the chair, balancing with a paw on Kate's shoulder.

"The case has moved in a direction where we lack background knowledge. It isn't something you can solve with an algorithm. The crime took place in 1969 during the Vietnam war. A unit went out on what they thought was a routine patrol, but something happened. Something that has had members of the unit fearing for their lives and those of their families. That's as far as we've gotten. We need someone with firsthand knowledge of what it was like to be on the ground fighting there."

Sal stared at them for a minute they said, "It was obscene. It was a war that never should have started. The U.S. shouldn't have been there. Have you ever been to the Wall? There are 58,267 names of those killed. Over 33,000 were 18 years olds. Kids! They were kids. Most did not know what it was like to be an adult yet. We drafted them. Talk about when your number comes up, you die. That old expression fit them perfectly. It was a war we could never win. Vietnam skewed jungle warfare there toward the Cong. They fought dirty, and they led us like lambs to the slaughter. What can I say? We lost the war and at the end, those last to leave barely escaped, having to be picked off the roof of a building."

"Were you drafted?" Kate asked.

"No. I knew my number was coming up, and I'd begun training to become a cop, so I volunteered and went into the Military Police."

"The crime we are trying to solve apparently took place in Vietnam during the war in 1969. A unit went out on what they thought was a routine patrol, but something happened. Something that had members of the unit fearing for their lives and those of their families. That's as far as we have gotten."

"Where did this crime take place? Do you know?"

Isaac spoke up, "I have the coordinates here." He handed Sal several sheets of paper.

"Are you any relation to Calvin Evans?" Sal asked him.

Surprised, Isaac said, "He was my father. He died several years ago. In fact, he's the reason I'm investigating this. How do you know my father?"

"I met him in Nam."

Kate looked at him. "Sal. That's the crime we're trying to solve now."

"Was that how you met my dad?" Isaac asked?

"Yea."

"While you were investigating this crime?"

"Yea."

"The threat is still real for all those in the unit who are still alive, as well as Everett because he's trying to find the details for his book. Have you also gotten threats because you investigated it?"

Sal said nothing and just stared at her.

"I saw you standing at the window of the kennel on Wednesday. You had a letter in your hand."

He looked at the men and at Kate, then stood and left the room. After a minute, he returned carrying a metal box, which he placed on the desk, unlocked and opened. Inside were letters.

"There's one a year," he said. "All mailed from DC. All typed on the same typewriter. All sent to the same address until this last one." He removed it from the box and put it in front of Kate.

She looked at it, then up at him. "It's addressed to you here."

"I'm so sorry Kate."

"All the more reason to stop him."

Blackler slammed his hand on the desk. "We've got to break this code, track this bastard down, and stop him. The General left the diary. We've got to pry the answers from its pages."

"Diary. What diary," Sal asked.

Kate looked at him. "Taylor kept a diary his entire life from the first days of Vietnam. In the first volume, there is a section where he says he witnessed a crime. He also recounts the threats made against the lives of members of his unit and their families if what they saw ever comes out. Taylor, however, is a straight arrow. His compromise is to detail the crime in his diary, but write it in code. He also secreted two photos in the book's binding. Unfortunately, the code needs a key and nobody has yet broken it."

"Harry?" Sal asked.

"Not so far."

"I need to see that diary and those photos."

Kate looked at Everet, who nodded. Kate turned back to Sal and said, "Get your tablet."

He went to his desk and returned, handing the device to Kate. Her fingers flew over the keys, stopping only to ask him for his password. Then she keyed in a few lines of code and handed it back to Sal. "I temporarily locked your tablet into our secure system. I upgraded your security and finally downloaded the diary and photos. I simply labeled the file with today's date and the letter 'd' followed by your granddaughter's birth date."

Sal took the tablet from her and muttered, "Design School. No wonder Claire went nuts." He stared at her for a minute. "You know you're scary."

"So, Harry keeps telling me. Welcome to the team."

CHAPTER 19

Sunday noon

"Sal, before you go off to read about the crime, we need your take on it? How did anybody find out about the crime if everyone in the unit had to swear to secrecy? How did you get assigned to investigate it? How did they know it was a crime and not an attack by the enemy? If the Bastard ordered his men not to say anything and they returned to camp saying nothing, nobody should have had a clue, but they asked you to investigate which isn't something that would have happened if anyone thought the Cong had done the deed."

Sal sat and stared at Kate, Everet and Isaac, and then with a sigh, began. "The first clue anyone had that something criminal had happened was when a local woman, one of those helping in camp, came back from a visit to her sister. The woman was hysterical. All she could say was 'all gone.' Her friends finally calmed her down enough to explain that her sister's small village had burned. Of course, our first thought was that the Cong was closer than we had first thought. But then she babbled something about graves. Now the enemy burning a village was a normal part of war. Burying the dead—never."

"After getting the location from the woman, my partner, Jacob, and I took a few men with us and went to check it out. When we got there, we saw someone had torched the village. There had been a few huts plus a small building that seemed to be a sort of temple. Everything burned."

"The woman had said that the graves were on the edge of the village where the jungle opened slightly. There were seven graves. Someone had tried to disguise them by dragging brush across them, but once one was located, we found the others, almost like a small graveyard. We uncovered the bodies and brought them back to the camp for the forensic guy to study. We were lucky to have someone with those skills. What he found were that five of the bodies were female and two males. Jacob questioned the woman who first told us about the village. It turned out that there was a temple with several small gold statues which were historical treasures. These the monks were to guard because of their age and history. The women were there to grow the food and care for the monks and the temple."

"When we had examined what it left of the temple, there was no sign of the treasures. But the shock came when the forensic guy reported to us on the bodies. It turned out that they did not die from the fire. Someone shot them before burning them. But that wasn't the most important fact. What he found when he examined the bullets was that they all the shots were from the same gun. Not only that, but that the gun was one of ours. This wasn't the work of the enemy. An American soldier had done this."

Sal stopped and seem to lose himself in thought. Kate asked, "How did you know to question Taylor's unit?"

"They were the only unit assigned to that specific area recently. We had the evidence from the woman in our camp that the village had been normal three weeks prior. Two weeks earlier, they ordered that unit to check the area. They reported back that they'd found nothing. When Jacob and I went to question the members of the unit, we found the lieutenant in charge had only been with them for three days. They had shipped his predecessor back to the states. The men were very closed mouth. They all held that it was normal and there was no sign of the enemy. They all claimed that they did not come upon the village when they were scouting the area."

Kate sat back to think about what Sal had told them. Why would a soldier, since he had said it was a lone shooter, and since the photos that Everet had located showed one man, shoot everyone in a village and burn it? Did he steal the treasure? Was he the soldier who went back to the states? There were too many questions. Taylor must have witnessed this. What ever happened that led to the graves Sal and his partner had uncovered, it had to be described in the diary. That must have been why Taylor had written it in code. He was afraid that if anyone got their hands on his diary, his life and that of his wife would be in great danger. Isaac and Everet questioned Sal about the finer points of his investigation and asked for details about the unit, but Kate had heard enough.

She told the men that she was going to get lunch started. Leaving them, she headed back to the house, but instead of starting lunch, she went to the library and closed the door. These details shook her, and she needed to be alone and think. How Nathaniel Taylor must have felt tortured to have witnessed this and not be able to say anything. They had to stop this killer. She saw now that not only had this been a burden carried by members of the unit, but it had also haunted Sal. She opened her tablet and settled in once again to read the section of the diary before and after the coded pages, trying to find a hint of the identity of the killer.

***

Harry returned from snowshoeing as Everet and Isaac came back into the house. "Where's

Kate?" he asked.

"She said she was coming back here to begin lunch."

"Back from where?"

"We've been learning from Sal what went on in Vietnam with the investigation into our crime. Kate knew that he'd not only been there as an MP, but had investigated it."

"I didn't know that. But the question is, where is my wife?" Harry walked to the French doors and looked out. Then, using hand signals, he got Dillon to move to the top of the deck slowly and sneak in the door without alerting the other dogs. Once the door was closed, he whispered, "Find Kate."

Dillon immediately headed for the library and Harry followed. Finding the door shut, he eased it open only just enough for Dillon to slip through. Harry waited a minute, then pushed the door wider and saw that Kate sitting in one of the overstuffed chairs. Her arms were now wrapped around Dillon, her head buried in his ruff, and her shoulders shaking. Everet, who had followed, looked over Harry's shoulders and frowned. Harry signaled him back and closed the door.

Then he explained, "The bond between Kate and Dillon is huge. When she is under stress, that dog is what she needs. She needs his comfort without having to justify the fact that she's upset. According to her brothers, when she lost her grandfather and father so close together, the two men who'd raised her, the only thing that kept her sane were the dogs, especially Dillon. He loves her completely and has saved her life multiple times. They are as close as it gets."

"And you're not jealous?"

"Kate loves me, but she's bonded to Dillon. When the baby is born, I expect his protection and devotion will expand to include one more. When I first met Kate, I realized I needed Dillon's approval to make our relationship work. Her father and grandfather, along with generations of these dogs, molded her into the exceptional woman she is, but whose existence they completely intertwined with her Samoyeds. I wouldn't have it any other way."

"I see."

"Let's go see about lunch."

The kitchen filled with delightful smells as rotini macaroni and cheese with broccoli filled two large baking dishes in the oven; the cheese turning a nice golden brown on top. A big salad bowl bursting with color sat on the counter, as Harry had added to the spinach base about every vegetable imaginable. Containers with Harry's homemade French and Italian dressings rested on either side. The smell of loaves of Italian bread heating in the warming oven and the olive oil for dipping added the perfect welcome.

They heard footsteps mounting the front

steps as Sal and Roger came through from the back hall. Everet, who was closest, moved to the living room to open the front door as the rest of the crowd arrived full of cheer from the snowshoeing. Talks of falls when trying to go uphill and stepping on their own feet kept everyone laughing. Tom finally said, "Considering how I did the first time I was on the short snowshoes, you guys were great."

"That's because they weren't chasing a killer." Kate muttered as she entered the room with Dillon.

Tom leaned in and hugged her. "And thanks to you, I had no permanent damage." He told the others, "What I learned from Kate was always to know what is right in front of your feet. The temptation is to look up and around, but it's the small things, right under your nose, that can kill you."

"What took you out?" Robert Blackler asked.

"Razor wire stretched across the trail." Everyone gasped. "It wasn't fun. Luckily, Kate was there to keep me from bleeding out. Plus, the guy who put it there is now in jail and will stay there for a good long time."

James asked Harry, "Is it true that you used to be in the FBI?"

"For a while. But after I got shot, I went out on my own and build a security company."

"Do you still chase bad guys?"

"Yup."

"Wow."

"I try not to chase them around the world any more. Most of my clients are companies that get hacked or have one of their employees try to rip them off. It's more about figuring out how the crime is being committed and then how to stop it from succeeding, rather than chases and shootouts."

"You need a lot of school for that, I suppose."

"A lot of math."

"Hmm."

Harriet Blackler gave Harry a thumbs-up behind her son's back.

"That's why Satu and I are off to MIT next fall." Seamus said. "We will work full time for Harry when we get out, but he lets us work part time now." Robert turned to Satu and asked her what they had done so far. She looked at Harry, who nodded, and then began telling him about all the criminals they had helped stop. By the end of lunch, Seamus and Satu definitely had a fan club. Robert was talking MIT for college and math for a major as the meal ended.

Kate had been quiet during lunch. Several times, Harry had reached for her hand to see if she was all right. She nodded, but then returned to contemplation rather than taking an active part in the discussion.

When lunch finished, everyone went off to

pursue their own interests. Harry, Everet and Kate stayed at the table with coffee and tea.

Harry looked at her and said, "Penny for your thoughts."

"Do either of you think that this case is nuts? Nothing about it makes sense. We've got an FBI agent and a retired CIA operative telling us that this is a dangerous case. We've got a hit man stalking us. We've got bad guys trying to run your Harriet's car off the road, and a retired FBI agent shot."

"I keep waiting for all of our friends to jump out from behind the furniture, yell 'surprise,' and tell us we're being televised for some stupid reality show. Why did Ramsey go to the trouble of sending us a text that took several reams of paper to print?"

Harry reached over and took her hands. "The reason you think it makes little sense is that nothing DOES makes sense. However, I'm used to cases not making sense at the beginning. Such as, when I go looking for a killer only to find that he killed because they finally caught him stealing, a career he's had for twenty years. I should have been looking for a thief. The only way to handle cases where nothing makes sense is to line up all the facts and see if any of them fit together. We may have found a piece of the information that is needed in this pile of nonsense, but it's going to take a lot more ingredients to turn this case into a delicious stew."

"This analogy is making me hungry again,"

Kate said with a smile now lifting her face. "All we have to do is to find the key, unlock the code, expose the crime and the bad guys, get the book published, plus all while keeping Everet and his family safe." Kate said, looking at the others. "I think I need another cup of tea."

CHAPTER 20

Sunday afternoon

"Look, it's going to snow again tonight. We'll have plenty of time to search for this key or try to break the code without it, but the sun is shining, Everet's kids have had a rough time, the dogs are restless and if I don't get out of the house, and get some exercise, I'm going to scream. I vote, after lunch, we get the sled from the barn, and let the dogs and the kids have some fun." Kate watched the men go from scowls to smiles.

"Get on your coats and boots everybody." Harry said as he headed out the back to head for the barn. Kate went to the door off the hall and signaled for Dillon, Liam, Shelagh, Kelly and Quinn to come in. She quickly snapped leads on Quinn and Shelagh. These two had not yet gotten enough training to be completely reliable off lead, especially in exciting settings. Then she headed back through the house to the front porch. People were flowing toward them from both other houses. Harry must have sent out a text. Both Quinn and Shelagh moved forward toward the crowd, but Kate quickly gave them corrections to heel before heading down the steps. Satu raced up to her and took Shelagh's lead. "I'll take her Kate. We don't want you pulled into a snowbank by these two bouncing pups."

Seamus took Quinn's lead and followed her down the steps. Harry emerged from around the corner of the house, pulling the sled, which had been his Christmas present, to Kate. On the seat lay the harnesses. They had originally gotten harnesses for three dogs, but Harry had since ordered more so that they could, once the dogs trained to the sled, run a team of seven.

Roger and Sal stepped up to help as the Blackler kids went on an orgy of hugging happy Sammies. As soon as they had laid the harnesses out, Kate asked Sal to get Rory to add to the group. She and Harry hitched Dillon and Liam as wheel dogs, then added Kelly and Shelagh, and finally put Rory in as lead. Setting the rest of the harnesses aside. She asked the guys to check on the amount of snow still left on the surface of the driveway. For the early runs, a packed surface would be easier to travel rather than powder snow, especially as deep as this was.

Both Kate and Harry had experience driving

the sled. They'd spent the end of their honeymoon, after the cast of thousands had left, putting the dogs through their paces. Quinn had even gotten to where she could harness him as lead. But today, with so many dogs who would love a chance to run, Kate decided the young pup, whose body still needed to develop more, could work as cheerleader.

Harry helped the Blackler boys get in to be first passengers as Kate went to rear of the sled. The plan was to follow the sidewalk up toward her grandmother's house, and circle around toward her mother's place then move onto the driveway and make a big circle across the main drive, angling left toward the barn and circle past the kennel, the dog yard and finally back to where they began.

The shouts of joy from the kids as the sled moved had everyone pulling out their cellphones to record the moment. Smiles were everywhere. The kids were waving and cheering. For the second trip, Shannon and her mother got to be passengers. Next, Harry took over and two at a time, the retired Sams got turns on the sled. Dedre and Teagan replaced the younger bitches and didn't show their age at all as they raced happily around the parking lot. This time, Kate and her mother got to be passengers. Listening to her mother cheer made her more determined than ever to make up for lost time. Maud, Dermod, Brendon and Shannon all had time to run.

On the last round of the day, Kate took Rory off as lead and gave Quinn a chance. He had settled down enough to stand quietly to be harnessed and then to perform beautifully in the lead. Once everyone got to ride, Kate and Harry got to be passengers for the final ride, and Sal, who'd been studying the skills involved in driving the sled, got his chance. As they came off the sidewalk and raced across the driveway, Kate saw a car turn into the driveway, despite the cones Roger had installed, blocking the entrance. It paused long enough for Kate to pull her phone from her pocket and record the car's information. Then, as they rounded the bend to head down toward the barn, Kate opened the video on the cameras at the entrance. Two men were sitting in the car. One pointing at the sled. They seemed to argue, but then as the driver pointed; she felt the sunlight disappear. The car reversed and pulled out of the driveway, heading back in the direction they came from. Kate glanced away from the screen and realized that Sal had driven the sled into the barn through the door that Roger had pulled open.

"How did you get here so fast?" Harry yelled to Roger.

"I had started back to the kennel when I saw those guys turn off and pause. You were sitting ducks out there and if you followed the pattern, they could have nailed you, with none of us being able to stop them. I just ran for the door and hoped that Sal saw me."

Harry gave him a high-five and said, "I can't thank you enough. I suspect you saved our lives."

"I've got this team of potential killers on video. I'm sending it to Sal and Harry, as well as my laptop. I attached the license plate. It's a rental, but we might get lucky with follow up."

Sal stepped off the back of the sled and stood. "I don't know which scared me more, the back of this sled or spotting those two morons in the car. But I know which one I want to try again."

Harry slapped his hand. "It's addictive. Let's get these guys out of their harnesses and back into the exercise yard—so they can sleep. They've definitely had their exercise today. Quinn, my man, you did me proud as lead." He reached down and undid his harness. Quinn licked his face and then bounced around the barn. Once we unhitched all the others, a general melee broke out with them, all racing around together. Harry and Roger lifted the sled to hang it on hooks in the barn ceiling and Sal hung the harnesses to dry. Then Kate snapped a lead on Quinn, who was still bouncing, and handed it to Harry. They took the dogs back across the parking lot to the house and when they reached the hall, let them out to join the others already in the yard.

"Do you think the family spotted the danger?" Kate asked.

"I don't think so, but we put ourselves out there like a target, waiting for them to strike. The driveway and parking lot are much too dangerous for the sled."

"Once this next storm finishes, we should take the snowmobile and clear a trail which begins at the barn and goes across the area behind our house and then up and around Gram's and finally circles back," Kate suggested, "to connect onto the main trail through the woods. That route would circle around and then return to the trail back to the barn. It would give the dogs a nice long run, the area would be safe from killers, and everyone could practice and learn."

"Sal knows how to ride the snowmobile."

"As do all my brothers."

"The dogs really enjoyed themselves today, especially the senior citizens. It amazed me to watch Shannon and Brendon get out and pull with the others. I hope it wasn't too much for them at their age."

"They weren't on wheel, which is where the strongest dogs must be. Remember how they keep up with the others when they race in the snowy yard. The benefit of the surface we were on was once the sled got going, keeping it moving was much less work—its basic physics."

They put away their outdoor gear and settled at the banquette with their tea and coffee. Kate pulled up the video on her laptop, and both watched the two men first focus on the sled. The passenger pointed and waved his hand, urging the driver forward. The driver shook his head and lifted his hand to point at the crowd watching them, then quickly reversed out onto the highway and left.

They looked at each other and Kate murmured, "Thank you, Roger."

"No, kidding. I suspect these guys thought Sal was Blackler. He has the height and, with his down parka, seems to have the bulk."

They looked up as Seamus and Tim came in the back with a bunch of grocery bags. "Hey guys, what's up?" Harry asked.

"Mom said that with all the extra mouths you two are feeding, you could probably use a grocery run before the storm hits." They put the bags on the counter and said they'd be back with the rest. Kate began unpacking groceries and chuckled. "They made sure the ingredients for all their favorite meals are here. I know what we're having for supper for the next few days."

Harry put the staples into the pantry and what meat and fish that didn't fit he stored in the freezer in the basement. The boys brought in the rest of their load and as they headed out, let Blackler in. Kate finished putting the last of the groceries away and noticed that their guest looked very upset.

"What's the matter?" she asked.

"Was it just my paranoia or did the driver of that car intend to run you down and kill you?"

"Let's just say we're happy that Roger is as fast

as he is," Harry said. He handed Everet a cup of coffee and then turned Kate's laptop so that he could see the screen. "Tell me if you recognize either of these two men."

"No."

"We'll have to assume that they were more hired muscle brought in to monitor the place. They saw a chance to take you out, thinking that Sal was you, but the opportunity disappeared before they could act on it."

As they were talking, the kitchen door opened and both Sal and Roger came in. They both went to get coffee before sitting at the table.

Sal pulled out his phone and set it on the table. Then looking up said, "I sent the video to Gurka. He pointed out that they did nothing illegal, but agreed that if Roger hadn't been so fast, there might have been a different outcome. He's got a lip reader on retainer and is sending her the video to see if they can get anything."

"Good. Everet doesn't recognize them so they are probably more hired muscle."

"Do we have a name yet for the person behind this?" Sal asked.

"No. Just his nickname. It doesn't help. We still need to go through all the paperwork that Oliver sent," Harry added. He looked at Blackler. "Are you sure that he didn't name the man later in another diary?"

"No. I checked every page, believe me."

Kate stared at the four men. "One thing is clear. Whoever is behind the original crime is working hard to stop his identity from coming out. He must have deep pockets if he can hire this many thugs to go after Alven, Ramsey, your wife and kids, and us. It also shows a desperation. I suspect that whoever he is, he's under a ticking clock. He let it go for years and years. Now it's vital to stop the information from surfacing. Why? What is happening that could cause harm by revealing something that far in the past?"

CHAPTER 21

Sunday evening

K ate was happy to leave the cooking of supper to Harry and headed to the bedroom to
take a nap. Her body was craving sleep, but
her mind was searching for keys to the coded pages.
She remembered when she and Harry first met; they
had to break a code to trap the bad guy. In that case,
they needed to find the book that served as the key.
It happened again in a case where a murderer tried
to kill her at a dog show while she was in the ring. In
both cases, the books would not have appeared unusual in the settings where they found them.

Hmm, she wondered. What book would a soldier have with him at all times. Just before sleep
claimed her, she thought she should ask Sal if there
is a book most soldiers carry.

###

She woke to a kiss, like Sleeping Beauty. Smiling down at her, Harry announced, "The food is being put on the table. It's time for Sleeping Beauty to join us for a delicious meal."

Kate stretched and, with Harry holding her hand, sat up and reached for her shoes. Harry leaned down and quickly had them on and tied. While he was bent, he leaned in to kiss her slightly bulging stomach. "Hello there, Munchkin. I'm so looking forward to your arrival."

She chuckled and patted her stomach. "I wore him out and we both slept well." They walked hand-in-hand to the dining room, where wonderful smells let her know how hungry she was. Everyone sat and plates were being filled by the time they arrived. They settled in to relax and eat while talk flowed around them of the storm that seemed to wreak havoc in the Midwest and was heading their way at a good clip.

"The first part of the storm should hit us by eight or nine o'clock tonight and according to the latest weather predictions, snow shouldn't end for at least twenty-four hours." Harry said.

Conversations about school and sports took up the rest of the meal, leaving Kate's eager mind get back to work on their case.

Kate stopped Sal as he headed back to the kennel and asked, "I know this is a strange question, but in a normal army pack, is there any book or pamphlet that all soldiers must carry?"

"No. Packs are heavy enough with everything else they have to tote on missions." He turned and took several steps to leave, but then stopped and pointed Kate toward the banquette. "You nudged a memory for me about your man, Taylor. From what I remember of the guy, he was a straight arrow, which surprised me when I ended up getting involved in breaking up a fight between him and one of the new guys who had just arrived. The newbie had grabbed Taylor's pack by mistake, at least he claimed it was a mistake. It later turned out that the guy was light-fingered and ended up being brought up on charges for theft six months later."

"However, back to the fight. He'd grabbed Taylor's pack and found a book inside. He took it and offered to return it only for a price. Taylor apparently went ballistic and went after the guy. After I stopped the fight and got the guy to cough up the book, it turned out to be a book of poems that his new bride had given him just before he left home."

"Do you remember what book it was?"

"Yeah, because it was one of the few books of poetry I'd read. It was a collection of poems by Robert Frost called New Hampshire. His wife had given it to him so he'd have a bit of New England in all that jungle. Luckily, the book had suffered no damage. I let both men off with a warning. It was the only problem Nathaniel Taylor ever gave me except his joining his unit members in their silence about what happened in the crime I was trying to investigate. "

"Have you had time to look at his diary?"

"I just started. The two photos are another matter. I vaguely remember the guy, but not his name. He wasn't among those I interviewed for the crime, just someone I'd seen around. But then the unit had just had a recent change in leadership. The lieutenant who'd been with the unit had transferred stateside. Apparently, he had connections. By the time they assigned me the case, he was history. That might be the guy in the photo, but I couldn't swear to it. I just noticed him around the base but never talked to him."

"Well, you've given me something to think about." Kate said as he rose and headed out to the kennel. Her Kindle tablet was on the table. Kate pulled up the entry for Robert Frost's New Hampshire and added the Kindle version to her library. Then she opened it up to look at it. She could see it was a replica of the original book. Unfortunately, it contained a lot of poems. Taking her tablet, Kindle, phone, and a pad of paper, Kate headed for the library. She settled into one of the overstuffed chairs and laid out the various electronic devices, placing the old-school pad and pencil in her lap. Pulling up the Diary on her phone, she copied out the first line of the coded information across the top of the page, and then put her phone back in her pocket. Then she opened the book of poems. There were almost fifty of them. This would not be easy. However, it was the closest thing to a key that she had come across. The work would be in finding if any of the poems held the key. She knew she wasn't the one to decode it. That had never been one of her talents. Either Harry or Agnes could do it easily. The trick would be to find the right poem.

An hour into the struggle, after trying all the standard decoding patterns and applying them to the first bunch of poems, and constantly comparing them to the line on her page, she realized it could take weeks to go through them all. She stared at the list of poem titles and opened her mind, seeking inspiration. Her eye fell on a poem called Fire and Ice. She clicked the link to read it. She had read enough of the Diary to know that the irony of this short poem might just appeal to Taylor as a New Englander in Vietnam. Plus, it was short, and could work well as a key. She closed her eyes and let the thought take hold. So didn't hear Harry when he came up behind her.

Before he reached for her, he whispered, "I'm behind you Kate, just letting you know in advance."

She started, but then laughed. "Thanks for the warning. I'm not sure, but I may have found the key."

"THE KEY? As in the key to the code?"

"Possibly." She told him about her conversation with Sal. "I've been going through the poems in order with no success since there are almost fifty of them. I just stopped and tried to insert myself into Taylor's head."

She pointed to the poem, and he read it aloud. Without taking his eyes from the screen, he reached for her pad. It only took a minute before he looked up at her, smiled, and said, "The decoded first line now reads, When the unit was out on patrol..."

"It works?"

"It works. Now all I need to do is to decode the four pages of tiny print and hope that somewhere he gives us a clue to the guy behind this."

"I'll leave you to it and go check on the rest of the team. While you were out snowshoeing, I found Sal was an MP while in Vietnam."

"I knew that. He hated that war."

"But what you probably didn't know was that he did the investigation on our crime. And, because he did that, they have subjected him to the same death threats as the others. The threats have been going to his old address. However, he got one on Wednesday, addressed to him here. They now can hunt him here and I assume the 'family' would include us."

Harry looked at her for a minute and then said, "So this investigation has become personal. We've got to end this now."

"Agreed. We also need to make sure that my

mother does not find out about this recent change of status."

"That's a given. Though it was her idea to bring the Blackler tribe en-mass to our door."

Kate chuckled and stood. "Well, baby and I will leave you to your decoding. Despite my nap, I am tired. I'm going to go take a bath and then go to bed. Don't stay up too late."

"I won't. I'll take care of the dogs. I want to check the news about the storm before I turn in." He stood and lifted her from the chair and enjoyed a long kiss before letting her go and getting back to work decoding. Kate left the door to the library slightly open for the dogs to find Harry.

Following her bath, Kate found herself more awake than she had been. Picking up the remote control, she turned on the television in the room's corner. She saw that there would be a full report on the upcoming storm in eight minutes. She turned to watch the news. She realized with all that had been going on in the last few days; she hadn't thought to check what was going on in the world outside. She was listening with only half-an-ear as she re-arranged the pillows on the bed so she could sit up more comfortably, when she heard, "The closely guarded short list of names being considered for the position of acting Attorney General is waiting until the FBI completes a thorough background check on each of the nominees following the problem that was encountered with the earlier nominee. Once the White House releases the names of the semi-final candidates, an advisory panel will work with the President in making the ultimate choice."

Kate reached for her phone and pulled up her search engine, typing in "former Attorney General nominee." A flood of articles popped up. Hints of scandal had apparently emerged within hours of the candidate being nominated. They criticized the FBI for not doing an in-depth investigation. The Bureau found no proof of the accusations, but rumors were enough for the President to pull the nomination. Kate looked at the name of the nominee. It surprised her to find it was Arthur Grumwald was a former director of the FBI.

What was it that Des had said about Justice giving Malcolm a hard time? Could there be a connection between Oliver, Alven and the man who is behind the crime. Kate hoped that there was something in the coded pages which would help nail this down and remove the threat.

Kate felt herself losing the battle with sleep. Whatever Harry found would have to wait until tomorrow. After she heard the latest about the storm, she turned off the TV and set the remote on her nightstand. Her phone buzzed with a text. *"Be careful when you break the code. If the wrong person finds out, your life will be in danger. Time is running out. A"*

CHAPTER 22

Monday morning

It was a quiet, swishing sound that Kate heard as her eyes slowly focused on the sight out her bedroom window. The snow was visible, but coming down at such a clip that she could already see it building on branches that had shed the snow from the earlier storm. Glancing over the edge of the bed, she didn't see Dillon. She pushed herself up to a sitting position and glanced at the clock. It wasn't quite six, but she could see the light on in the dog yard. Since the light was motion sensitive, she realized Harry must have let the crew out early.

Sliding on her fuzzy slippers, she pulled warm clothes from the bureau and dressed quickly. On her way to the kitchen, she spotted a light coming from under the door of the library. "Have you slept at all?" she asked her very rumpled looking husband. His desk covered with papers which were covered with his distinctive tight scrawl.

"I'll sleep later. I only have a paragraph left. I want to make sure that the decoding is perfect because this is going to be explosive. I don't want any misinterpretations of the facts."

"Have you come across the name yet?"

"No. However, I have come across a description of the man and his background. That, combined with the photo, should get us something. When I finish this paragraph, I'll do the new snow in the yard while you feed the pups and then I'll go catch some sleep."

"I know you're used to pulling all-nighters, but we've got a house full of people, a killer who knows where all the players are, and I suspect, a very short timeline. After you get some sleep, I'll talk to you about an idea I had last night." Without explaining, Kate headed to the kitchen to start breakfast for the crowd. She was gathering dog dishes when Isaac walked in. "Harry just told me he broke the code."

"Yea. He pulled an all-nighter to get it done."

"He said that he was going to use the snowblower to clear the edges of the dog yard and then sleep. I volunteer to use the snowblower. I've been using one for years so I'm familiar with how they work."

"Great. It is just outside the door at the end of the hall. The cord plugs in on the wall to the left of the glass door opposite Harry's office. I'll feed the dogs and let them out again once you're done. Thanks for doing this."

"No problem. So far, this is the nicest assignment I've ever had. It's a great place to stay, with nice people and fabulous food."

"We aim to please." They both chuckled, and Isaac headed down the hall.

She was just finishing up an apple strudel when Sal came in with his coffee mug at the ready. "I see Evans is pitching in. He seems a good guy." Looking around to be sure that they were alone, he said, "I finished reading the diary entry for the day of the crime. I wished I'd known about the coded entry back then. It was like working a case with both hands tied behind my back. Can Harry break it, or Agnes?"

"Actually, he was up all night doing just that. He's just gone to bed. I'm hoping he'll allow himself a couple of hours of rest before he's back working the case. However, the person who broke the code was you."

"Me? I know nothing about codes."

"No, but the story you told me about Nathaniel Taylor's fight over the book of Frost's poetry gave me an idea. I downloaded the book to my Kindle and finally figured out which poem was the key to the code. Without you, we never would have found it."

Sal stared at her and then smiled. "Thanks. That makes me feel less guilty for allowing this bastard to know where we're located. With all the people that pose a threat to him in one place, I thought that I'd set us up as sitting ducks."

"Actually, with everyone involved here, it's easier to guard. Our resources are all together. The weather is helping as well."

Kate stacked the dog's dishes and signaled the pups to sit. Sal took half and began on one side while Kate came from the other. The dogs finished quickly. After gathering the bowls, Sal grabbed a fistful of biscuits and headed for the French doors as he saw Isaac dragging the snow blower back into the hall. Soon, the dogs were racing around the cleared path. The oven timer went ding as he walked back to the kitchen and Isaac came in. Roger followed him through the hall door as the sound of footsteps descending the stairs signaled everyone gathering together and ready to eat.

Roger showed the kids where all the dishes and cutlery were and then went to fill his coffee mug as they set the table.

"Hold it a minute, kids. With this snow, we may end up with a crowd," Kate said. "Sal, could you make the table larger and boys? Could you pull some more chairs from the closet right behind you?" No sooner had they opened the table to seat twelve than there was a sound of feet mounting the front porch and greetings being called from the living room.

"Kate," Tim asked, "do you mind if I turn on the TV to keep track of the storm?"

Kate just waved for him to fill her largest teapot for the non-coffee drinkers in the crowd and took the tray of sausage and apple slices from the warming oven. Tom, Ann and Gwyn came in next, carrying a basket of warm muffins. Once everyone sat and relaxed, the conversation turned to the storm.

"Where's Harry?" Claire asked.

"He's sleeping. He had to work late into the night on a case and so he's catching up on his Z's."

Everet pulled out the chair next to Kate and looked at her. "Was he able to..."

Kate nodded, but then said, "We can work on this later. Harry will be up in an hour. For now, just relax."

The storm seemed to ramp itself up over the next few hours, and Isaac and her brothers worked to keep the level of snow in the yard comfortable for the dogs. Eventually, Kate just brought all the dogs in and let the snow build for a bit. Her brothers and Sal took turns plowing out of the driveway and keeping at least one exit clear at each house. Accumulation was coming down at 2 to 3 inches an hour.

It was almost noon when Harry, still slightly sleepy, emerged from the bedroom. Sal had just walked into the kitchen and kept walking until he reached Harry. He asked, "Could I talk to you for a minute?"

"Sure." They both headed for the library. Isaac looked at Kate and then stood to follow them. Everet watched them leave, then looked at her? She nodded at Everet. "Go with them. Lunch will be ready in about half an hour."

She heard a buzz on her phone and opened it to find an email with an attachment from Harry. She tucked the phone back into her pocket. She'd look at the decoded pages after lunch was ready. Food first with this crowd. Reaching for the remote control sitting on the island, she turned on the television near the kitchen table. She turned on the weather channel and saw the local update would be in five minutes. She moved to an all-news station where reporters were discussing names of possible Attorney General nominees. The commentator was interviewing a reporter attached to the White House. He said, "Rumor has it, though it is unconfirmed that the final three men being considered are Marco Weinbaum, Edward Cantwell, and Alessandro Macrino. Both Weinbaum and Cantwell are former members of the Justice Department, with each having served under multiple administrations. Al Macrino's experience is primarily corporate law. The former administration appointed him to the Ninth Circuit bench. He would be an easy confirmation for the President because of his connections on both sides of the aisle, but the question is, will a level of resistance come from the far-left members of the senate who haven't liked some of his recent decisions favoring corporations over workers. The President is pushing for thorough background checks on all three following the allegations which cropped up with his last nominee. Though, we must point out, we have found no confirmation for those allegations. Back to you, Jim."

The kitchen's rare empty status gave Kate a chance to pull up her laptop and type in all three names into a search. Two were the right age, so she opened a new tab and typed Cantwell and Macrino's names into a search for war records. Her watched beeped with the reminder she'd set to check the full weather report.

Any hope of this being a quick storm was disappearing. The accumulation rate remained at two to three inches an hour. All businesses, schools, and public buildings were closed. The governor had ordered that only emergency vehicles be out on the roads. Towns were designating parking only on one side of the street to allow plows to clear lanes as quickly as possible. All shelters were open, plus schools and churches were being used as emergency shelters for those who were in need. They gave emergency numbers for medical personnel needing transport in order to keep the hospitals staffed. As Kate listened, she felt relieved that the likelihood of anyone causing trouble today seemed to fade with the bad weather.

She was just taking a lasagna casserole out of the oven when she heard a sound in the hall. Seamus was pulling the snow blower down toward the dog yard door to the as Satu let in the pups. Kate heard her command, "Shake," and smiled. Satu had an excellent voice for dog commands. Maybe Kate could lure her over to the dark side and have her handle Kelly as a special. They would look superb in the ring with Satu's long stride, which came from keeping up with Seamus and Tim.

Kate popped loaves of Italian bread into the warming oven and, after pulling out her largest salad bowl, began shredding spinach and several kinds of curly lettuce into the bowl. Next, she chopped vegetables, added dried fruit and tossed the whole thing. Finally, she added a sprinkling of nuts and wontons on top. Lunch was ready to go.

Kate pulled a stack of plates from the cupboard, and over her shoulder asked Satu to go knock on the door to the library and tell the men that lunch was ready. A minute later, the room filled with men, teenagers, and women all talking at once. Ann had brought pies, and Tom walked in with a crock pot filled with baked beans while Gwyn brought a basket filled with hamburgers, hot dogs, and salads for supper.

Ann leaned across the island and said in a voice that Kate could just hear over everyone else,

"I thought I'd bring the fixings for a quick and easy supper. The time line with the end of the storm and all the clean-up necessary will need quick snacks for the workers. I figured I could later do a more formal meal."

Kate reached over and squeezed her grandmother's hand. "Thanks. The best part is not having to think of what to serve." She turned to the dogs and told them to 'down for dinner.' Harry came up behind her to give her a hug. "How did it go in there?" she asked.

"We now know why this guy is so desperate to keep this quiet. Unfortunately, Taylor didn't give us a name, just a pair of initials."

"Were the initials either MW, EC or AM?" she asked.

Harry stared at her for a few seconds. "How did you know?"

CHAPTER 23

Monday noon

"Kate, this is delicious." Harriet said. All the kids chimed in. The snow was helping them in one respect. They would have fewer missed days counted against them if school was closed for storms. Claire and Ann began talking about storms that had created problems in their youth. They discussed the time the governor had to close the entire state because of the danger of the deep snow.

Harry ate quietly at Kate's side, a hundred questions on the tip of his tongue, but knowing that this wasn't the time or the place to ask them. When everyone finished eating, Ann suggested Kate go lie down and rest while they clean up. Kate smiled and took them up on the idea.

Harry made an excuse to go get something from his room and followed his wife. When he closed the door, Kate turned and said, "The President has a short list of candidates for the Attorney General position. The former FBI director, who he first nominated, apparently became the victim of a smear campaign of innuendo, and half-truths. His name had to be withdrawn. Two of the men being considered are lawyers who have been part of Justice most of their careers. The other candidate is a former corporate lawyer recently appointed to the ninth circuit by the former administration. He would get support from the other party, so would be a shoo-in for the job. However, the President is gun shy and has both justice and the FBI doing background checks. However, the type of checks they do might not turn up this crime because it was never solved and the lieutenant's identity never came out. The FBI might need some help from influential Army specialists."

"Well, the army owes you a favor, Kate. Also, I hate to suggest it, but why don't you contact your favorite former spook and your great-aunt and get some information on who might help us who were in Nam when this crime happened. That someone sealed this unit's information is suspicious. If you get a minute, read the decoded description of the crime and see what stands out to you. I need your brains." He leaned in and kissed her, tucking the blanket in around her.

Kate lay for a while, letting her body relax and hopefully getting junior to settle into a nap. Picking up her phone, she began with Alven. She texted him, *"What do you know about Alessandro Macrino? Early career? Army service? Family connections? Business connections? Skeletons? Harry broke the code."* She hit send and then called Sadie. She didn't spend too much time on chit-chat, but asked her to do the same type of research as she'd asked of Alven. Finally, she called Maeve.

"Hey Kate, how deep is the snow out there? The city is almost at a standstill. The subways are still running, but buses and taxies are not moving."

"We're doing fine here. The dog yard needs constant attention from the snow blower so that the dogs don't get hurt or have it built up so high that they go exploring. I'm wondering if you had any luck finding out more about General Taylor's time in Vietnam?"

"Yes, I did. I was just on the phone with my old friend Jason, who apparently knows Sal. He said they were MPs together. Anyway, I didn't get a full name on the guy who was the lieutenant in charge of the unit, but the first name was Al. I don't know if that helps."

"Yes, it does. Now I've got another job for you. The President is considering three men for the job of Attorney General. They are being screened, but one of them may have more to hide and the obvious places to check may not work for those doing the checking."

"I see where you are going. Yes, I still have con-

tacts. In fact, with a full name, I can get back to my friend and go a little deeper. I'll get back to you later today."

"Thanks, Maeve."

Kate put her phone on the nightstand and closed her eyes. She'd done all she could. Now she needed sleep.

***

She had slept for almost an hour when her phone buzzed with a text. Pulling it to her and wiping the sleep from her eyes, she read the message. *"Oliver sent you info on AM hidden in the stuff on Taylor. Reread with that in mind. They've scheduled O's surgery for tomorrow. Tell H to keep it to himself."* A.

The blankets flew off as she sat up, grabbed her shoes and used the chair beside the bed to help with shoe tying. Slipping on one of her warmer sweaters, this one with puppies romping around the bottom, she headed to the library to check the fax box for clues about a killer. Isaac was sitting reading Everet's book on her Kindle, which she'd left on the desk. Looking up, he smiled and said, "Blackler is a fantastic writer. I feel as though I know Nathaniel Taylor and my best friend. I think I would have enjoyed that."

"I've heard that from several people. But if we could put the General aside for a minute, I need some army expertise. Did Harry share my suspicions about Macrino?"

"Yes. That's going to be a tough battle to fight."

"And that is why I need the Army. Remember the problem you had uncovering sealed information on the unit?"

"Yes. They redacted documents about the unit and therefore I didn't see who was who."

"Vietnam was over fifty years ago. Since then, we've come out with a key to the information locks called The Freedom of Information Act. A FOIA request for that information might take time unless you have some help. I have a few contacts in the Army and my great-aunt has more. Spell out exactly what we need with dates, unit identification, and all the specifics you have and I will forward it to my contacts."

"You are a genius. I should have thought of that before."

"You're army trained. Like Harry and the FBI, you guys think in straight lines. My mind never worked like that. The shortest distance between two points is often a squiggly line that moves around barriers."

"I'll get right to work on this." Isaac said and headed up to his room to work uninterrupted.

Kate went in search of Harry and the others. The kitchen was empty. She looked out the window and saw that the dog yard path had been cleared recently. The dogs were mostly sleeping in groupings. As she stared, Dillon made eye contact, and she watched him rise quietly and head for the hall door. Liam was right behind him. Kate smiled. Sal had told her not to be alone without those two dogs at her side. She quietly opened the door and let the dogs into the hall. As she passed the kitchen island, she saw a note from Harry telling her they were out practicing since there was a break in the snowfall. Kate pulled out her phone and checked the weather radar. It looked as though they had about an hour before the next part of the storm would arrive.

She laughed. The snowshoeing bug had truly bitten her family. She admitted it was fun, especially when she wanted to do some wildlife photography, but mostly, she used it to train cops and search and rescue teams. With weather like this, it was the only way to get around.

She filled the kettle and started it warming for tea, then headed to the library to find Oliver's fax. She needed to reread the papers with the new information in mind. It had sounded very confusing when she'd thought it applied to Taylor, but it might be more logical with a focus more on Macrino. She had only gotten comfortable when her phone dinged, letting her know that someone was entering the driveway.

The windows looking out toward the front gave a perfect view of an SUV pulling up in front of the porch. Two men in matching dark suits got out and headed for the door. Kate found out what was going on and opened the front door, but engaged the lock on the storm door at the same time. The pair approached slowly, checking out their surroundings as they mounted the steps to the porch.

They spotted her flanked by the two white dogs, who were not wagging their tails but standing still and focused. Kate didn't smile but tilted her head, waiting to hear what they had to say.

"Does Harry Foyle live here?" the man on Kate's right asked.

Kate responded, "Who's asking."

"Look lady, does he live here or not?"

The man on Kate's left stepped forward and grabbed the handle of the storm door and twisted it while pulling. Kate mentally thanked the builders for putting such a well-made security door in as a storm door. Something was definitely wrong. If she were to guess, these men were agents, but they were not using protocol when they spoke to her. They were acting more like bullies than agents. Slipping her hand into her pocket, she pulled out her phone and got ready to press speed-dial for someone who might know what was going on.

She stood her ground and asked, "Tell me gentlemen, are you from the Bureau, because if you are, you've broken protocol and I have no intention of answering any of your questions until I find out what is going on. I'd like you to tell me, who is asking?"

"Lady, you are in for a pile of trouble. Just open this door and get us Foyle, now."

Sighing, she pushed the button and after two short rings, someone answered, "The AIC Bullock's office, who is calling?"

"My name is Kate Killoy and if possible, I'd like to speak to Malcolm now. I have a pair of men who might be FBI agents have just threatened me."

"One moment please, Miss Killoy."

Kate heard someone put her phone on hold, but only a few seconds later, she heard Malcolm Bullock's voice ask, *"Kate, what's going on?"*

"Malcolm, I've just had two men drive up in a government issued SUV, and demand to see Harry without identifying themselves. Then they tried to enter the house without invitation. At the moment I am alone with Dillon and Liam at my side, so I thought I'd call for guidance."

"Are you sure they're agents?"

"No. For all I know, this is an audition for the road company of Men in Black. Maybe they'll talk to you?"

Kate turned to the men on the porch and said, "Gentlemen. Since you have yet to introduce yourselves, I thought I'd call someone who might get a better answer to my question of who you are." She pushed the button on her phone and said, *"You're on speaker, Malcolm."*

"Alright, who is in charge? What is your name? Who sent you and what do you want?"

"Who's asking?" the first man said.

"Malcolm Bullock, AIC in the Washington, DC office of the Federal Bureau of Investigation."

The second man stepped to the edge of the porch as he said, "Oh, shit."

"Unless Shit is the name of one of you gentlemen, I'm still waiting for some identification," came the request from the phone.

The man in front pulled out his phone and keyed in a number. Then he spoke into the phone requesting to speak to the AIC about a case involving Harry Foyle.

From Kate's phone came the sound of a buzz and a woman's voice saying, *"There is a man on line 2 asking to speak to you about Harry Foyle, Sir."*

"Tell that man to give his name to Kate and answer my questions."

The agent muttered something into his phone and disconnected the call.

"Sir," the man in front said, "Agents Grody and Figueroa. We're from the New Haven field office. We have been told that former agent Foyle may have evidence in a case being reviewed by the Senate and we have instructions to bring him in along with any evidence."

"Do you have a warrant?"

"Er..., no, sir. We figured he want to come in and help."

"Agents, do your homework. Rogue FBI agents have almost murdered Harry Foyle several times, as has his wife, who is standing in front of you. You should also know those dogs beside her are police dogs. I suggest that if you want Harry Foyle's help on your investigation, you hire him. He's smarter than you are and has more friends in high places. Apologize to Mrs. Foyle and go back to your office and work through channels. If you need to force a testimony or, better yet, you ask nicely, for help. Kate, Have Harry call me when he gets back."

"I will do that. Thanks Malcolm." She ended the call, nodded to the four men on the porch and closed the door—locking it.

CHAPTER 24

Monday afternoon

K ate looked down at the dogs leaning against her side and took a deep breath. "I wonder who sent the clown car?"

Pulling out her phone, she texted Harry about what happened and then went back to the library and settled in, going one page at a time through the box holding the fax sheets. What she found was that a page would begin with details about Taylor and then suddenly the phrasing would change to a more cryptic way of expression. They used initials instead of names when referring to various individuals. Grabbing a highlighter from Harry's desk, she began again, slogging her way through the pages. She marked each part she felt would be a better fit in a case involving the criminal. Page after page, she found individual paragraphs that covered some detail of the crime. She was about halfway through the stack of papers when she heard the kitchen door open.

"Kate, where are you?" Harry yelled.

Kate used a post-it to mark her place. "I'm in the library."

Harry raced in and wrapped his arms around her. "I was so worried when I realized that we'd left you all alone. We had gotten as far as the border with the state park when my phone went off. Who were those guys? What did they want?"

"They were from the New Haven field office. I had to call in Malcolm because they didn't follow protocol. By the way. That's a very good storm door. It didn't even rattle when they tried to get in."

"Get in?"

"They were after you. I suspect something connected it to the case. Malcolm wants to talk to you as soon as possible. Oh, and this is not to be repeated to anyone, including Malcolm, in case someone is listening in. Oliver's surgery is tomorrow."

"Thank goodness. Why the secrecy?"

"I suspect that if our nemesis finds out that Oliver could soon be a threat, he'd try again to kill him."

"Why would he think Ramsey is a threat?"

"This is why." Kate picked up the stack of papers she'd been working on and pointed out the sections she'd highlighted. "Alven told me that Ramsey had sent information about the killer in the fax. I went through it again and noticed that the text changes styles in certain paragraphs on each page. I've been going through the pages and when I'm done, we can read them straight through and find what he was trying to tell us."

"You're amazing."

"No. It's more a case of the boredom of a pregnant woman who is used to being out and about now stuck inside thanks to the storms."

"I'm sorry, Sweetheart. We're all out playing and you're stuck here fending off FBI idiots. Did they say who sent them?"

"No. In fact, I was getting suspicious that the man we're after might have friends in high places if he can order government agents to do his bidding."

"You might be right. I'll call Malcolm now and see if he has any ideas."

"Fine. I'm going to finish this up while it's quiet. I'll let you know if I find any informational gems." Kate went back to her pages and saw a story developing. Each paragraph added more to the information Oliver collected about AM. Oliver had a very low opinion of the man.

"Kate, I may need your help in getting this FOIA request sped up. Here's a copy of what I've requested if your contacts can expedite it."

Kate stopped what she was doing and picked up the list, looking it over to see what he was requesting, when her phone rang. Checking her phone, she saw it was Maeve.

"Hi, Maeve. Was your contact able to get us information?"

"Kate. This man is dangerous. I need for you and Harry to be very careful. Very careful. If half of the reports I've gotten are true, he would have no problem getting rid of you."

"I think he tried with Harry about an hour ago. Two clowns from the New Haven field office showed up at my door and ordered me to let them at Harry. Luckily, the crew was all out in the woods practicing snowshoeing. When they didn't follow protocol, I had to sic Malcolm on them. I had locked them out since I was alone, but I had Dillon and Liam with me."

"This guy has his fingers in many pies. He is a danger to Malcolm too."

"Do you think your contact could put through a FOIA request for Isaac Evans, of CID? Someone blocked him when he tried going through channels. He's working the case with us."

"Send me the request and I'll see what I can do."

"Thanks. I'll keep you posted."

Kate quickly sent a copy of the request to Maeve and then returned to the papers on the desk.

It took another half hour to finish highlighting the paragraphs, but since she was reading as she went, she'd slowed toward the end. The list of crimes Ramsey Oliver laid at this guy's door was horrendous. He must have had some mob connections because the style of many of the 'hits' was familiar. She'd had experience fighting the mob and was well aware of their capabilities.

Kate opened the closet and pulled out a ream of paper. Then, using cut and paste, she assembled the document from Oliver without the distractions of added text. When she finished, she made a half-dozen copies and went in search of the team.

The kids and adults were sitting around the kitchen table talking about snowshoeing. The dogs were let in and Kate watched as all the old-timers were lapping up love with plenty of hands to rub their heads. For once, Quinn and Shelagh weren't stealing everyone's thunder. Harry had made hot chocolate and warmed up some pies and muffins. It was just what the crowd needed.

Keeping her folder in her lap, and snuggling Dillon, she accepted the hot chocolate from Harry and a piece of apple pie. All the wildlife they'd seen impressed the kids. James said he was going to begin a list of every new species he saw. Apparently, Isaac had told him about his father's love of birds and the life-list he'd kept. They were still discussing binoculars and cameras with night vision. Kate smiled. It was good for the kids to be exposed to these men

who had such unique life experiences. Dog showing had given her that, since people who show dogs
come from every walk of life.

When the group broke up, Kate signaled the
men to wait. As soon as the others left, she passed
on the information she'd gotten from Maeve. She
told Isaac that Maeve would pass his FOIA request
to her friend, who might speed it up. Then she
put the folder on the table and passed the stapled
packets to the others. "This was what Ramsey Oliver
was sending us. He hid it in plain sight, but once
I got so I could spot the style changes, it all came
together. This man is truly a bastard, as his troops
so clearly said. I suspect he has a mob connection
because of the style of the hits. Harry and I have experience with hits. In fact, I suspect that we could
have involved this character in the scheme we halted
several months ago. At least, he seemed know how
to insinuate himself at the highest levels of the government."

Sal sighed. "I hope you're wrong about this,
Kate. That guy almost killed you in the middle of
your wedding."

"I'm just glad we had these guys on the job,"
she said as she snuggled Dillon.

The men looked startled. "That's a story for
another time. If you each could take one of these and
read it through, when we can talk to Ramsey, hopefully soon, we'll have a better handle on this."

Harry placed a hand on her shoulder. "I told them about the visit from the Bureau. If this guy can call in that level of official help, we've got to iron up our invisibility cloaks."

"Have you talked to Malcolm yet?" Kate asked.

"No. I should call him now." He moved to the banquette as the men began reading the pages Kate had given them. She glanced at the pages while keeping her focus on the phone conversation. It had taken a strange turn. She stood and walked over to stand behind Harry. From what she could hear, Malcolm was calling Harry Henry and was asking about Beth and the new baby. It talked about an assignment that might require some travel, so Henry should check with his wife. It ended with Malcolm telling 'Henry' that he'd get back to him with the specifics later.

Harry disconnected the call and looked at Kate.

"I'd say that either there was someone in the office or he suspected they tapped his phone,"

Harry returned to the table and joined the others in reading Ramsey's report.

They had been sitting there for a half hour when Kate's, Harry's and Sal's phones all announced that a car had pulled into the driveway. Kate stood and dashed to the front window. The car passed by their house and pulled up in front of her grandmother's place. A man stepped out and walked behind the car, which put him out of view of the camera. Kate turned to say something to Harry only to discover that she was alone, except for a dozen Samoyeds that had let in without her noticing. She rushed to the kitchen to pull up the cameras on her laptop, with its larger screen. Going from one camera to the next, she landed on the camera which showed the porch on her grandmother's house and the entrance to K and K. As she watched she noticed a slight movement at the right side of the screen, a figure stepped out of the shadows with his hands on top of his head and stood perfectly still. A few seconds later, the four men who'd minutes ago had been sitting in the kitchen, stepped into camera range. All four stood with guns trained on the man. Since there was no sound, Kate couldn't tell what they said, but Harry grabbed the man, whirled him around and pulled off his hood so he was looking directly into the camera.

It was Des.

CHAPTER 25

Monday late afternoon

"You're lucky you're not dead," Kate yelled as Des walked in the front door. "Of all the stupid tricks to try…"

"Hi, Kate. Actually, yell at Malcolm. He said to check your readiness for an attack."

"You're both idiots."

"Agreed. Hey, Quinn. How's my boy?"

It thrilled the puppy to see his old friend and, with no thought to the scare he'd put into Kate, just bounced up with tail wagging to snuggle his old pal. Heads appeared on the staircase and Kate called out, "False alarm. Apparently, the FBI wanted to test our readiness to defend ourselves against the idiot who's after us. This is agent Deshi Xiang from the DC headquarters of the FBI. Des, this is Everet Blackler, his wife Harriet and their children, Shannon, Robert and James. And the only other person you don't know is the man on your left, Isaac Evans, CID."

"Hello, everyone."

"Okay, the niceties are over. Why did Malcolm think we needed you here?"

"He wanted me here to keep you safe. He thinks you may have the answer to what's going on. Justice is about to get a new Attorney General, but there's something off about the whole deal. Rumors are rampant. Oliver was bringing him information that could upset the nomination. He feels that there is a publicity bomb ready to go off, and he doesn't want the Bureau or the President caught in the crossfire."

"Who is doing the background checks on the candidates?"

"We are."

"What areas have you checked?"

"All of them."

"What about their war records?"

"What war records? None of them served in the military."

"That is not true."

"What?"

"Macrino was in Vietnam."

"There was no listing of him ever serving."

"They covered it up."

"Why?"

"The reason they covered it up is the reason there is a threat against us. Something happened in Vietnam. A crime involving Macrino. Through connections, he could return home and get the record sealed. He threatened those who knew the truth and a number have met with 'accidents' over the years.

"We can't get the President to change his mind based on accusations about a crime that happened fifty years ago."

"How about eyewitness testimony?"

"Who? Why hasn't he come forth?"

"He's dead."

"Eyewitness testimony from the grave. Kate, you're good, but even you can't pull that rabbit out of a hat."

"If I had the testimony of a respected member of the military whose reputation they spoke of as pure gold, would it help. If I had it in writing, in his own hand. What if I had photographic evidence to follow up the charge?"

Des sat and stared at her.

"This is behind Ramsey Oliver's shooting?" he asked in a whisper.

"Yes."

"You have proof that Al Macrino is a criminal

when he is about to be made Attorney General. What is the crime they alleged him to have committed?"

"Crimes. Murder and grand theft."

Des stood and began pacing. "You know, Killoy, you have made my world very difficult since we met."

"Sorry about that."

"Kate. These people do not fool around."

"We are well aware of that, including the children upstairs who had their lives threatened this week. Believe me, Des, I don't go looking for criminals to threaten my life. I haven't set a toe off this property in almost a week. I am a pregnant woman, being constantly reminded that snow and ice can be dangerous. I'm confined to the house for my safety and that of my baby. I can guarantee I have done nothing to invite a killer into my life."

"I'm sorry, Kate. Foyle, I think I need one of your special scrambling phones to call Malcolm. We have to get the President to create an emergency so that we can postpone the announcement."

"I'll bring you the phone and you can make yourself at home in the library. Kate and I will be in the kitchen making supper. We have many people to feed."

Sal went out to the kennel to help Roger with the dogs. The kids went back to work on their school assignments. Maeve called to say that her friend had success, and that he was faxing the papers to Harry. Isaac went to Harry's office to play with the cats and wait for the information to come through. Kate took a long breath and sat at the banquette while Harry let the dogs out. The second part of this storm was due to start up again in an hour, so hopefully the pups would have fun while they could.

Kate's phone buzzed with a text. *"Tell Malcolm's boy that there are three unknowns who just arrived in town. Talk to Gurka. You should warn him. These types like to use sniper rifles and automatic weapons with large capacity magazines. Stay away from windows. Keep the dogs inside as much as possible tomorrow."*

Kate set down her phone and dropped her head in her hands. It was all starting again. Killers with guns were invading her world. Not even the oceans of snow could keep these men away.

Harry reached for the phone as Kate lifted her head to stare out the window. Sliding into the seat beside her, he reached an arm around her shoulders and pulled her close.

Everet walked into the room. "I am so sorry I brought this all down on your head, Kate."

"You didn't. Alessandro Macrino did when he murdered those women and stole the treasures the monks guarded. The way you can fight this criminal, Everet, is by writing this story with truth in every detail. You owe it to General Taylor and every member of that unit. They spent their lives living in a hellish fear because this creature thought he could do what he wanted and get away with it. He's a walking psychological casebook for insanity. The Bible quotes Jesus as saying, 'And the truth shall set you free.' All those lives threatened or taken need you to use what we've found and write the best book you've ever done. We each have a task here. Yours is as author/biographer. Make the General and his wife proud. Oh, and keep your head down and your wife and kids close until we solve this."

"Good pep talk," Harry said.

"I get preachy when I'm scared and trying to talk myself into finding bravery."

"Guess what? You've found it."

Everet went back upstairs, and Harry picked up her phone. "How does Alven know all this? How does he know that hit men have invaded our town or that Des has arrived or that Oliver was about to be attacked?"

"I didn't know that Alven was a spy when I was growing up, but I knew he was a sort of techno-logical wizard. I would overhear conversations with Dad and Gramps about some source that only Alven could reach. I thought he was a researcher since he could find information for K and K that nobody else could. The more I think about it, the more I'm convinced that Alven can hack into any system he wants. He probably knows about the men in town by hacking into the traffic cams looking for out-of-state cars. He can probably hack into our system here. And, I suspect, he did the same thing to the system at the hospital in DC. Alven may not be a spring chicken, but he's brilliant. When this is over, if we all survive, you need to talk to him and maybe bring him in as a consultant."

"You have the most interesting friends."

"Yes, I do. But my question is, where do we go from here." Kate looked at Harry, seeing his expression drawn and worried.

"I'm not sure how to fight this," he said.

"We've been up against similar situations before. If we can protect Everet and his family, I think we should let the world know what this man did. We may need to call the freedom of the press in this case. I think what might work is for a news organization to interview Everet about the horrific crime he uncovered while researching his forthcoming biography. A crime that concerns a major figure in the news today. He could do a Zoom interview. There could be a description of the crime. It could show a sample threatening letter if Sal will agree."

The door to the hall opened, and Isaac walked in carrying a fistful of papers. "Your great-aunt is worth her weight in gold, Kate. I've got copies of the records showing Macrino as lieutenant in charge of that unit, as well as the request to hide the information in the first place and the names of those making it happen."

"Great. I think it's time we get together and plan out a strategy."

"After supper," Harry said.

"Supper. Right. Food and stuff. We should do that first and then have the 'A' team meet in the library to work this out."

We filled the next hour and a half with food preparation, and lots of people and dogs. Des, as well as Kate's brother's, Tom and Tim, talked about problems with the latest draft picks by their favorite teams. Ann, Claire and Harriet discussed Agnes' upcoming wedding and comparing it to the one Kate and Harry had last Thanksgiving weekend. As for the members of the team, they were pretty quiet. It seemed to be a case of not having the ability to engage in small talk when a major crisis occupied your brain. But despite seeming to be four-hours long, the meal ended and everyone retired to their favorite places.

"Kate, why don't you lay it all out because you've been on the front line of this so far?" Harry asked her as the team settled into the chairs in the library.

"Okay. Since not everyone has been in the room when different facts came to light today, I'm going to go over what we've got so far. To begin with, the diary had the coded description of the crime. We eventually got those pages decoded which spelled out an attack on a tiny Vietnamese village, of primarily women and children, with monks charged with guarding a stash of religious treasures during the conflict. According to what Taylor learned on the night of the crime and from some investigation later, Lieutenant Alessandro Macrino raped several of the women. When the monks tried to intervene, he shot them, along with the women and children. Macrino then searched the village, found the artifacts. After burning the village to disguise the crime, he took the stash and returned to his unit. He insisted they bury the bodies and threatened the other members of the unit to guarantee their silence. They took his threats seriously since there were two of the unit members killed within the next forty-eight hours."

"Before the week was over, Macrino got himself transferred back to the states, along with his stolen goods. Within a month, a judge intervened and his name and evidence of his ever being in the unit were now hidden."

"Sal, can you tell us about the investigation that the army tried to carry out once they discovered the crime?"

"I was one of two MPs assigned to the case. Though the paperwork showing the units assigned to that area conveniently disappeared, some people had long memories. The new lieutenant assigned to the unit knew nothing. Members all claimed to know nothing as well. I will say one thing about

PEGGY GAFFNEY

Taylor. He never lied to us, but he gave us nothing with which to work. Eventually, the case got listed as unsolved. It remained my only unsolved case until now. However, my determination made me a target for the threats." He reached for the metal box beside his chair. Opening the box, he reached in and pulled out a fistful of white envelopes. "They're all exactly alike. Typed on a manual typewriter. Each stating that the only thing that would keep me and my family alive would be my silence about the investigation. One would arrive each year on the anniversary of the crime. I kept track of the members of the unit. Several of them, or their family members, met with deadly accidents over the years. Too many for it to be coincidence. What terrified me this past week was getting this year's letter addressed to me here instead of the address where all the others had been. It meant that the bastard was still keeping track of all of us, over fifty years later."

Everet spoke up. "Apparently Nathaniel Taylor's conscience bothered him. He recorded what he had seen in his diary but wrote it in code in case anyone found the book. He had to protect himself and his wife, especially since he had made the army his life. When his wife left me the journals, it was specifically to write and publish his autobiography. There was a notation in the will that I didn't pay attention to, but with all this coming out, appears important. Mrs. Taylor stated her husband wanted the journals to be used to give a clear picture of what actually happened during his career. However, he specified that this could only happen following her death. I don't know if I would have been as clever as Kate in breaking his code, but since they did not give me anything else, he carried with him. I didn't know about the book of Robert Frost's poetry. It is amazing that she could not only track down the book with the key, but find which of the poems he used."

"Well, Sal inadvertently helped with that," Kate said. "Isaac, what were you able to find with your FOIA request?"

"The judge who concealed the details about the unit turned out later to be indicted for working with the mob. He was also Macrino's uncle according to information that Kate's aunt's friend could dig up."

Des shook his head, "Oh, no, don't tell me that Maeve is in on this."

Harry grinned and shook his head. "Tell me, Des, did the thorough background check on Macrino turn up his mob affiliated uncle?"

"No. Apparently, someone scrubbed his background completely. My question is, now that you've uncovered all this, what are you going to do with it?"

"Well, according to my source," Kate said, "three mob hit men have arrived in town in the last twenty-four hours, so we've got our work cut out for us. I don't know about the rest of you, but this pregnant lady is going to get a snack and have a cup of tea before planning our method of attack. Is anyone else hungry?"

Everyone stood and followed her to the kitchen.

CHAPTER 26

Monday later that evening

When they returned from their break, they agreed they needed a plan. Kate pointed out that the danger would only continue if Macrino kept his crime a secret. If the truth comes out, his power disappears. The question is how they were going to do that, and still stay alive.

"The book, and revisions to put in what we discovered, and the time and work involved in publication, will take too long for this," Everet said.

"Wait. Do not count out the book yet. What we need is to align the facts so that it creates a compelling story in a brief clip to be delivered to the public. That means all the information about Macrino's background, time in Vietnam, the crime, the coverup, the criminal threats, and that his name is being considered for Attorney General: all this has to be done with graphics of the diary, the coded pages side by side with the decoded ones, along with a mention of Frost's poem, the black and white photos, and the redacted paperwork showing that Macrino was in Vietnam. It's got to be pulled together into a tight story and we've got to get a name reporter to do the interview."

"Now Everet can't go to a television studio for the interview. It would be too dangerous. However, this is the twenty-first century and we can zoom interviews with you just sitting and talking to the screen on your phone or tablet. What we need is for you to write the script. Time for yourself, Everet. Make sure you can get all the highlights in within the least amount of time. They have to work around commercials, intros, questions, etc. Also, make the list of questions. If we're going to get this out asap, then we're going to need the questions to fit our story. While you're working on that, I'll see what I can find in the way of an interviewer."

Kate disappeared back into the kitchen. She needed a nationally recognized reporter or commentator to get out the information fast. Before she could settle, she heard the phone ringing in Harry's office. Quickly dashing down the hall, she picked up the phone and at the last minute remember this was business and answered "Harry Foyle's office, Kate speaking."

George Nason's voice surprised her. *"Oh Kate, I'm glad I caught you. I have lined up an interview for Harry with Patience Snyder. She has massive national coverage. She's really hard to get, but she'd heard of Harry from something he did about the mob, and a theft at the Greek embassy, plus some other cases she was going on about. She'd like to interview Harry as soon as possible. I'm sure that he has interesting cases that would appeal to her viewers. She's prime time and it would really get his name recognition out on a national level."*

"George, is there any way I could get in touch with her. We have a case now that I think would be just the ticket for this interview. Do you have contact information? If so, I'll call her for Mr. Foyle and make the arrangements."

"Fantastic. Patience was my wife's roommate in college, and they stayed in touch. Though Patience usually does hard news, when Elizabeth told her what Harry and you did, she jumped at the chance to interview Foyle. I will email Mr. Foyle all the contact information. I hope this will be successful. Harry and I might argue, but the actions of his business were fantastic. It's just what the business world needs."

"I'll contact Miss Snyder right away. Thanks, George."

Kate ran from the office to the library, bursting in on the discussion. "Harry, where's your phone?"

"Right here. Why."

"Give it to me, now."

Staring at Kate, he handed over the phone. Kate seized it, opened the email, and began copying information. Then she dialed a number and waited. "Miss Snyder, my name is Kate Killoy and George Nason suggested I call on behalf of Harry Foyle. Yes, an interview. Well, Mr. Foyle is working on a case right now that, when we reveal the information, will definitely come under the heading of expose. Would you be interested?" While she was talking, she wrote the name Patience Snyder on a piece of paper and turned it for all the men to see. Their jaws dropped.

"The team will be ready to go over the information with you in the morning. What would work with your schedule? I can have Mr. Foyle contact you. His client? The author Everet Blackler. Yes, there was a scandal attached to him for several years and we tied it to this case. Let's just say it was one of several attempts to keep information on this crime from coming to light. It was a cover-up at some top levels. However, there thing very important. We must keep the details of this expose confidential until the broadcast. They have made several threats, plus an attempt on Blackler and his family. For their safety, we should not warn the subject of the investigation before the broadcast. It could cost lives. Um, yes, my name is Kate Killoy." Kate listened for a minute and then said, "Yes, I was part of both those cases along with Mr. Foyle. Thank you, but right now the focus needs to be on bringing this criminal to justice. Nine o'clock tomorrow morning. I'll let Mr.

Foyle and Mr. Blackler know. Thank you."

Sal stared at her and shouted, "You go to the kitchen to make tea and come back with a nationwide interview with Patience Snyder! Are you real or is this a joke?"

"Let me explain. I went to make tea but heard the phone ringing in Harry's office. I went to answer it in case it was important, and found it was George Nason, Harry's last client. George, it seems, has developed hero worship for Harry's business since it saved his company. George's wife was Patience Snyder's roommate in college. Apparently, they were chatting, and the wife told Patience about Harry saving the company. Patience decided that it would make a good interview for her, along the line of creative ways to stop corporate crime."

"Well, I hear this and a bell goes off. I tell George that the case you are working on now is right up Snyder's alley. George sends a text to your phone with all the woman's contact information. I thank George, race in here and line up Patience Snyder to do the interview with Everet so he can reveal Macrino's crime. You guys will get the i's dotted and the t's crossed tonight and be ready with the graphics, bullet points, etc., ready for the lady at nine o'clock tomorrow morning."

"Oh, she knows about you being pulled in by the bureau and then the case disappearing. Be prepared to include that as an example of a false flag to keep you from finding the truth. If I were you, I'd start with an author finding a coded message in the diary you were using for source material, the unexplained incarceration, solving the code, finding out about the crime, finding the criminal behind it and the covered up, the FOIA request to revealed, and finally the attempt on your family's lives."

"Kate, sit," Harry told her. "You're going to explode if you keep going."

"You're right." She leaned back in the chair. "I've been so worried about the shooters, and such. Who would have thought that the hero of the hour would be George Nason?" She giggled and then broke out in a laugh.

Sal looked at her. "That's the guy with the roses?"

"The very one."

"Roses?" Des asked.

Now Sal was laughing and finally Harry joined in after he gave a brief description of one of his most embarrassing moments.

Kate leaned back and rested her head against the chair. When her laughing ended, a series of yawns followed.

"Okay, Kate. I think you have earned your rest. You can leave all the Y chromosomes to put the presentation together. We'll need you tomorrow to help us set up the broadcast." Harry stood and pulled her from the chair. Her strength seemed to have left her after the excitement of the phone call. She wished the guys goodnight, and she and Harry headed to their bedroom. He tucked her in. "Kate, you are amazing. You take a friendly call from George and turn it into the solution to our problem."

"It was just luck." Kate mumbled, sleep claiming her.

"No, my love, it was your wicked brain taking over and creating gold from straw. Sleep tight and we'll try to get everything organized for the morning. I think you were wonderful." Harry looked down and saw that Kate was already sound asleep. Chuckling, he headed back to the guys. They needed to put this thing together quickly. Their lives depended on it. He let Dillon, Liam, and Quinn into the bedroom. "Watch over her, guys. We need her quirky brain to survive this. Keep Kate safe."

He noticed other dogs had already settled into their usual places for the night. The snow battered against the windows and French doors as the storm raged unable to do anything about the weather; he returned to the library to put the information together that would hopefully stop Macrino.

CHAPTER 27

Tuesday early morning

It was still dark when Kate opened her eyes to check the time. Her 'early to bed' the night before now had her feeling energetic. She moved carefully so as not to wake Harry and slipped her feet over the edge of the bed and onto the floor. The dogs had already moved to the French doors, ready to check the world outside. She realized she must have slept through the last pass of the snowblower, because there was barely an inch of new snow on the path. She eased the door open and three white fluffy bodies shot across the deck to begin the day's race around the snowy mountain.

Quickly, she ran to the living room and pushed through the crowd of canine bodies pressed against those French doors. Shifting bodies, she opened the door and, like water in the rapids, the dogs shot through, eager to be part of the race.

Kate watched the show, smiling, and then headed to the kitchen. Even though it was early, there were lots of mouths to feed and much to do. As the kettle heated, she pulled the phone from her pocket and reread the description of the crime Harry had decoded. The brutality of the crime, primarily aimed at defenseless women, hit a cord with her. Macrino had serious mental problems, and she'd bet that one was a basic view of women as something he could use, abuse and destroy. If she never met this creature, it would be years too soon.

James came around the corner from the living room, dressed for the day and looking hungry.

"You're up early," Kate told him.

"I looked out the window and saw the dogs circling the snow mountain so I figured either you or Harry would be up."

"Milk, juice or hot chocolate?"

"Hot chocolate. It's cold out."

"It is a day that needs a good, hot breakfast to start. Why don't you hand me a dozen eggs from the fridge along with the milk and that bag of shredded cheddar cheese from the drawer under the bottom shelf and I'll get breakfast started. People will be up early because we've lots to get done today."

"Why is today different?"

She looked at the boy across the island and said, "Because today is the day we fight back."

He looked at her for a long minute, then smiled and said, "Good."

By the time others descended looking for food, Kate had the scrambled eggs and cheddar casserole, bacon, sausage, fresh fruit, and muffins laid out along the island with a stack of plates at the beginning of the line and silverware and napkins. Sleepy people worked their way down the line, but once they sat, conversation built.

It was just barely six o'clock when Harry and Des wandered in. Their conversation ended as Kate lifted a second casserole, hot from the oven, to replace the one that was history. Both men dug in.

"Sorry I slept late," Harry said. "I didn't mean to leave you to do breakfast alone."

Kate laughed, "I didn't. James was my sous chef. He's very good at following recipes. The blueberry muffins are his, start to finish."

Everet, who was filling his plate, stared at his younger son. Then he reached and grabbed two of the muffins. James grinned. His father leaned in toward him and whispered, "How about you and I take over cooking dinner a couple of nights a week?"

"Yeah! Let's do that," James whispered back, grinning.

Kate smiled to herself, happy to have given James a love of cooking, as her grandmother had done for her and her brothers. Everet collected 'good dad' points as well.

While everyone was eating, Harry stood and cleared his throat to get everyone's attention. "We are beginning the first step today to fight back against this monster who has been making life miserable for a lot of folks. We have found the details of the crime that was committed during the Vietnam War that is behind these attacks. It was a horrible crime, though I won't talk about it now. The upshot is that the information in the general's diary, which was in code, but now decoded, will become public on national television." Everyone's attention was now focused on Harry.

"At nine o'clock, we will get a call from Patience Snyder and her crew to go over the details of her interview." Here everyone began talking at once. The famous, respected commentator meant excitement flowed like an avalanche through the room. Kate let out a whistle and silence ensued.

"Much to do and little time, everybody. Let's get back to the plan," she said.

Harry grinned and then said, "Okay. This will be a Zoom interview. Miss Snyder will be in her studio and Everet and I will be here. The producer emailed me they will send a digital background to give the effect of us being in the studio during the interview. Seamus, you and Satu will handle the technology at this end so we don't have any dropped signals or other problems. Having our own server will be helpful. We sent a list of suggested questions, plus copies of the diary, the decoding and the part of Everet's book covering that period of General Taylor's career."

"If word leaks about the interview, that will be the time when we are most at risk. Toward that end, you must be silent. No using your phones even to text. The bad guys will use that to find you. In fact, if your friends can live without you for a day, I'd suggest that you go dark starting now."

The three Blackler kids pulled out their phones and turned them off. Kate watched her brother Tim do the same, but in slow motion. She raised her eyebrows while looking at him, and he nodded sheepishly and stuffed the phone back into his pants.

Des stepped up beside her. "Malcolm thinks this is the best or worst idea you guys ever had. He has notified the President in confidence that one of his candidates will have his reputation destroyed in prime time tonight. He recommended a need to speak to the President of Ukraine or Italy on a vital matter as a reason to postpone the announcement."

"Sounds good. You might have Malcolm call him about a minute before the interview to warn him, so he watches." Kate suggested.

"Tonight is Snyder's regular night for the program where she does her take on what's happened during the week. Millions of people tune in to get her view on things. People trust her. This will be everywhere and picked up by everyone. Harry told me they are giving them the entire show, except for commercials."

"They've got a lot to cover. Not only the crime in Vietnam, but the reign of terror carried on since then, including the attack on Everet's wife and children. All this to cover up the original crime."

Kate stepped up as Harry finished. "My source has warned me that three thugs, he spotted in town, are potential hit men. So far, the snow has kept them at bay. He warned me they could carry assault weapons and sniper rifles. The warning suggested staying away from windows. We will keep the dogs inside as much as possible. I don't want to worry anybody, but a sniper with a rifle could shoot from the highway and hit someone here. Luckily, the highway is very busy, so it is not a likely place for an assassin to stand. There will be no outdoors activity today. The storm should finish within the hour. Once the driveways and parking lot are clear, there will be no exposing people to danger there. We will keep all the kennel dogs inside until the danger is over. I'll be keeping the dogs inside most of the day with only a short time outside to burn off energy. The broadcast will be from the file room in the basement. Once inside, we can lock the door, ensuring safety and no interruptions. That's about it. Meals at normal times. Be aware of your surroundings and be careful."

Harry looked. "Okay, Satu, Seamus, Everet, Des, Isaac and Sal, let's head for the basement. The call from the network is due in five minutes."

Claire suggested that she, Ann and Harriet retire to the large bedroom where Harriet and Everet were staying and work on their knitting projects, since there was a sofa and comfortable chairs in the room and the windows didn't put them in danger.

Tim took the kids up to work on the computers in the play area at the top of the stairs as Tom and Gwyn headed back to K and K to get some work done.

Roger disappeared back to the kennel. He told Kate he would pass on the information to Gurka about the three, armed strangers in town. I would ask Sean to keep an eye out for out-of-state cars.

A few minutes later, Kate's phone rang. It was Maeve.

"Katie, how are you doing? Did the information my friend sent help?"

"Yes, it did. Thanks, Maeve. It has been a wild twenty-four hours and today seems to be more of the same. We decided that the only way this guy can hold power over his victims is if they stay quiet. Tell me. What do you usually watch on television on Tuesday nights?"

"Television? Tuesday nights? The news, the nature show, Patience Snyder, and then the news again be-

fore going to bed. Why?"

"No specific reason. That's an excellent lineup. I may watch that myself tonight. The storm has almost let up. I think the dogs are getting a little tired of having two-thirds of their yard taken up by a snow mountain. When that melts, I'm going to have to keep them in the barn run most of the time, which has gravel or I'll be washing dogs daily. It's going to take at least a week of sunny and dry weather to get the surface dry enough so I won't be dealing with brown Samoyeds."

Maeve laughed. "That is the downside of having a dozen dogs with long white double coats."

"You've got to love hair. I've got to let the dogs out for a few minutes, so I should get about it. They're on restricted play because being confined in the yard makes them excellent targets. Alven warned us to keep low profiles today."

"Kate, be careful."

"I am. In fact, Mom, Gram and Harriet are upstairs knitting. Tim is playing computer games with the kids and everyone else is working down in Harry's storage room where the computers and servers are. We're all home bound."

"If Alven is using his toys to look after you, I feel better. He has some stuff that even the spooks in DC haven't yet discovered." Maeve laughed and then said goodbye.

Disconnecting the call, Kate smiled. She

never had to spell things out when chatting with Maeve. She didn't know if Maeve took on any special cases for MI-5 anymore, but she'd talked to some of her old partners and she knew they missed Maeve's talent and instincts.

Walking to the hall door, she called for the dogs to follow. As she went, she explained to the dogs that they were to go out and do their business quickly, and then come back in. Harry laughed when he heard her explaining exactly what was going on, but she'd done so all her life and she would probably never change. He couldn't argue with the fact that they listened to her and responded to everything she told them to do. When she reached the door, she put her hand on the knob and, looking at them, all said, "Okay. Quick, like bunnies. Out." She swept the door open, and they flew out. Kate stayed out of view, not presenting a target. She figured that three to four minutes should be enough time for them.

As she waited, her pocket buzzed. She pulled out her phone. A car paused at the top of the drive. She clicked buttons on the app and recorded the license plate. She didn't have a good angle on the driver's face, but she waited until there was a break in traffic. As the driver glanced to the right, she hit the button, capturing his face. She continued to watch the video camera they'd installed and saw a trooper's car slow down to pull into the driveway. Spotting the law, the car gunned its engine and sped into traffic. The trooper followed the driver. Kate hoped he pulls him over and give him a ticket for reckless driving. She quickly sent the photo and license to Roger to pass on to Gurka. and that a trooper had chased him off. Roger got back to her that Gurka had up'd patrols in this area for the next forty-eight hours. Kate smiled. The grumpy sergeant really had a heart of gold. She told Roger to be sure they alerted the troopers about these characters as armed and dangerous.

She looked out into the yard and noticed that several of the dogs were now relaxing in small groups. Time was up. She opened the door and gave a quick whistle, stepping back at the same time and plastering herself against the wall. A dozen slightly damp bodies filled the hall. She closed the door and walked to the whelping room, followed by the crowd. Pulling the towels from the basket in front of the dryer, she reached down and, working quickly, rubbed anybody within reach. After only a few minutes, they were all dry enough to return to the house. Tossing the now wet towels into the dryer, she left the whelping room and turned left toward the kitchen, then stopped. Holding up her hand, she told the dog, "Wait." Turning around, she went to the back door and threw the deadbolt. Then, reaching into her pocket, she texted Roger what she had done. A few seconds later, thumbs up emoji responded, and she headed back down the hall with the dogs. It wasn't paranoia if there really was a threat. She'd be the first to admit. It frightened her...

CHAPTER 28

Tuesday noon

L unch was relatively quiet, as they had worked out the bugs for the broadcast. Filming would be at four-thirty and broadcast during her regular slot. Harry worried something might happen between the time of the taping and the broadcast, but they had no control over that. Patience Snyder had promised them that if they gave her the exclusive, it would run—uncut. Everyone knew that television studios could make things happen or not, with decisions turning on a dime. They had to trust that Snyder and her producer would make it happen.

Satu walked into the kitchen and, leaving a piece of cardboard on the island, went into the library. A minute later she was back with an 8 1/2 by 11 head shot of Patience Snyder. Kate watched as she pasted the head shot to the cardboard and sketched out a body beneath it. Then she headed to the basement. Kate couldn't keep her curiosity from getting the better of her and followed her through the door of Harry's file storage room. Seamus was sitting at the table, covered with blue paper. He folded his hands on the table and he sat erect. Satu used a yardstick to align his line of sight with her cardboard cutout. Then she had him move to the chair on his left, followed by the one on his right. "Perfect." she told him. "Let's eat."

Turning, she spotted Kate in the doorway. "I studied Patience Snyder's position when they did the dry run. This spot aligns perfectly. If the guys look at the cardboard cutout, they will seem to make eye contact with their host and it will give a feeling of them all being in the same room. That is the look we're trying to achieve. Digitally, we can project the studio behind the guys and the blue just helps disguise any distraction in her fancy table."

"Fantastic. You guys are great. Let me go feed you so you'll be ready for the show."

Both of them dashed up the stairs ahead of Kate, whose dashing days were on pause while transporting junior.

As Kate emerged from the basement, Sal was chatting away with her grandmother and all the kids were asking about what they'd done downstairs. Harry decided Satu was the one to give the blow-by-blow description of the setup and how they were going to make it look like Harry, Everet and Sal were all sitting in the studio in New York City. Using computers, they could literally create the illusion that the three men were being interviewed face-to-face about the crime and the criminal. If Macrino turned on the television, hopefully he'd think his enemies were not in Connecticut. Kate hoped that would work.

Ann had taken over as cook and the hamburgers and hotdogs were being loaded onto platters and passed around the table. The relief bringing this threat to an end seemed to give everyone an appetite. Salad and chips followed the picnic fare along with her brother Tom's special baked beans. Kate didn't know his secret ingredient, but they tasted wonderful.

Apparently, Tim and Shannon had a grudge match going with one of the video games which Kate had developed. They'd each won a round so the afternoon would be the playoff. The kids were arguing who was better, and the boys were trying to decide whether to go with family loyalty or guys support guys.

Kate's phone buzzed with a text from Gurka. *The guy who had been checking out the driveway racked up two moving violations in his eagerness to get away from the trooper so he was now cooling his heels in lockup until his court date, which, with the back-up from having the courts closed for snow the last few days, might be awhile. So that made one fewer threat.* She quickly sent; *It would be lovely if we could get rid of all the threats this easily. But I'm afraid that probably won't happen.* Then she shared the information with those at the table.

Following lunch, the group headed off in different directions. The men put together outfits that would look good for their television appearance. Ann was sure that there were at least two suit jackets and a sport coat that would fit Sal. This way, he wouldn't have to travel to his empty house and maybe encounter an assassin lurking around town. Kate was sure that Sal and Gramps were close enough that something would fit.

Harriet and her mother returned to the second floor where they were now discussing working together on a book. Kate finished the cleanup and took the dogs down the hall for a quick trip outside. As she headed for the hall, Harry called her to wait. He walked through the herd of dogs and joined her as she headed for the door to the yard. He checked the yard before he sent the dogs out and then went to the whelping room to get the towels. About four minutes later, the dogs were let in and dried. He checked to be sure that Roger had locked the back door when he went back to the kennel. Then they brought the dogs back into the kitchen. Once they settled, he took Kate with him to their room.

They had barely gotten inside when he wrapped his arms around her and just held on. Kate held him and whispered that they were going to make it through this.

"Hang on, just hang on. Believe that we will make it," she said.

"I sat at the table going over what we had to tell Patience and the genuine horror of the crimes sank in. Macrino has no conscience at all. I kept seeing that photo as he stared at the bodies burning and suddenly, I thought of your danger and it terrified me. I knew you were upstairs by yourself and it took every ounce of professionalism I could dredge up not to jump up and run up the stairs to you."

"Then we'll go with the simple solution."

"We'll lock the house up tight and I'll go downstairs during the broadcast. You'll be able to see me while you deal with the interview. Will that help?"

"Absolutely." He reached out again and drew her close. They stood like that until Harry felt comfortable choosing what to wear. Kate insisted he wear his new suit with the blue silk shirt she had given him for his birthday, along with the coordinating tie. "Remember." she said, "George Nason is telling everyone that you are a fantastic businessman and a great solver of problems. Live up to George's brags."

Harry took her breath away as he stood before the mirror, fully decked out. His emerald green eyes, the dimples that peeked out as he smiled, and his overall male beauty had her falling in love all over again.

When they joined the others in the living room, they impressed Kate. They had decided that all of them would be part of the broadcast. Each would cover some aspect of the tale, so all dressed in their best. Kate spotted Sal in one of her grandfather's sports jackets. It looked good on him. Gramps would be pleased, she was sure.

Satu said that they should go down a few minutes early so she could make sure everyone's line of sight with Miss Snyder worked. Harry and Sal walked around the house checking all the entrances. Then they all trooped downstairs.

Kate took a seat near the door, where she could see Satu's monitor. She had to look back and forth several times for her mind to accept the sight of Harry and the others sitting in the television studio with Patience Snyder and not the truth of them sitting just a few feet from her. Technology was amazing.

They were almost ready to begin when the director said, "Our sound engineer is picking up dogs barking. It's faint but people will hear it on the broadcast." Harry and Sal looked at her. She stood. "I'll take care of it. There won't be a problem."

"Who was that?" Patience Snyder asked.

"That's my wife, Kate Killoy. She raises and trains Samoyed dogs for show and also trains dogs for various competitions and police work. In addition, she's a designer."

"Wait, does she design those sweaters with the gorgeous dogs? I have one with my Westie on it. It's amazing."

"She's very talented," Harry said. "She also, if we're giving credit where it belongs, was the one to find the key to break the code which led to uncovering the crime." The men murmured in agreement.

"Ready to go in 5, 4, 3…" his count went silent as the music came up and the camera focused on Patience Snyder.

Kate smiled at Harry's praise as she hurried quietly up the stairs to see what had the dogs in a twist. Actually, they didn't sound that loud for being inside. Quietly opening the door, she stepped into the kitchen but saw no dogs. She'd only taken one step when she her mother's voice, obviously upset, arguing with someone. Stopping, she listened.

"You can't think you'll get away with murdering all of us. And why do it? What do you gain? They'll catch you and send you to prison."

"Nah! Not me. I've got someone who'll keep me out of jail. I can do anything I want. My boss has power. He can keep me out of jail."

Kate held her breath and peeked around the corner. A man, still wearing a ski jacket, was holding a gun on her mother, Harriet, Shannon, Tim and Robert. They were sitting on the sofa as he stood in front of the fireplace.

"My son and my son-in-law will make sure you go to jail. That's what they do and they're very good."

"Well, they're not here, are they?"

Kate held her breath but heard Robert pipe up, "No, they're in New York City going on television and exposing a criminal along with my dad."

"In New York City, huh? How are they doing that?"

Kate caught Robert's eye and nodded, flipping her hand to have him continue since he had the guy's attention. Then, ducking down behind the island, she moved to the hall door. Staying low, she worked her way to the glass door and undid the latch, easing it open. Dillon must have caught her scent because he turned from the pack and headed in her direction, quickly followed by Liam. She let them in and then eased the door shut.

Pulling her phone from her pocket, she quickly texted Roger and Gurka that one assassin was in her house holding captives. Then, staying low, she returned to the kitchen and took a position behind the island. The dogs were beside her, but not visible to the man in the living room. She saw him pull out his phone.

"Well, my boss will stop this. He can shut down that show. He can shut down the entire network. Your brave daddy will have done it all for nothing, kid."

Kate rose from her position. "Oh, I wouldn't say that. Alessandro Macrino is going to be toast by the end of the day and on his way to prison. And you, he will think you have failed him. Do you know what Al Macrino does with people who fail him? You can kill us all, but you can't save yourself. You're a dead man walking. You'll never escape his punishment."

"And who are you, pretty lady? How do you know who my boss is?"

"I'm your worst nightmare. I'm the lady who uncovered ironclad evidence that Judge Al is a murderer and thief. I'm the lady who is going to stop you. One of your buddies is already in jail. The troopers arrested him."

Kate saw that she'd got under his skin. He pushed away from the fireplace and stalked around the couch, heading straight for her. Reaching to her sides, she used her hands to signal the dogs to move to the ends of the island and hold.

"Well, it sounds like you should be the first one I eliminate."

"My God, Kate. No." her mother screamed.

CHAPTER 29

Tuesday afternoon

T he man stopped halfway across the dining room with the gun pointed right at her. "Lift your hands slowly so I can see them."

Kate realized where she was standing and without moving her arms she slipped her hand into the tilting drawer in front of her, then making fists with both her hands raised them and slowly walked around the island leaving Dillon and Liam in position, but out of his sight. She walked slowly forward, not taking her eyes off the man until a movement behind him caught her eye. James peeked out from the door of the bedroom with Kelly's head poking out from under his arm. Glancing to her right, she noticed that all the dogs were no longer at the French doors. She opened her left hand in a hold motion. She prayed James remembered the chat that they'd had at lunch yesterday about what each hand signal means to the dogs.

"That's far enough," he told her and stepped forward to reach out to check that she didn't have a gun. "Pretty gutsy for an unarmed bitch. You're even pregnant. Lady, you're an idiot. I should shoot you right now for being dumb."

"Oh, I wouldn't do that if I were you. I'm not unarmed. If you even hint that you're going to harm me, you'll not only be dead, but they'll need a garbage bag to collect all the pieces."

"You telling me you're not pregnant and are really wearing a bomb?"

"No, I'm pregnant. I can't deny two months of throwing up. Dillon, Liam, heel."

The dogs shot from behind the island to sit side-by-side on her left side. Both growling hackles up in attack mode.

"You think your fluffy doggies are going to protect you?"

"No. I think my trained police dogs are. If I am threatened, they will tear you apart because I won't be able to tell them to stop. Ergo, the garbage bags."

He started laughing. He pointed at her and laughed harder.

While distracted by his laughter, Kate nodded to James, who then opened the bedroom door, releasing the rest of her dogs. As they raced toward her, she signaled for them to sit in a line. Though it wasn't mealtime, if she got through this, she'd make sure they had a ton of treats. She braced herself and smiled back at the man then barked out the command, "Split." In an instant, Dillon and Liam positioned themselves on either side of the man, three feet from him.

He stopped laughing, now looking back and forth between the two dogs, suddenly realizing that if he shot one, the other could get him. "Call them off or I swear lady, I'll shoot you, them, and everyone in this house."

Though it hurt her to keep the smile planted on her face. "I wouldn't count on it. I train cops. And the first thing I teach my officers, both human and dog, is always to have a backup plan. You could shoot me, and if you're really fast, you might shoot both dogs, but you'd still have to deal with my back-up plan."

"What back-up plan?"

"That one," she said and, lifting a finger from the fist of her left hand pointed over his shoulder.

He pointed the gun at her and stole a glance over his shoulder. She saw his body convulse as he took in the line of ten dogs behind him, none of them moving, and all of them watching him. His head swung back to Kate as she yelled 'stick' and threw the fistful of flour she held in her right hand into his face while dropping to the floor.

Dillon leaped and grabbed the gun from his

hand, roughly from the sound of the scream which came from the shooter, as Liam slammed his body into him, knocking him to the floor, and stretched out his jaws to press them on his target's throat.

"Hold." Kate yelled as she scrambled up from the floor. "Tim. Zip-ties in the drawer at the end of the island." She stood and placed her hands in front of her and Dillon immediately went to sit before her and offered her the gun. She let him place it in her hands and then with a flick of her fingers she had him move to heel position.

Her brother ran up to her with a fist of the plastic ties. The man was screaming in pain while holding his hand. "Bind his hands behind him and bind his feet together. James, come check to see if he has any more weapons. And Liam, 'Galway' - release and hold." Kate felt relief as she remembered her grandfather's release word for Liam. She didn't need her dog getting carried away with all this drama in front of the kids and eating the guy.

Taking a long breath, she turned to look across at those in the living room. Her mother was being held by Harriet as she cried, tears shaking her body. Shannon ran to help Tim with the zip-ties, telling him to double them up in case one breaks. Robert was standing, held tight in his mother's free arm.

Roger burst through the kitchen entrance, gun at ready. Taking in the situation, he nodded at Kate. "All those years of training and practice seem to pay off, Killoy. James, could you go let in the troopers who are hiding on the front porch?"

The room was suddenly overflowing with troopers and, it appeared, a bunch of FBI agents as well. Sean ran up to her. "Thank God you're in one piece. Agnes would kill me if anything happened to you. Not only are you her best friend and favorite cousin, but — The Dress."

Kate chuckled. "We mustn't forget—The Dress." Gurka raced up and grabbed Kate in a hug. She got the feeling that she had been added to his collection of daughters along the way. "Who should we talk to first? How did this happen?"

"I came in toward the middle. You should start with my mom, Harriet Blackler, her sons, and daughter and my brother Tim. Somehow, this guy got in and rounded up everyone he could find while shutting the dogs outside. I do not know how that happened. I was down in the basement. I only came upstairs because I heard the dogs barking."

Gurka headed toward the living room. She turned around as the troopers lifted their prisoner off the floor and one asked, "Kate, what's this white stuff on his face? Is it dangerous?"

"It's flour, Billy. I threw it in his face to gain a couple of seconds for Dillon to grab his gun."

"Still using that 'stick' routine.?"

"Hey, if something works, don't change it.

Plus, it gives Dillon a chance to practice before parade season opens."

"Excuse me ma'am," the man behind Billy stepped forward.

"Ah, Agent Grody I believe. May I ask what you are doing here?"

"You are due an apology from us for our earlier visit."

"I will accept that on one condition."

"A condition? What condition?"

"I need every detail about who sent you last time, why, and everything they told you. They set you two up. I, for one, am curious why someone went to the trouble."

"Well ma'am. That's FBI business…" he began.

Kate held up her hand to stop him. "You can either tell me, or you can become a subject of this investigation, which includes murder, theft, the attempted killing of a former FBI agent, an attempt on a CIA former operative and threats to both FBI and cops. I'd think fast about which side of this case you want to be on when this house of cards falls."

His partner had stepped up behind him while Kate was talking. "Is there any place where we can talk privately?"

"Figueroa?" his partner said in a panic.

"No. I'm not throwing away my career on the

promises of some future Attorney General."

Kate waved to Sean to let him know she was taking the two feds into the library. She sat herself in Harry's chair as the men took the wing chairs while looking around the room with admiration. They also noticed the framed commendations that both she and Harry had earned hanging on the wall behind her.

"The assistant to a judge who is being considered for a position by the White House approached us." Grody began.

Kate held up her hand. "Let me make this easier on you. Judge Alessandro Macrino is about to be arrested for multiple murders and theft. They will probably lay other crimes at his door in the coming months, so if you are trying to protect his name, I wouldn't bother."

Once they realized they had no chance of being included in those aiding the judge, the facts started coming fast and furious. They were still talking half an hour later when the door burst open and Harry burst in, followed by Des. He raced around the desk and swept her into his arms. "God woman, I can't trust you out of my arms for a minute without danger descending on you. You are going to turn my hair gray."

"Killoy, are you crazy? Wait till I tell Malcolm. You took down another killer using that trick of Dillon's."

"Liam helped, plus when faced with ten more of them, the guy almost had a heart attack. The medics might want to get his hand checked. Dillon wasn't entirely gentle when he removed the gun."

"Who are these guys?"

"They are Grody and Figueroa from the New Haven Field Office. They have been giving me information about how Macrino recruits members of law enforcement to help him with his crimes. Here are some notes on what we've been discussing. Gentlemen. Let me introduce Agent Deshi Xiang from DC headquarters. Malcolm has already spoken to them once, Des. I'd better go reassure my mother so I'll leave you to chat."

She and Harry headed back to the living room. She had to brace herself to approach her mother. She knew that she'd frightened her terribly, but didn't have a choice. She held Harry's hand hard as they reached her. Her mother opened and closed her mouth several times, but no words came out. Finally, she just reached out and swept Kate into her arms, holding her tight. Finally, she spoke. "I was so frightened. When you walked up to that killer and challenged him, I thought I would die."

"I'm sorry, mom. It had to be done. He is a gun for hire. He'd have killed us all and just thought it a job well done. I had to convince him it wasn't in his best interest to do it. That if he made what was the obvious choice for this time, he would die, and that it would be a very painful death, not just a bullet. If I hadn't stopped him, mom, not only would you and I be dead, but Shannon, Tim, Harriet, Robert and James and of course when the men heard the shots downstairs, they would have rushed up and shot one at a time without a chance. You realize I had no choice."

"You frighten me so."

"Claire, she has been doing this to me since we met. I love her, but she scares me constantly."

"Alven says there's at least one more of these jokers wandering around town. Before we let down our guard."

"Another?" Claire grabbed Harry's arm.

"One at a time, Claire. We've got this one on his way to jail and another arrested yesterday. We'll find the final gunman. What I want to know is how did this guy get by our alarms."

Tom walked up as they were talking. "Gwyn asked me as she left for work today, who was skiing out beside our place. It didn't sink in until she left. The answer was none of us. By the time I followed the tracks, I spotted the troopers sneaking in, out of sight of the camera at the road. Roger met them and led them around it so that your phone wouldn't warn the shooter, Kate. That's how they ended up on your porch when you took the guy out."

"God, I hope they don't get poison ivy. There

is a big patch of it in that area." Kate said.

Tom laughed. "I'll tell Gurka to make sure they are careful in removing their pants and boots."

Claire looked at her daughter and said, "Your father used to terrify me with the chances he and your grandfather took working against criminals. I knew I'd have to worry about Tom when he took over the company. But the last thing I expected was to have the same worries with you."

Harry looked at her and said, "I don't think her father or grandfather would have been the least bit surprised. This is the Kate they raised. I know they'd be proud."

CHAPTER 30

Tuesday evening and Wednesday early morning

A large group gathered after supper to watch the Patience Snyder Show. They rarely used the big screen television that hid in living room cupboard when it wasn't a playoff season. The cupboard was open and the television brought out and angled for all to see. The chairs filled, along with couch spaces, so they brought chairs from the dining room and kitchen.

Kate had insisted that the troopers get their pants and shoes sprayed for poison ivy and many decided that they'd just stay on, eat one of her mega meals and watch the show that would explain what it was all about. Kate and Harry had squeezed into one end of the sofa next to her grandmother, Sal, and her mother.

All conversation stopped when the theme

music began and the camera showed Patience Snyder sitting at a table filled with Everet, Harry, Sal, Des, and Isaac.

"Tonight's story differs from our usual fare. It's a story that covers over fifty years. It started with a diary and ended up uncovering a crime of horrendous brutality. It is the fallout from that crime that brings us here tonight."

The interview began and Kate marveled at the fact that Satu had made the whole thing blend seamlessly to where the guy's hands appeared to rest on the same table as Snyder's. She began with Everet and an abbreviated version describing how he came to own the diaries and the discovery of the coded pages, and the photos hidden in the binding. Next came Sal in his role as an MP in Vietnam who investigated a crime involving this unit and the lack of cooperation from members, some of who told him directly that if they said anything, they and their families would die. We later discovered that one member of the unit not only left prior to the investigation, but got his identity and even his army presence hidden by someone in power.

Harry spoke of being brought in primarily for his decoding ability and his eventual ability to break the code and read the details of the crime, including time, date, what happened, who were the victims, what he stole, as well as the initials of the man that the unit referred to as 'The Bastard.' He also covered the subsequent threats to members of the unit. That he killed two members of the team under mysterious circumstances within a week convinced the rest of the unit to stay silent.

Des told about retired FBI agent Ramsey Oliver who had been working to solve this last case they had assigned him before leaving the Bureau. He had apparently found something of importance and asked for a meeting with the Director to discuss it. A killer shot him in the head on the steps of the Hoover Building on his way to the meeting and remains in a coma.

Finally, Isaac discussed the steps he took to uncover the identity of the missing man, that someone had redacted from all documents by using a FIOA request to get copies of the original records.

Kate noticed that each time he brought something up, graphics appeared on the screen. The original redacted documents hiding the name of the unit's leader and the document, unredacted, with the man's name and a photo of his face. They then placed the face photo on the screen next to the photo of the soldier following his massacre of the villagers. When the camera came in for a closeup of the face of the man standing, watching the bodies burn while wearing a cocky smile, and put it next to the photo from the FIOA paperwork, the faces were a match.

The identity revealed to be none other than Alessandro Macrino. Because of this cover up and subsequent crimes, he hid his guilt, almost getting appointed to one of the highest positions in the government. The program then shifted to a live shot of the FBI arresting Macrino at his home in Arlington, Virginia and taking him into custody.

Patience Snyder interrupted the sign off of her program with the breaking news from the Connecticut State Police of an unsuccessful attack on the families of Everet Blackler and Harry Foyle just prior to the broadcast. They gave credit for stopping the attempt on the lives of the family members to Harry Foyle's wife, Kate Killoy Foyle, who, with the help of her police trained Samoyed dogs, could stop the attempt without a shot being fired. The show concluded on that note with a thank you from Patience to all involved in finding justice after all this time.

Kate could not keep her eyes open for much of the broadcast and had lost the battle with sleep completely before they mentioned her confrontation in the afternoon. When Satu asked, "Kate, how do you like being the heroine of the hour?" everyone looked her way and saw was sound asleep.

Harry eased off the sofa and bent to scoop up his exhausted wife. Making his excuses to their guests, he headed for their bedroom with the soundly sleeping lady of the hour. He tucked her into bed and let the dogs in to keep her company.

As he went to return to the living room, he heard Kate's phone buzz with a text. Lifting it from the nightstand, he opened it.

"Kate. Good job today. Tom and John would have been proud of you. However, it's not over. There's still one more hunter. I've spotted him on skis and I'm warning you, this one knows his way in the woods." A.

With a sinking heart, Harry took her phone with him back to the living room. He would have to share Alven's warning with the others. This blasted battle wasn't over.

***

The first thing Kate noticed as she woke was the silence. Opening her eyes, she saw dawn breaking with a hint of sunshine and a complete absence of falling snow. She rolled onto her back only to find the other side of the bed, still warm but empty. Her gaze went to the French doors, only to see a plume of snow flying over the snowy mountain in the center of the yard. Dillon, Quinn and Liam sat transfixed as Harry rounded the far corner and began moving the snowblower in their direction. Tired as she still was, she forced herself to stand and head for the bathroom, grabbing warm clothing along the way. She needed to get dressed and start the day's work.

Having dressed in record time, she opened the door to the living room and looked toward the kitchen. She spotted Harry pulling the snowblower into the hall. Turning left, she pushed her way through the mass of bodies pressed against the French doors and opened them. She held tight to the handle of the door as the force of joyous dogs in motion flowed out. Shutting the door, she headed for the kitchen only to be met by a somewhat sleepy Des, followed by Isaac, both muttering about coffee.

Harry had the ingredients for pancakes assembled on the counter. Reaching for the large mixing bowl, Kate got to work. Harry came in from the back hall accompanied by Sal and Roger. While the men went to get their coffee, he pulled two large griddles from the drawer under the stove and then reached into the refrigerator for a container of blueberries. Kate grabbed the container and used her hand add to the batter. Then she handed the bowl to Harry and went to heat the kettle for tea.

The front door opened with Kate's family as the Blacklers descended the stairs. Kate had a pound of bacon from the refrigerator, along with a bag of sausage cooking by the time everyone settled at the table and the banquette. Once everyone was eating, Kate spoke up, apologizing for sleeping through the broadcast last night. Everyone agreed she had earned her sleep, but she missed the mention on national television of her adventures with the dogs in taking out the guy who tried to kill them.

"Me? Roger will tell you that's just a stunt that I use with my drill team obedience demonstrations. It's come in handy a few times, but I don't teach it as a defense technique."

Tim reached over to tousle her curls and said,

"I don't care if it's regulation or not. I, for one, was not happy at the prospect of dying and when I saw you take out that monster after scaring the shit out of him when he saw the lineup of silent dogs, made me want to stand up and cheer."

"Me, too," yelled Robert, and everyone laughed.

"Well, I'm just happy that it's over and nobody got hurt," she told them while picking up her tea.

"But it's not over," James piped up.

"What?" Kate said, while scanning the faces of those at the table. What she saw had her appetite disappearing.

Harry settled into the chair next to hers and reached into his pocket to pull out her phone. "You got a text last night after you were asleep from Alven. It seems there's another assassin, and this one knows how to survive in the woods. Alven has spotted him on skis."

Tom interrupted, "Yesterday, right before everything happened, Gwyn had to leave because the State Police found a body, and they needed a forensic pathologist. When she left, she mentioned she'd spotted ski tracks that seemed to come out of the woods from behind K and K and headed toward your place. I headed over to tell you, but by then, the troopers were on your porch, so I joined them. However, the guy you took out apparently did not use skis because we found none. The tracks I saw may belong to the third assassin who saw what was happening and just retreated to the woods."

Claire spoke up. "Do you think he'll still try to come after us even though they've captured his boss?"

"They will bring Macrino to trial. Many of those testifying against him are sitting at this table. In answer to your question, Claire, I think he will be desperate to eliminate every single person who could put his boss in jail for life," Des said.

"He has to be stopped," Satu said. "But think about it, Kate. We've done this before."

"Not with someone who seems to have winter sports skills."

"Yes, but there are more of us than of him. And, we have both Alven and Rex," said Satu.

Kate stared across the table at this girl, who had become such a vital part of their lives. "True. And we have you and Seamus."

At this, both of the teenagers grinned.

Blackler looked at her. "Am I missing something?"

Harry looked around the table, kissed his wife on the top of her head and said, "Okay. Roger, call Gurka and Sean. We need to have a meeting as soon as possible."

Kate smiled. "Eat up, people, it's about to be a very busy day."

CHAPTER 31

Wednesday morning, later

As soon as the meal ended and the table cleared, laptops popped up everywhere. Kate looked around. "I designate the dining room table as mission central. Set up the laptops there so that Satu can begin chaining them together. This will allow multiple 'eyes on' stations manned by those not out in the field."

They had only begun when their phones announced visitors and soon Gurka and Sean were coming through the front door. Harry met them and called them into the library for a strategy meeting, which included all those who'd been on the broadcast and the troopers, Kate, Tom, Satu and Seamus. "The reason I asked you to come this morning," Harry began while looking at the troopers, "is that we have learned we have another assassin whose mission is to take us out, and this one has wilderness skills and is in our woods."

"How do you know this?" Gurka asked.

"Alven."

"Okay. Do you know where the old spook is?"

"In the woods."

"Got it. We've got to hunt down a skilled assassin before he kills you guys. I take it the pressure is on to eliminate anyone who can testify against Macrino."

"That's about it," Tom said. "I spotted his ski tracks going right up to the dog yard fence yesterday. He'd escaped detection by approaching from behind K and K."

"The question is, would it be possible to do a sweep of the woods to track him down and arrest him, all the while trying to remember that he is an armed killer?" Harry asked.

Sean turned to Kate. "How many troopers have passed qualification for winter search?"

"Statewide, 18."

"Plus," Harry added, "several of us have been training on snowshoes for almost a month. All of those who were training are qualified with small arms, except for Agnes who I don't want to include."

"We will not include my 'bride-to-be' in any of this, please," Sean said.

"We will have Rex available for surveillance. I

called my security guy and he'll be here in an hour to set up several more permanent cameras, plus he told me he had some portable ones we could set up in the field along known trails. Kate and Satu can man the base and keep us all posted."

Des looked around. "Isaac, do you know how to do this or like this city boy, would get lost if I went farther than the kennel?"

Isaac grinned. "I grew up in the Blue Ridge Mountains, which don't get a lot of snow, but get enough to make skills like this handy. Plus, I did some winter tracking in the army. I'm more of a short ski guy than snowshoe."

"I've got a pair of those you can use," Tim said.

Gurka stood. "I'm going to have to get an okay for this while keeping it quiet and notify all the barracks. I'd better get moving."

The group split up. Seamus went to check out Rex, making sure he had a fully charged a battery and two backup batteries. He'd been practicing switching out batteries to get his speed up. Robert and James followed him into the whelping room, fascinated with the robotic drone. backup

Kate left the meeting and, since she still was a pregnant woman, headed to her room to use the bathroom. While there, she sent a text to Alven with their plan to go after the other assassin. A three minutes later her phone buzzed with a text.

"Kate. Have Satu use the code I'm sending to link me into her feed. It will connect her to the six portable cameras which I've posted around my base. This will give more 'eyes on' locations. Tell Tom there are four vests in my basement storage locker, leftover from the last case I did with your dad and grandfather. They will fit the big guys. I located this guy's car hidden off the old logging road. It is now disabled. He won't be able to escape."

Kate sent her thanks and went to find Satu. Sean was on his phone as she passed through the living room. She assumed he was talking to Gurka. He looked up as she went by and put up a hand to stop her. "Gurka has all eighteen on board. Since they haven't been able to practice this year and with this super amount of snow, everyone wants to be involved. They'll meet here at noon."

She held out her phone and showed him Alven's message.

"He's trapped," he said, grinning. "Good, I'll go get the vests. Sal, Roger and I are going to set up a food and mapping station in the barn and check out your two search and rescue snowmobiles. There are two departments with snowmobiles as well, so we'll be able to haul people and equipment as needed."

"Good, I'm going to get this coding to Satu. Let me know if there is anything you need."

The dining room table was now a sea of laptops with wires running down the center of the table. Harry had her brother Will's recipe for chicken stew cooking in large vats on the stove. This would give everyone a hot meal before heading out on the first search. Though Kate trained the troopers for just this sort of work, she was handing over the job of directing the troops to Gurka.

She found Satu and showed her the piece of computer code that Alven had sent. The girl's face spread in a grin and, taking Kate's phone, she sat and immediately copied the code into their system. Suddenly Kate's laptop filled with a spread of six views of areas she recognized in the woods. The shots were clear and would allow them views of areas of the state park which backed up onto her land as well.

Seamus must have been showing what the drone could do because the door to the back hall opened and Rex floated over Kate's island and landed on the back of one of the dining room chairs. Satu immediately transferred to Rex's view and the dining room now filled the screen.

Ann walked in, followed by Gwyn carrying baskets of breads and muffins. Gwyn, who hadn't been here during the last search, stopped when she saw the fascinating drone lift one of its 'hands' and wave at her. She laughed as she spotted Seamus lurking in the back hall.

By noon, the driveway and the entire parking lot for the kennel soon filled with police cruisers. Men and dogs gathered around the tables in the barn that now held a large nutritious luncheon. Kate spoke to them as they ate, reminding them of the safety measures she'd taught them. The dogs were all to wear protective boots and the men would wear the white coveralls stored in the training equipment closet over their regular clothes. This would make them blend in with the snowy background and make them tougher targets. They distributed walkie-talkies and Sal pulled down the maps of her woods and the state park and the two neighboring properties. They blocked out areas and Kate reviewed specific natural dangers found in each. By the time they consumed the food, she felt ready to turn over command to Gurka and return inside.

Des and Harry had been talking. They explained she was to keep Des at her side at all times. Even though they wouldn't call her to testify, if the assassin could grab her, he could hold her as a bartering chip.

Since Liam would partner with Sal, Kate thought that perhaps she should have Dillon's work with Harry. But before she could say anything, her mother, who had been helping clean up the leftover food, interrupted. "Harry. My John used Rory as his partner for years. I know they did winter searches together. I also know that Kate's father would want you to partner up with his dog. I'm sure that you'll work together perfectly."

Harry looked at her for a long minute and then reached out and took her hand. "Thank you,

Claire. Knowing Kate as I do, I feel that I have a glimpse of what her father was like. It would be an honor to work with Rory. If John trained him, I will feel very safe with him as my partner."

Kate watched her mother reach out and hug Harry. Then she handed him Rory's lead and, reaching into her pocket, pulled out a set of leather boots for the dog. Then, with a hug for Rory, she picked up a basket full of things to be returned to the kitchen and left.

"Okay, people. The day is disappearing. We've got about seven hours of sunlight. Let's make the most of them." Gurka said.

Harry turned and reached for Kate, pulling her into his arms and kissing her quickly. "I want you to head back to the house now. Keep Dillon and Des with you at all times."

"I will. Be safe." Kate tapped her leg, letting Dillon know they were heading back to the house. Des walked back to her side. As they passed through the kennel, they saw Roger fitting boots on dogs. The troopers, now dressed in white with head coverings, reminded Kate of James Bond type movies. She exchanged hugs with some of her trooper friends who she'd worked with for years, then waved to all and headed for the house.

She unlocked the entrance to the back hall and then after they were in, locked it again. As she reached the dining room, Satu showed Kate her work station and pointed out that she'd be working with three screens this time plus her tablet. The tablet was on the same program as her phone and would have all her usual cameras for their property's security. "Harry's security man came while you were in the barn. You now have a camera pointing behind K and K plus cameras with views from the second floor of the house with wide angles showing all the access from the woods and from the road. I wrote the new codes on the card I taped on your tablet. Check them out before we get too busy."

Kate sat and flipped through the codes quickly, noting that with the high angles from the second story of her house, she could see her entire woods in just three clicks and it only took two to get the whole expanse of the woods between the family houses and the highway.

Des came up beside her and placed a mug of tea on the table. "Harry told me that one of my jobs today was to make sure that you have a cup of tea whenever you need one."

"Thanks, Des. What have you heard from Malcolm about Macrino's arrest last night?"

"He is presently being held in jail, but he's got a whole phalanx of lawyers trying to get him out. We're pushing for him to be held without bond because of the recent attempts on the lives of people related to his case. He'll keep us posted."

"I hope they can keep him locked up. He does

not need access to these killers."

Kate looked up as she noticed movement at the other end of the table. She saw her mother, Harriet, Everet, Shannon and the boys settle into viewing stations. "The more eyes on the cameras, the better," Claire told the others as they settled into their chairs.

James and Robert shared a station and James looked at Kate and nodded. "You can count on us, Kate. We'll find this guy and stop him."

"Thanks, James. That makes me feel better," she told him with a nod to him and Robert.

"Okay," Satu said. "Rex is in the air. Man, your stations."

CHAPTER 32

Wednesday afternoon

The screens filled with views of the woods. The men were wearing lapel cameras tied into the system as well. What that meant was trying to look at every screen at once would be a challenge.

Kate heard the front door open and then lock again and glanced to her left to see her grandmother sliding into a chair next to her mother. More eyes on the screens.

As she switched her view to the body cam's, Satu clicked in a few numbers and a box appeared in the upper corner of her laptop. A card appeared in her right hand with each camera number and the name of the person assigned it. "Do we have a two-way sound system this time?" she asked.

"You bet," Satu said, grinning. "Say hi to your

husband."

"Harry, can you hear me?" she asked as she clicked the box with his camera.

"I sure can," he answered. *"As you can see, Rory and I have almost reached the end of the green trail. We found ski tracks so we're pretty sure our guy is up ahead."*

"Be sure if you lose the trail, to check for signs of someone trying to wipe out traces by using branches. Also, beware of traps. Tom told you about those, so look both down and ahead. Rory will spot them and hop over if they stretched them across the trail."

"Got it. Ah, I just spotted Rex sweeping the area ahead of us. We'll be careful. Hang in there and drink your tea," he said, laughing.

Kate looked at the cup of tea she'd forgotten. It was now sitting on a small round disk that was plugged in somewhere in the mess of wires on the table. When she lifted her cup to drink, she found it was a hot as if it were just made. Her husband thought of everything.

"Kate!" she heard a shout. Alven's voice boomed over the connection. She glanced at Satu and she whispered #14. Kate clicked on the square and asked, "Alven?"

"Yes, Katie. I may have gotten a sighting on our target about an hour ago. He kept disappearing on me,

so I suspect that he, like your boys, camouflaged in white. Let the troopers know. He's distinctive though, because he's wearing a black pack with a red band running vertically down it. He has snowshoes, but they're trail shoes with long tails. Pass it on."

Kate immediately locked into the 'all call' and passed on Alven's information about their target. Acknowledgments came bouncing back over the line. Rex had just finished a sweep of the land above the gully when something flashed for a mere second and disappeared. "Seamus," she called hitting his connection. "Have Rex repeat the sweep of the last minute. I thought I saw something."

"Will do," he answered.

Kate watched as the drone reversed its course more slowly. She'd almost convinced herself it was her imagination when she saw it again. "There. Move the camera in closer to the left side of the Hemlock tree. The big one."

The camera slowly enlarged the view, going in for a close-up. That was definitely a piece of red showing between the lower branches. It wasn't a red normally found in nature except on tulips and some roses, not found here with this snow. Seamus was slowly bringing the drone down almost to ground level for a swift look around. All at once, the screen filled with what appeared to be the pack that Alven described and a pair of skis.

"Seamus, do you think Rex could lift that

pack?"

"There's only one way to find out."

The camera showed the drone's claws reaching to grasp the pack and lift it. Quickly ascending, the drone flew back toward the launch site in the cupula atop the kennel. A minute later Seamus yelled, *"I've got it."*

Everet, who'd been standing behind his wife, said, "I'll get it," and raced down the back hall. Minutes later, he returned with the large backpack. He pulled two of the kitchen chairs over near the dining room table and then unzipped the pack. They all gasped at the item on top. Kate had only seen photos of AR-15 automatic rifles, but there one was. Alongside it was stacks of magazines filled with bullets. Everet carefully lifted out the rifle and set it next to the pack. He took out all the magazines, about a dozen with ten bullets each. Below that were three different handguns, one of which looked like a smaller version of the rifle. Next came lined gloves, long underwear and a box with a dozen packages of beef jerky. There were some other things to eat, but that was the main contents of the bag.

Kate had remained focused on the screens while the pack was being unloaded. But when she heard James say, "Wow." She turned. Grabbing her phone from the table, she quickly snapped a photo of the pack's contents. Then she texted it to Alven, Harry, Gurka and then sent a blanket text saying that Rex had swiped the assassin's stash. Kate then suggested that Everet repack it and put it in the closet in the library. "I'm not worried about the guns and ammunition, but with a dozen Samoyeds, his stash of beef jerky might be one temptation too much."

Everyone laughed. Kate gave the coordinates of where the pack had been found to everyone so that they would know this was a place where he had been. Rex, with a new battery installed, went back on the search. Alven texted, *"He's heading toward the old lumber road. He probably doesn't realize I disabled his car."*

Kate did an 'all call' broadcast with the information from Alven. Gurka replied that they'd focus on closing in on that area. She kept her eyes on all the various screens as much as she could. Occasionally, she'd spot Harry with Rory. They moved beautifully as a team. Her dad would be proud. When her focus swept back to Rex's camera, she saw a flash of something by a large granite outcropping. She called to Seamus to circle that area. She watched with her total focus on the drone's camera. After a minute, she spotted another flash of red. Asking to have Rex slow down, she told Seamus to have Rex go in for a closer look. What she saw gave her chills: it was the assassin, moving slowly, wearing trail snowshoes with their long tails dragging. But what frightened Kate was the backpack the man was wearing with the red stripe. It was identical to the one sitting in the den closet.

Satu sent the feed to everyone. They could all see their target and the searchers worked to get closer.

Kate's focus now switched to all the other cameras, especially the ones surrounding the house.

"Satu," she asked, "does connecting the house security feeds to this setup cancel the sound warning?"

"Yeah. The computer has a maximum of different feeds it can carry at once."

"Got it." Kate bounced from one view to another, searching. Back and forth. Then she saw it. The faint line of ski tracks on the snow from beyond the kennel and along the fence line.

"Kate, can I let Quinn and Shelagh in? I'm tired of looking at screens?"

"Sure, James. Just keep them away from the wires over here."

She stood up and ran from window to window, checking the areas close to the house. She saw nothing.

"Kate, what's the matter? What's wrong?" her mother asked.

"Not three, but four. There are four assassins. The two we have, the one they are about to get, and one more who is here. I don't know where. But he's here."

She hit Harry's feed. "Harry. There's another assassin. There are four. He's somewhere near the house. His tracks showed up on the camera coming in the way the shooter took you out of here when he tried to kill you last November. I haven't spotted him yet, but we've got his pack with his automatic rifle and a bunch of other guns. We need help."

"Coming, Kate."

She texted Roger. *"Another assassin near the house. I don't know where. Watch out."*

She ran to the French doors and called the dogs. All came racing in. As she went to close the door, it snapped back, almost knocking her to the floor. An immense man stood before her. A man whose photo she'd seen. Gianpaolo Rapino, the hit man Alven said was deadly.

"Not so fast, lady. You and I are going to talk." He grabbed Kate's arm and pulled her to him as he shoved a gun against her head. He looked at those around the table and nodded at Des. "You must be the Fed. Put your hands on top of your head and stand slowly." As Des did what he said, he nodded at Robert. "You, kid. Go get his gun and do nothing stupid."

Robert, who'd been sitting plastered against his father, stood and looked over his shoulder. Everet nodded, and the boy walked around the table to Des. Des nodded at his chest and Robert pulled back his jacket and lifted his gun out of its holder. "Take it to the door and throw it outside," Rapino ordered. The boy slowly walked to the door and threw the gun into the snow at the bottom of the deck. Then he hurried back to his father.

"Good, Now we can sit and wait. I need Foyle, the old MP and the army cop. Along with you two, then they'll be nobody to testify."

"Now you, Princess, are going to take all your doggies and put them away or I'll just use them for target practice while we wait." He lifted the gun from her head and shoved her forward.

Kate signaled the dogs to go with her and walked through the kitchen to the back hall. "In, everyone. Liam in, Dillon, in. Good boys." Her eyes swept the dogs before her, tears slightly clouding her view. Ten. There were ten. Shelagh and Quinn weren't here. She turned and started back toward the others. As she moved, she saw her bedroom door crack open. James peeked out. He had a firm grip on Quinn, who was pushing to get through the door. Shelagh stood at his side, looking at the stranger.

"Sit." Rapino pointed the gun at the chair by her computer. She placed her hands on the table to steady herself as she sat, balancing her baby weight. She slipped the phone she'd left beside the laptop up her sleeve. Once seated, she rested her hands in her lap. Des, whose chair was in front of hers, turned toward her, but the hit man yelled, "Turn around and face me, fed."

As Des turned, Kate whispered, "Block me." Then, not wasting time, she pulled the phone from her sleeve and without looking at the keyboard, opened the text app and messaged Harry. *"Killer inside, Des gun gone, Dogs locked up. He waits for you, Sal and Isaac."* she hit send and then, slipping the phone into her pocket, prayed.

Rapino stood, his gun pointed at them, and reached into his back pocket to pull out a package of beef jerky and bite off a chunk. "You don't mind if I eat. All this exercise has made me hungry." He laughed and stuffed the rest of the stick into his back pocket and then focused back on Kate.

"They said you took out Junior last night using those dogs. One bit him. Is that true?"

"He got a slight bite to his hand when my dog disarmed him. He'll live."

"Maybe it's a good thing you put those doggies away. I wouldn't want one to disarm me. I'd mow down the lot of them. Now we're going to wait until the others come."

Kate felt as though her brain was empty. She didn't know what to do. What if they didn't get her message and just walked right in? She was staring at Rapino when she saw her bedroom door open again. James peeked out, still holding Quinn, who wanted to come play. She didn't dare move or even focus on James for fear the hit man would catch on. She realized she was holding her breath and forced herself to breathe as the sound of a key in the front door lock had everyone turning that way. Harry burst through the door, slammed it shut and raced across the room to her, never once looking at the man with the gun. Harry swept her up and behind him as he pointed a gun which had appeared in his hand at Rapino.

"It looks like we have a stand-off, Mr. Hero—or not. You won't shoot me in cold blood in front of your wife and friends whereas I wouldn't think twice about it." He smiled and bit off another piece of the beef jerky, shoving the rest back into his pocket.

Kate watched while peeking around Harry's shoulder and noticed the bedroom door ease open. Her heart jumped, and she drew a breath as her old friend stepped out from her bedroom and pointed a fancy automatic weapon at the killer and said, "You're right. Harry's too nice a guy to shoot a man down in cold blood in front of his family and friends. I, however, do not have that problem."

"Asch, where have you been? I've combed every inch of these woods for you."

"You should know that old spooks are invisible. I now regret not putting a bullet in you last week. It would have saved both time and aggravation. Now you're going to set the gun on the floor, and kick it toward the front door and while you're bent over, you can add the gun in your ankle holster to the pile. I can promise you that people will only thank me if I remove you as a nuisance in this case right now."

As he bent down, Kate watched Rapino's face. He would not give up. He was going to shoot. She saw the muscle in his arm bunch as he flexed his hand. He went to pull the trigger—and screamed.

CHAPTER 33

Wednesday late afternoon

The gun flew from Rapino's hand as his arms reached behind him and he swung around. Hanging onto her prize, Shelagh had a good grip on the beef jerky and part of the hit man's rear end.

"Shelagh, leave it!" Kate shouted. Reluctantly, the bitch let go, still focused on the treat.

Harry and Des leapt forward, knocking the man to the floor and pulling his arms behind his back. Des pulled cuffs from his pants and quickly immobilized the man. Robert ran to the kitchen island and came back with zip-ties so the men bound his feet as well. Harriet raced to her great-uncle and embraced him, her tears of relief spilling over.

Claire and Ann grabbed each other as the front door swung open and Sal, Isaac, Gurka, and a half-dozen troopers filled the room.

Kate bent forward and reached for the man's back pocket. "James, you can let Quinn go now," she called. The bedroom door opened, and the puppy raced around, happy to see so many people who could pet him.

"Quinn, Shelagh, come," Kate commanded. The two young Sams raced to Kate and sat straight in front of her. She glanced at the hit man who was watching her and smiled. Then she peeled the plastic wrapper off the jerky and, breaking it in two, gave it to the Sams. "Good puppies," she told them.

***

Ann, Harriet, Shannon and Gwyn made supper. Kate was interviewed by Gurka and two agents from the New Haven Field Office of the FBI. It amazed them she captured four known hit men without a single shot being fired. They took the backpack as evidence. After Everet went to retrieve Des' gun from the edge of the deck, Kate had let the dogs out of the hall and into the yard so that their excitement wouldn't impede the interviews. Shelagh was so proud of herself she was racing around and jumping off the top of the snow mountain to show off. Quinn was happy that he'd gotten a treat for sitting quietly with James. In the middle of the agent's interview, Malcolm called. Des had filled him in and he wanted Kate to give Shelagh a special pat from him.

They ended up feeding all the searchers, the investigators, the troopers who arrived for the arrest, and the usual crowd, so it took all the seats and an extra table was added to make room for everyone to sit.

Alven sat by Kate, making sure she was okay after the stress of the last week. He talked through supper of how her grandfather would have loved to have been part of the search. The troopers celebrated the outcome. They enjoyed having Rex overhead to give them a bird's-eye view at spotting the shooter.

The Blacklers headed back home after supper since tomorrow was a school day, with the roads now clear. Isaac and Des headed back to DC together so they could report in to their respective bosses. Alven, who'd dropped his dog off at home before coming to Kate's, wanted to get home to feed him. He was also looking forward to sleeping in his own bed tonight. When they left, everyone else followed.

By eight-thirty in the evening, Kate and Harry found themselves curled up on the sofa, surrounded by their dogs, enjoying the peace. Harry's phone rang. Looking at the screen to see who was calling, he smiled and pressed the button to answer, putting it on speaker.

"Oliver?" Harry asked.

"*Foyle. Malcolm tells me I missed all the fun.*"

We couldn't have done it without your help.

"You figured out my weird fax.?"

"My wife, Kate, did. In fact, she also found the key for the code and captured assassins in her spare time. When I come to DC, I'll bring her. You've got a lot in common."

"They won't let me talk much longer without resting, but I look forward to seeing you soon."

"Take care, Ramsey."

Harry smiled, happy that his old friend would live. Relaxing, he turned on the television to replay the interview Kate had slept through the night before. Before beginning, he handed her a cup of tea to drink while she watched. She realized the tea was his attempt to keep her awake through the entire show. It worked, and it startled her when they mentioned her take-down of yesterday's assassin.

Turning off the set, they walked around the house, locking up and bedding down the dogs. Then, they retired to their bedroom to get ready for sleep.

"To think, my only goal for this week had been to get all the furniture arranged on the second floor." Kate said.

"Well, you did that, and it looks great."

"True, that worked out very well. I'll get to try out the laundry chute tomorrow, washing all that bedding."

"There's no rush on laundry. You should sleep in tomorrow, since you won't have the pressure of fighting criminals."

"Are you kidding? Sleep in? Not a chance. You've forgotten about the chaos that is my life. Following last month's fashion show, my business doubled the number of boutiques that want to carry my line. Also, next month, the architect should have the plans ready for the expansion of the barn to add the garages and double the size of my studio. Plus, thanks to the lady who inspired the fastest furniture delivery ever, I added one more task to my to-do list."

"The best-known model in the country, perhaps the world, is getting married in two months. The news media is calling it the wedding of the year. And, the biggest secret of all is who will make—The Dress. Once that leaks out… and it will leak out, the fact that your wife is designing and making—The Dress, means the press and paparazzi will invade this place."

"We're going to need more security than we did for criminals to keep them out. Sorry, but tension is only just starting. The stress of this last week is going to look like a retreat at a spa compared with the insanity and chaos of Agnes Forester's wedding. Brace yourself. We're about to have a high-class three-ring-circus. Crime will look like a walk in the park compared to what's coming,"

Kate hugged her husband laughed. "Just you wait, Harry Foyle, just you wait."

ACKNOWLEDGEMENT

Thanks to my wonderful editor, Sandra McDonough, who is my first reader, for her tight edits, and her fellowship in the world of Samoyeds.

ABOUT THE AUTHOR

Peggy Gaffney

Born in Connecticut, Peggy Gaffney has wanted to write since she took her first creative writing course at the age of twelve taught by a Yale professor and where she was the only child in the class. But it has been her more than fifty year love affair with

Peggy Gaffney with her Samoyeds Dillon and Quinn.

showing Samoyed dogs which inspired her to create the Kate Killoy Mystery series of suspense for the dog lover. Her many generations of Samoyeds have taught her to love their smiles and to live with tons of shedding hair. Her main character Kate is a knitting designer who shows dogs, two things the author is very familiar with since she's also published ten knitting books mostly for dog lovers and continues to show her Samoyeds.

She lives in Connecticut with her family as well as her two cats and her Samoyeds, Dillon and Quinn.

A WORD ABOUT REVIEWS

I am so glad that you could join Kate and Harry on their latest adventure and ask you to share what you enjoyed about the book by writing a review.

Ratings and Reviews are very important to an author's livelihood. It is the only way that we, as creators of the stories, learn what you think of the book. And yes, every book in a series needs **reviews —lots of reviews**. These are very important to a writer's career. It helps if you can let other readers know what you enjoy about these adventures full of math, dogs, crime and quirky characters.

Thank you for reading this seventh story in the series and I look forward to sharing with you many more adventures of Kate, Harry and their wonderful Samoyeds.

If you are new to the series, take a quick peek into the first book of the series, *Fashion Goes to the Dogs*, where Kate and Harry first meet and begin their adventures.

FASHION GOES TO THE DOGS

*A Kate Killoy Mystery - Suspense
for the Dog Lover*

Chapter One

"**K**ate, we need to leave now." My cousin Agnes charged past me out of the pre-dawn darkness, grabbed my shoes from the shelf where they lived safely out of puppy reach, and tossed them at me. While I was still struggling to tie my shoes, she pulled my coat off the rack, shoved me out the door and into Henry, her Ford Explorer. Before I could even ask where we were going, we were headed south on the Yankee Expressway, known to the locals as Connecticut Route 6, toward the interstate. She reached between the seats and grabbed a large Dunkin' Donuts bag, which she plopped onto my lap.

"There's two cups of tea and croissants with

orange marmalade. It was the best I could do on short notice."

Having grown up with four brothers, my first instinct was to argue, but the smell of those buttery croissants on my still sleep befuddled brain was too tempting to ignore. In half the time it normally took, we turned up the ramp onto I-84 and were heading west.

Once the bag's contents, including both cups of tea, were history, I felt awake enough to speak. "Where the hell are we going?"

"Into the city."

"I hate to inform you, Rambo, but taking someone across state lines against their will is kidnapping, a federal offense. I've got two businesses to run in Connecticut and don't have time to watch the sunrise over the Hudson with you."

"It's all taken care of. Sal is getting coverage. You were smart to bring him on as kennel manager. He told me he could manage without you in the boarding kennel this weekend. This week's numbers are low because, next week, everyone and his brother will be boarding their dogs when they go away for the long Thanksgiving weekend. Since it's Saturday, you're not scheduled to teach training classes. Also, I checked, and you don't have any entries in the dog show at the Big E this weekend, so that's not an issue. Last, according to Ellen Martin, you could take the month off from your knitting studio and still submit the number of new designs you've created for the business since summer. Your studio manager is about to start kicking your butt."

I stared ahead, silent. I had to admit, I'd hit a dry spell. Following the second funeral, I'd just stopped thinking, doing, or caring. If it didn't happen by rote, it didn't get done.

In the Killoy family, I was not only the sole girl of the five children, but the only offspring who possessed a passion for the world of dog breeding and showing, especially Samoyeds. My mother and all four of my brothers lived and breathed mathematics. That was Dad and Gramps' field too, but their true passion was the dogs.

I, meanwhile, showed no aptitude, let alone genius, for numbers and it absolutely appalled everyone when I snubbed MIT to study fashion design. But Dad and Gramps stepped up to the plate and supported me, turning the second floor of the dog-training barn into a design studio for my business. The fact that my designs were aimed at people who showed dogs also helped.

Losing Gramps to cancer had been heartbreaking, but I'd seen it coming and I still had Dad. Sharing our love of dogs, the three of us had been a team all my life. Since I was seven, we'd spent weekends together at dog shows. They had taught me my craft the way no one else ever could. Always together, we became "The Three Amigos" of the dog-show world. With Gramps gone, Dad and I had just begun to build a new connection, working as a pair. We had even begun taking an interest in the new litter of puppies and their show potential.

We'd actually been in the puppy pen, laughing at their antics, when the aneurysm hit him. They told me later there was nothing I could have done. Dad was dead before he reached the hospital. My world caved in as though the ground had been cut out from under me. I stood at his graveside, oblivious to the crowds that had gathered. I was alone and, after that, nothing seemed worth the effort.

We'd driven for about half an hour when I finally roused myself. "Why?"

Agnes didn't take her eyes off the road. "So, I can help a friend. As for why you're going, I need someone who looks like you."

"Looks like me how?"

"I need someone who looks like a kid. You've got to pretend to be a kid who likes dogs but knows nothing about them. Act like you're very shy so you won't have to talk, your voice would give you away."

Her eyes were glancing at the clock every few minutes.

"I'm twenty-four."

"You look twelve."

"Bitch."

"Agreed. Though I think I qualify as veteran bitch. Look, Kate, you've been trading on that 'little-girl' look in the ring for years. I just thought I'd take advantage of it for once. You run around the ring with your braid flying and your cute innocent expression, and all the judges think it cool to put up the young handler with the great dog. Tell the truth. Don't you think it's about time to start playing on a level field with the grown-ups?"

"Any more advice, Dear Abby? What else can't you stand?"

"Well, someone's got to tell you this stuff. Your mother doesn't notice you exist. Ann is too sweet to criticize her granddaughter, and everyone else thinks it but likes you too much to say anything. It needed saying. You adored your dad and grand-dad, but they kept you frozen in amber and didn't let you grow up. If they'd tried this type of control with your brothers, there would have been war, but you were their sweet little girl. They could keep you young and play with you in the dog show world for-ever."

"They didn't..." I began what I knew was a flimsy protest.

"You haven't changed a thing about yourself since you were twelve.

Even in design school, people thought you were some young kid in a special program. People didn't take you seriously."

I moved as far from her as possible. Pressing up against the door, I stared out the window. I wanted to scream and shout that she was wrong. She wasn't. What's more, I'd known it for a long time but just didn't want to admit it because the thought of change scared the hell out of me.

With work, everything was fine. I could run the kennel and teach the classes, no problem. And my design business was done online. No challenge there. No, I knew she meant that I should have a social life as a woman. Truth was that terrified me. The world of sex, drugs and rock' n' roll was not even in my solar system. I glanced at her determined expression and knew I was about to be ripped from my protective cocoon and thrown into the cold, cruel world. After more miles of silence, Agnes sighed and glanced my way.

"Remember when we were kids, and I'd ask you to do things and not ask why?" I nodded. "This operation is like that. I'm involved in something I can't discuss, but I need your help."

The words "Go to hell" popped into my head, but "fine" came out of my mouth.

We were making excellent time. She crossed onto I-684, heading into White Plains. It was good we'd gotten this far so early because the sun was coming up–and that meant a gazillion cars would flood the highway any minute, traveling in the same direction we were. I twisted in my seat to look at Agnes. She was biting her lower lip as her thumb twisted the Claddagh ring she always wore. She was nervous, which was unheard of for her. She could handle any situation with style and aplomb. Hell, her photo was on a billboard in Times Square. I'd never seen her stressed. I went back to staring out the window. We ate up the miles as we transitioned from the Saw Mill River Parkway to the Henry Hudson Parkway, which ran along the Hudson River as both the city and the sun rose before us.

Before I knew it, we were swinging into the parking garage of Agnes' condo. I headed toward the elevator, but she yelled, "Come on," and ran for the street.

Five minutes later, we slowed to a stop at the entrance to Central Park nearest Strawberry Fields, an area named in memory of John Lennon. Agnes grabbed a gaudy scarf from her pocket, tying it around her head like a turban, and turned her reversible white coat inside out so the white fake-fur collar stood out against a now bright-purple coat. Then she put on the ugliest pair of glasses ever designed and slipped the strap of a camera over her head.

We'd barely gone forty feet into the park when I noticed a group of men moving toward us. "Don't speak and follow my lead," she whispered.

Then, in a voice that dripped of a supposed Georgia birth, she ordered me to pose in front of a statue as she morphed into the quintessential obnoxious touristzilla. My eyes focused immediately on a gorgeous Afghan Hound walking at the side of Bill Trumbull, a handler I'd known all my life. "Oh my God, darlin', will you look at that pretty doggie!" Agnes gushed. "Oh, I've got to get a photo of that. People back home won't believe that you can see something that beautiful just walkin' in the park."

The men had all stopped because we were blocking the walkway. I automatically moved toward the dog, which was an exceptional blue-gray color with a white blaze. "I just know that you gentlemen won't mind if my baby sister poses for a picture with your magnificent doggie. Step a little closer, sweetie.

Stand right behind the—excuse me, what kind of dog is this?" Agnes raised her camera and waved me into position. I stood beside Bill, but he didn't show any recognition.

"It's an Afghan Hound, madam. You may touch the coat, young lady." He reached out to stroke the dog. "Feel how sleek it is—like your own beautiful long hair." He reached out and stroked my hair, giving it a slight yank partway down.

"Oh, thank you so much." Agnes gushed. "Come on, darlin' we don't want to be late meeting Cheryl for breakfast." I turned and waved shyly at Bill, then hurried to join Agnes. As soon as we were out of sight, we exited the park. She waved down a cab and gave the cabbie an address I didn't know. As we started forward, she looked back to make sure we hadn't been observed. Once we were in traffic, Agnes grabbed my shoulders. "Turn around and let me see your braid." Her hands worked their way down to the spot where Bill had yanked it.

"Ouch." She pulled something out of the braid along with a clump of hair that had recently been attached to my head. Turning, I saw her slip a mini memory card into her bag.

"What the hell is going on?" I was now getting worried. "Bill acted as if he'd never seen me."

Agnes didn't answer; she just looked out the window.

We pulled up in front of a brownstone building with a plaque on the door that read Marcel. As we got out of the cab, I looked at her. "Those men with Bill were not the kind I'd like to meet in a dark alley. Are they a danger to Bill or to us?"

"Neither, they're bodyguards."

I looked at her in surprise as we climbed the front steps, but her frown told me the subject was off limits. When we neared the top, she turned to me, grasping my shoulders to hold my attention. "Since you were twelve years old, what has been your one goal in life?"

I laughed because this had been the family joke forever. "You mean my fantasy, to have my fashion show here in the city during Fashion Week?"

"Well, what if it weren't a fantasy? What if it were a challenge? What if I told you that since we were coming into the city today, I thought it might be a good time to kill two birds with... well, you get the picture? Kate, it's about time you show the world that you really are a serious designer.

Fashion Week is in February, right before the Westerland Kennel Club show. I pulled some strings— well, a lot of strings—and you'd better be ready to put your ass on the line, kiddo, because your fashion show is in the works. I suggested it at the board meeting of the Canine Genetics Foundation. They were looking for something to use as a charity event to raise research money during show week. It will happen the last evening of Fashion Week. You'll meet with the sponsors later today to finalize the plans and sign the contracts."

My foot slipped on the top step and I grabbed the railing to keep from falling flat on my butt. Her words slowly sank in and began to have meaning. "I get a fashion show of my designs... here?"

"Actually, I think Marcel might object to that use of his front steps, but the ballroom of the host hotel should do. It's scheduled for the Saturday of their show week, which, as I said, happens to be the last day of Fashion Week, so all the buyers will still be in town. You'd better close your mouth or Marcel will think you're an idiot."

"Marcel who?"

"There is only one Marcel. He's my step one in the plan to pull you out of your cocoon and turn you from a frumpy, dog-enrapture child into a sophisticated fashion designer. That has got to happen before you sit at the grown-up table today to sign the contracts for the show."

Agnes pulled me inside to meet Marcel and in a flurry of activity, my transformation began.

Like Alice after falling down the rabbit hole, I felt disoriented. Each successive change was tearing me farther away from the only Kate Killoy I had ever known. Saying goodbye to my braid broke my heart since my hair had never been cut. The resulting stylish hair-do, clothes, and make- up created an entirely new person. As she stared back at me from the mirror, I didn't recognize her. She was beautiful. She scared me to death.

Agnes and her agent, Arden, supervised all the contracts for my show.

The deal guaranteed a winning result for all. The Agnes & Arden show took over the room, charming everyone while they pointed to the many places I, and everyone else involved, should sign. Once the stack of contracts was complete, they left, pulling me in their wake. Each gave me a high-five and welcomed me into the world of high fashion. I had ceased thinking hours ago and was running on auto-pilot. All I could do was smile and mutter my thanks. Reality began forcing its nasty way into my brain and I questioned whether thanks were premature. Had I just signed contracts that could be the death knell of my career?

We'd spent so much time today in Agnes' fairytale world that I was surprised when we arrived at a place I actually recognized.

Reilly's was my great-aunt and -uncle's favorite pub. We pushed open the door, and there they were. I was so happy to see familiar faces I almost burst into tears trying to hug them both.

Maeve held me at arm's length, just staring at me, but Padraig leaned over me to whisper in my ear. "You are the spitting image of Maeve the day I fell in love with her. It would thrill John and Tom speech-less if they could see you now. In fact, they're prob-ably doing a jig up in heaven now, knowing their lit-tle girl has grown up."

I wanted to cry, but was afraid the tears would turn my newly applied makeup into a horror mask.

Supper turned out to be a noisy affair with friends of Maeve and Padraig, coming over to our table to be introduced to Agnes and me. For some reason, many thought I was a model, too. Only their oldest friends recognized me right off.

Reilly's attracted mostly retired members of what I called 'The long arm of the law club.' Patrons was both active and retired NYPD, FBI, CIA and MI-5. Maeve had been working for MI-5 when she met Padraig. They moved to New York where Padraig's family business was, but Maeve had kept her hand in on an informal basis.

Partway through dinner, a man whose name they did not mention joined us at the table, pulling up a chair next to Agnes. As I watched, she slipped him the memory card. He apparently knew everyone there, because he jumped right into the conversation. After about five minutes, he said his goodbyes and disappeared. Agnes leaned back, relaxed and ordered a cocktail, the signal, I guess, for a job done.

I wasn't sure if I was just overly conscious of my new appearance, but I knew that we were being watched. The watchers sat at a table to our left. At first, I didn't pay much attention. I know the effect Agnes had on the world's male population. However, as one hour passed into two, this felt creepy. The younger one, who was dressed much more formally than any of the other men in the place, neither spoke nor ate. Every time I glanced in his direction, his eyes—his beautiful green eyes, I noticed—focused on me. He didn't look like the men shadowing Bill, but…

When we stood to leave, I took Agnes' arm. "Those two guys at the table on the left have been watching us since we arrived. The guy in the double-breasted suit hasn't taken his eyes off me since we came in. Could he have recognized us from the park? Should we worry?"

She glanced casually in their direction. "No, you needn't worry. Nobody could recognize you as that little girl in the park this morning." She grinned at me. "Brace yourself, Kate, I'd say it's a case of you having your first admirer."

When we turned to go out, I frowned and glanced back at the table. Both men were still watching. From where I stood, I couldn't read the expression on the younger guy's face, but when I looked at his older friend who had focused all evening entirely on Agnes, what I saw wasn't admiration. His look was pure, unmistakable hatred.

Made in the USA
Middletown, DE
11 February 2022

60371337R00217